SAMARQAND:
PRELUDE

Books by Mitchell R. White

Brannigan Mysteries
Secrets of Silvergrove
Forget-Me-Nots and Forgotten Graves
Blue Iris, Blood Morning (Summer 2025)
Daisies for My Wife (Fall 2025)

Summers Rose Investigations
End in a Dead Heat
So Easy It's Criminal (Summer 2025)
Tacos, Sunsets, and Murder (Summer 2025)

The Hollister Files
The Case of the Shadow Sisters (Fall 2025)
Salt Money, Blood Money (Fall 2025)

Writing as M. R. "Doc" White, Ph.D.
Samarqand: Prelude
Samarqand (Spring 2025)
Redeeming Lost Pegasus (Winter 2025)
Bloodwine Warriors Trilogy (2026)

Samarqand: Prelude

Mitchell R. White

WHITE JADE
BOOKS

SAMARQAND: PRELUDE

Cover Art and Design by M R White.
Interior Text Design by M R White.
First Electronic Edition: April, 2025
First Paperback Edition: April, 2025

ISBN 979-8-9927943-6-6 Electronic
ISBN 979-8-9927943-7-3 Paperback

WHITE JADE
Publications, LLC

To All Those Who Look to the
Heavens, and Dream...

"He who controls the spice
controls the universe."

— Frank Herbert, *Dune*

"Madness, and then illumination."

— Orson Scott Card, *Xenocide*

"Reality is shaped by the forces that destroy it."

— D. Harlan Wilson,
The Kyoto Man

Foreword

Samarqand is a world that has lived in my head for forty-five years. In 1980, I was in the middle of my doctoral work at the University of Utah. Research can be a pressure cooker, and to relieve steam I took up several outdoor activities. However, I couldn't afford many days away from the lab, and in the Intermountain West, days are consumed rapidly while enjoying the beauty.

I found a small listing in the Continuing Education catalog: How to Write Speculative Fiction. I still read 2-3 such volumes every week, and I had the cheek to assume I could write. The instructor's name: Orson Scott Card. I opened my Omni Magazine and there he was.

I had to try. If nothing else, I would see a real celebrity explaining his methods. I ran to the Registrar and signed up.

That led to the toughest 30 months of learning I ever experienced. You think Thermodynamics is tough? Quantum Chemistry? Pfft. Wait until Mr. Card has taken five minutes in a public form to eviscerate your fiction piece, tearing your heart out and eating it. Without breaking a sweat.

He was right, of course. My early attempts were, in a word, drivel.

I'm a rather stubborn type, though. Rather than pick up my ruined work and missing body parts and retreating to the lab, I kept trying. I eventually got a "Good Job" on one short piece. Written underneath was "Not long enough." Oh well, can't win them all.

I succeeded in convincing the Chemistry Faculty that they should stamp my forehead and launch me into an unsuspecting world. I left Card's imagination abattoir and went to find a life. And I did.

I tried writing serious fiction soon thereafter. I started more times than most smokers quit. It never quite worked. Oh, I had ideas and images. That's not a story, though…

Then I remembered a quote: Success is not the result of spontaneous combustion. You must set yourself on fire." Arnold Glasgow reappeared in my life at the proper time: Retirement.

Retirement is a funny career. I have lots to do, and not enough. So I opened my "Trunque of Junque," collected over four decades and dug in. I started wandering around the Internet looking for new tools that could help. Boy, did I find tools! I thought a good spellchecker was magic before then. Now I have more than I need, all at my fingertips. It's easy to get lost in the tools, actually.

I could concentrate on what Scott Card taught: Storytelling. Actually, that word is misleading. It's "storyshowing" that the good authors do. Awkward word, though.

I started plotting and drafting the hard science fiction novel "Samarqand." I wanted to understand the location more, and find characters that would have an exciting adventure there. Before I knew it, I had written a novella, a novelette, and three character origin stories, all to explain to me what Samarqand is and had been before the novel starts.

This volume collects and refines those stories. I felt you might like to see them. Here they are.

Enjoy! And thanks for reading; that's all writers really want…

Table of Contents

Echoes

Seeds

The air in the office was thick with the smell of stale tobacco and something vaguely metallic, like old machinery oil. Grigory Pasnov, Komisar of Political Perfection, sat behind a massive, scarred desk that seemed to absorb the weak light filtering through the grimy window. Across from him, Vladimir Ianovic Golovin, Political Officer designate of the **КРСС Ванкуишер**, stood stiffly, his posture betraying years of ingrained obedience, despite the subtle flicker of ambition in his eyes.

Pasnov pushed a chipped glass of vodka across the desk. "To a successful mission, Comrade Golovin." His voice sounded like stones grinding together from too many years of black-tobacco cigarettes.

Golovin took the glass, nodding curtly. "To success, Komisar." He downed the vodka in one go, the harsh liquid burning a path down his throat. Pasnov watched him, unblinking.

"Success, Comrade, is not merely finding resources, though that is… desirable. Success is *control*. Remember Krasnaya's principles in the void, Comrade. The crew is…diverse. Many come from backgrounds… less than ideal. You understand." Pasnov's eyes narrowed. "Keep the ship *tight*, Comrade Golovin. Discipline. Ideological purity. No deviations. No… *weakness*."

Golovin lowered the empty glass to the desk like a man adjusting a chess piece. "Komisar, you insult me by suggesting otherwise. The **Vanquisher** will be a microcosm of Krasnaya Rechka itself, unwavering in purpose, steel in its spine. Deviations will be corrected. Promptly." A hard edge crept into his voice. "I assure you, Komisar, I will not fail."

Pasnov grunted, a sound that could have been agreement or dismissal. He gestured curtly towards the door. "See that you don't, Comrade. Krasnaya watches."

Eckhard Schulz's office was bright and airy, overlooking a sparkling artificial lake. The walls were decorated with star charts and landscape prints of Alpenheimsee's rugged mountains. He smiled warmly at Captain Clement Hoffmann, raising his glass of clear schnapps.

"To the voyage of **Neue Bund**, Clement! And a safe return, of course." Schulz's tone was genuinely cheerful, lacking any hint of threat.

Captain Hoffmann, a man with a weathered face and kind eyes, clinked glasses with the Director. "To discovery, *Herr Direktor*, and good news to bring home." He took a small sip, savoring the crisp, fruity spirit.

Schulz leaned back in his comfortable chair. "**Covenant** is a proven vessel, Captain. And you have, as always, assembled a capable crew. I have every confidence you'll perform admirably. We are eager to understand more of the lost colonies, to reconnect and, where possible, to offer assistance and trade. Heimsee thrives on connection, Captain, not conquest." He chuckled. "Though, of course, commercially advantageous discoveries are always welcome." His smile widened.

Hoffmann nodded, a thoughtful expression on his face. "We understand our mission, *Herr Direktor*. Explore, observe, and re-establish contact. We will proceed with caution. And respect, of course. Heimsee's reputation precedes us, and we intend to uphold it."

Schulz raised his glass again. "Then, Captain Hoffmann, *fahrt wohl und Glück auf!* Safe travels and good fortune!"

Race

Transition was never smooth. Not on the **Vanquisher**. Space twisted itself inside out, a nauseating lurch that rattled the old ship's bones and Maksim Bernatski's teeth. Then, silence, broken only by the protesting groan of stressed metal and the low hum of internal systems struggling to normalize. They were through.

Maksim gripped the arms of his command chair, forcing his stomach to settle. On the main viewport, the starscape resolved into unfamiliar constellations, stark and silent against the black. Dead ahead, bathing the bridge in a soft, mellow orange glow, hung their destination: a K2 subgiant, unnamed in their patchy, outdated charts. They were significantly farther out than projected: almost thirty-five astronomical units, a testament to the **Vanquisher**'s decaying navigation systems and the uncertainty of the jump path itself, reconstructed from fragmented pre-Collapse data.

A low growl emanated from the political officer's station to his right. "Farther out? Again? Captain, this inefficiency is…"

"Is prudent, Comrade Political Officer," Maksim cut in, keeping his voice level. He refused to rise to Vladimir Golovin's perpetual bait. "We are charting unknown territory with aging equipment. A cautious survey from the outer system is paramount for safety." He saw the flicker of annoyance in Golovin's eyes, the tightening of his thin lips. Golovin craved speed, decisive action, something glorious to report back to Komisar Pasnov. Maksim suspected the man dreamed more of promotion ribbons than the actual success of their mission. He felt a familiar knot of apprehension tighten in his gut – Golovin's ambition was a dangerous fuel in the confines of their aging vessel.

"Prudence is one thing, Captain," Golovin clipped, his voice regaining its usual condescending edge. "Timidity is another. Krasnaya expects results, not excuses."

Maksim ignored the barb, turning to his sensor officer. "Status report. Any planetary bodies detected?"

"Scanning now, Captain. Initial sweeps show… multiple gravitational anomalies. Refining data."

"Very well. Set Condition Three watch rotation. Maintain standard survey protocols." Maksim pushed himself out of the chair, feeling the familiar aches of a long jump cycle. "I'll be in my quarters. Alert me to any significant findings." He needed rest, needed distance from Golovin's simmering impatience.

He managed four hours of fitful sleep before the alert klaxon jolted him awake. Heart pounding, he slapped the intercom. "Bridge, report!"

"Captain!" It was the frantic voice of Ensign Petrov from Communications. "Another vessel detected! Jump signature appeared less than ten minutes ago! They're… they're inside our position, Captain! Bearing zero-niner-five relative, distance estimated twenty-seven AU from primary!"

Maksim was throwing on his uniform jacket even before the ensign finished. He raced through the cramped corridors, the metallic tang of recycled air sharp in his nostrils. He burst onto the bridge to find controlled chaos. Golovin was already in the command chair, barking orders.

"Full power to main engines! Course zero-niner-five! Best possible speed! We will intercept!"

"Belay that!" Maksim's voice cut through the tension. Heads snapped towards him. Golovin swiveled in the chair, a faint smirk playing on his lips.

"Ah, Captain. Just ensuring we don't lose the initiative. This intruder thinks they can sneak into *our* system?"

"Comrade Political Officer," Maksim said, forcing calm he didn't feel, stepping towards the command station. "What exactly are you doing in my chair, issuing engine orders?"

Golovin rose and stretched to his full height, blocking Maksim's path. "Assisting, Captain. Securing Krasnaya's claim. We were here first. Every second counts." The man's breath smelled stale, laced with caffeine stimulants.

Maksim felt a surge of anger, quickly suppressed by a colder wave of fear. Golovin held the real power, delegated directly from the Komisar. A confrontation here, now, was suicide. He glanced past Golovin, catching the eye of his Executive Officer, Simen Agdestein. Simen stood unmoving near the navigation console, his expression unreadable, but Maksim saw the deep frown lines etched around his mouth, his gaze fixed on Golovin's back. Maksim gave a minuscule shake of his head. *Not now, Simen.*

He took a deep breath, stepping around Golovin to his rightful place. "Helm, modify course to zero-niner-five. Maintain eighty percent power. Navigation, plot intercept trajectory, but prioritize fuel efficiency. We don't know who that is or what their intentions are." He could feel Golovin's glare burning into the side of his face. The race had begun, and already, the political officer was trying to run them off a cliff.

The transition was seamless. A barely perceptible shimmer, a momentary distortion on the main viewport, and the **BASN Neue Bund** settled into the outer reaches of the Ipak system as planned. Captain Clement Hoffmann allowed himself a small smile, the scent of freshly brewed coffee pleasant in the air. Twenty-six astronomical units out; minimal safe distance achieved, navigation precise.

"Excellent work, bridge crew," Hoffmann announced, his voice calm and warm. "Textbook jump. Helm, maintain station-keeping. Sensors, begin full planetary survey sweep. Let's see what this system holds."

Acknowledging calls echoed around the efficiently designed bridge. Data streams flowed across consoles, the quiet clicks of keyboards a soothing rhythm. Hoffmann stretched, feeling the pleasant release of tension after the jump sequence. "Astrid, you have the conn. I'm going to grab some dinner before things get interesting."

His Executive Officer, Astrid Cantara, a sharp woman with intelligent eyes, nodded once. "Aye, Captain. Enjoy your meal."

Hoffmann had just reached the bridge lift when a sensor technician called out, his voice sharp with discovery. "Captain! Multiple contacts. Four planetary bodies confirmed. One, well, it appears within the primary habitable zone. Large moon detected as well!"

A ripple of excitement rolled through the bridge. Hoffmann turned back to the bridge deck, a broader smile touching his lips. "Well now, that *is* interesting. Plot a course for the potentially habitable world, Astrid. Standard approach vector."

"Plotting now, Captain," Cantara confirmed.

Then, another call from Sensors, more urgent this time. "Sir! Another vessel detected! Engine signature just registered... behind us! Bearing three-one-seven relative, range approximately four AU and closing! They're burning hard, Captain, high-energy signature, possibly an older drive system. Krasnaya configuration, maybe?"

Hoffmann strode back to the command chair, dinner forgotten. The relaxed atmosphere evaporated, replaced by focused alertness. "On screen, tactical display."

A schematic appeared, showing the **Covenant**'s position relative to Ipak and the four planets. A blinking red icon marked the second vessel, its projected trajectory a direct line towards them. *Krasnaya?* Hoffmann felt a prickle of unease. Krasnaya Rechka had a reputation: insular, aggressive, unpredictable. Still, a survey mission... Perhaps they were simply eager.

"Helm, modify course," Hoffmann ordered in a calm voice. "Take us on a tangential approach towards the large moon orbiting the habitable planet. Let's use it for a closer sensor scan before committing to a planetary approach. Engines, make eighty percent and keep them stable."

"Course modified, Captain," from Navigation. A curt "Aye Sir!" from Power.

Minutes passed in watchful silence. Then, Navigation spoke. "Captain, the trailing vessel is altering course. They appear to be adjusting for intercept."

Hoffmann frowned. That was; less than friendly. A standard hail would be normal procedure. Breaking into a high-g intercept without standard hailing protocols sent a clear message — and not a sociable one.

"Very well," he said, his voice hardening. "A stern chase is a long chase. Engines, increase power to ninety percent. Maintain course for the moon." He turned to Cantara. "Astrid, I'm going to get that meal after all, and perhaps some rest. Call me in eight hours if I'm not back on the bridge before then. Keep me apprised of any changes." He trusted his crew implicitly. Whatever the possibly-Krasnaya ship intended, the **Covenant** would be ready.

Three days. Three mind-numbing, tense days chasing an unidentified ship through the void. The **Vanquisher** strained at ninety-five percent power, all the ancient propulsion system could give. The engines emitting a low, jagged thrum that vibrated through the deck plates. They hadn't gained much on their quarry, which maintained a steady lead, its trajectory aimed at the promising fourth planet.

Maksim felt refreshed, to his surprise. He'd kept to his watch schedule, ensuring adequate rest. Golovin, however, was a wreck. Hunched in his station chair, his uniform rumpled, eyes bloodshot and twitching, he looked like he hadn't slept since they entered the system. He lived on stim-packs and suspicion, his gaze constantly flicking between the tactical display and Maksim.

They were approaching the orbital path of the large moon now, its cratered, grey surface looming larger in the viewport. Both ships would need to begin deceleration soon.

"Captain," Golovin rasped, his voice raw. "Order the flip delayed. Burn longer. Close the distance when they decelerate."

"Comrade Political Officer," Maksim replied, keeping his tone measured. "That's tactically unsound. It wastes fuel and puts us in a vulnerable position during our own deceleration burn. We still don't know who they are."

"I want a close sensor sweep!" Golovin slammed a fist on his console. "I want to know who dares intrude on Krasnaya territory!"

Before Maksim could argue further, the Communications officer spoke up, sounding surprised. "Captain, we're receiving a transmission! Universal emergency frequency... audio only. They're hailing us!"

A spark of relief ignited in Maksim's chest. Finally. "On speakers, Ensign."

A clear, calm voice filled the bridge, speaking Standard Galactic. *"—naya vessel, this is the Bad Alpenheimsee Naval Survey ship* **Covenant**. *We are on a peaceful scientific expedition under Heimsee charter. Please identify yourselves."*

Heimsee. So, not pirates, not military aggressors. Just another survey ship. Maksim opened his mouth to order Comms to respond, to establish peaceful contact —

"Belay that order!" Golovin roared, surging to his feet. "Maintain operational silence! Helm, continue deceleration burn as planned, but maintain vector for closest possible pass!"

Maksim bit back a furious retort. Like a master tactician sacrificing pawns, Golovin was deliberately pushing them toward confrontation. He saw Simen, standing near the weapons station now, take a half-step forward, his hand clenching. Maksim shot him a sharp, warning glance. *Stand down, Simen.* The rest of the bridge crew found their consoles intensely fascinating, avoiding eye contact, ignoring the raw power play unfolding.

The **Covenant** grew larger in the viewport as they rounded the moon. Maksim estimated the closest approach would be around twenty thousand kilometers – close, but not dangerously so, unless someone did something foolish.

Then, the unthinkable happened. Golovin lunged past Simen, shoving a startled weapons technician aside. The tech landed on his backside, sliding against the wall, where he sat in stunned silence. Golovin's hands flew across the console, overriding the safeties. Four brilliant crimson beams lanced out from the **Vanquisher**'s dorsal laser emitters, streaking across the void towards the **Covenant**.

8

"GOLOVIN! WHAT HAVE YOU DONE?" Maksim surged out of his chair, horror and fury warring within him.

Golovin spun around, his face contorted in a triumphant sneer. "My duty, Captain! Securing this system for the glory of Krasnaya! I have the authority," he spat, his voice rising, ensuring everyone heard. "Komisar Pasnov granted me full operational override in situations demanding decisive action! This planet is ours! Not for those sniveling Heimsee cowards! Interfere again, Captain, and I'll have you thrown in the brig. Or worse." His eyes glittered with malice.

Maksim stood frozen for a heartbeat, the bridge silent save for the hum of the ship. He felt the eyes of the crew on him, waiting. He sank back into his command chair with deliberate slowness, the upholstery feeling cold beneath him. He tasted bile. He forced himself to turn to the trembling weapons tech. "Guns. Report. Any hits?"

The young man swallowed hard, squeezing past Golovin like the officer had leprosy. He frantically checked the weapons readouts. "N-negative, Captain. All shots missed. I think."

Maksim let out a breath he hadn't realized he was holding, forcing his clenched fists to relax, driving tension from his shoulders. Golovin scoffed, turned his back on Maksim and stalked off the bridge, leaving a wake of fear and uncertainty behind him.

"Still no response to hails, Captain," Astrid Cantara reported, her voice tight with controlled tension. The **Covenant** smoothed through space, the grey bulk of the moon filling the main viewport. The red icon representing the Krasnaya vessel paralleled their course, catching up slightly, still maintaining an unnerving silence.

Captain Hoffmann watched the tactical display, his brow furrowed. The projected closest approach was now under twenty thousand kilometers. Close, but manageable. Still, the lack of communication, combined with the aggressive pursuit; it set his teeth on edge. "Maintain readiness, Astrid. Take us to Yellow Alert."

9

"Aye, Captain. Yellow Alert."

Cantara turned from the tactical display, a thoughtful expression on her face. "Captain, I've been running deeper searches through the pre-Collapse archives based on the star's spectral signature and potential planetary configuration. There's a high probability match in one old, damaged data collection. This system was charted. Maybe colonized. The planet is likely Samarqand. The moon would be Spice, if the planet name is right."

"Samarqand…" Hoffmann murmured the name. It resonated with vague memories, a whisper from history. A lost colony. He leaned closer to Cantara's console, distracted by the implications. "Can you confirm?"

"Cross-referencing stellar drift and remnant navigational markers. I make the probability ninety-two percent, Captain. This is almost certainly the lost Samarqand system."

The confirmation hung in the air, thick with possibility, just as klaxons blared, shattering the moment.

"LASER FIRE DETECTED! INCOMING!"

Hoffmann jerked upright, shock rendering him speechless as crimson beams flashed past the viewport, terrifyingly close. Training, ingrained and immediate, seized the bridge crew before he could utter a word.

"Engaging evasion!" snapped the Helm officer, hands flying across the controls. The **Covenant** lurched violently as thrusters fired, angling them away from the incoming trajectory.

"Damage report!" Cantara demanded, her voice sharp but steady.

"No hits! Repeat, no hits! One laser bolt passed within fifty meters of the port stern quarter." Relief was obvious in Cantara's voice and the faces of the bridge crew.

Hoffmann's mind caught up, adrenaline surging. An unprovoked attack. Raw aggression. He gripped the command chair, his knuckles white. "Helm, get us behind Spice! Continue full evasive pattern!"

The **Covenant** shuddered again as it dove towards the protective bulk of the moon. The red alert status flashed its insistent demand on the displays.

"Red Alert status canceled, reverting to Yellow Alert," Cantara announced as they slipped into the moon's shadow. "We are shielded for the moment, Captain."

Hoffmann took a deep, steadying breath. His crew's performance had been flawless, reacting instantly to save the ship. He felt a surge of pride, followed by cold anger at the Krasnaya vessel's actions.

"Suggestions?" he asked, turning to his senior staff.

Clara Diamanda, the sharp-eyed Sensor Technician Lead, spoke first. "Landing on Samarqand is inadvisable, Captain. We know nothing of the surface conditions, potential defenses, or the disposition of any surviving population. And now we have a confirmed hostile vessel in orbit."

Hoffmann nodded. She was right. Rushing down was indeed foolish. "Astrid?"

"The Krasnaya ship holds the orbital advantage for now, Captain. Direct confrontation is unwise. We need a position where we can observe without being easily detected."

Observe. Assess. Plan. Hoffmann scanned the tactical display, his eyes drawn to the L1 Lagrange point, nestled between Samarqand and its primary star, Ipak. A natural collection point for dust and asteroids. Good cover. Glare from the star at their backs.

"Navigation," Hoffmann ordered, his voice firm, decisive. "Plot a course for the Samarqand-Ipak L1 point. Wide trajectory, use planetary and lunar gravity assists to mask our acceleration signature as much as possible. We'll find some rocks to hide behind and see exactly what our aggressive friends intend to do down there."

The **Covenant** altered course, melting into the vastness of space, a silent observer preparing for the next move in a now-dangerous game.

Discovery

From orbit, Samarqand was deceivingly serene. Two sprawling continents, brushed with emerald green and deep umber, nestled beneath swirling cloud patterns. Myriad islands, scattered like jewels across a sapphire ocean, completed the idyllic portrait. It was easy to forget, suspended in the sterile confines of the **Vanquisher**'s command deck, that this world had been lost, silent, for centuries. Maksim focused his gaze on the eastern coast of the larger continent, at the coordinates his sensor team had identified. There, nestled beside a cluster of buildings that had once constituted a thriving village, lay the skeletal remains of a spaceport. Long disused, yes, but structurally intact according to their scans. Minimal planetary defense signatures, all dark. Minimal threats, it seemed.

He pushed aside a flicker of unease. Something about the silence of this world felt… heavy. He glanced at the village again, picturing the people below, descendants of lost colonists, unaware of Krasnaya's imminent arrival. A pang of something akin to pity, unfamiliar and unwelcome, tightened in his chest. He pushed it down. Duty first.

"Comrade Political Officer," Maksim said, turning to Golovin who hovered impatiently nearby. "Surface scans are complete. We can confirm the spaceport is viable for shuttle landings. Minimal planetary defense detected within a twenty-kilometer radius."

Golovin's eyes gleamed with something predatory. "Excellent! How soon can we secure it?"

Maksim turned to Sublieutenant Sergiu Popescu, the compact, granite-faced commander of the seven KR Marines assigned to the **Vanquisher**. "Sublieutenant, deployment readiness?"

Popescu stood ramrod straight, his gaze unwavering. "Shuttle prepped and combat-ready, Captain. Marines are at Condition One. Deployment within one hour."

"Very good." Maksim nodded. "Sublieutenant, your orders are to land at the designated spaceport, secure a perimeter sufficient for follow-on landings, and establish a forward operating base."

"Understood, Captain." Popescu's acknowledgement was curt, efficient.

Golovin stepped forward, interrupting. "I will accompany the first shuttle."

Maksim raised an eyebrow, a flicker of surprise crossing his face. He had expected Golovin to remain in orbit, orchestrating events from above. "Comrade Political Officer? Are you certain? Initial landing zones can be... unpredictable."

Golovin waved a dismissive hand. "Nonsense, Captain. My presence will ensure the proper... *enthusiasm* on the ground. And," he added, his voice dropping to a conspiratorial murmur, "I wish to be... personally involved in establishing Krasnaya's claim." He gestured to two nearby ratings, mechanics from the engineering crew. "They will accompany me. We will maximize the shuttle capacity."

Maksim calculated. Three extra bodies in the shuttle, beyond the seven Marines. It would be a tight fit, but not exceeding safety margins. Objecting would be pointless, he knew. Golovin's mind was set. "Very well, Comrade Political Officer. I authorize the additional personnel on the shuttle manifest. Sublieutenant Popescu, ensure all personnel are aboard and ready for launch within the hour. Shuttle departs precisely at oh-nine-hundred ship's time. No stragglers." Maksim's gaze locked onto Golovin's, a silent, steely challenge. *Try to delay this, interfere, and you'll answer to me.*

Golovin, surprisingly, did not object. He snapped a curt nod and turned, almost running from the bridge towards the shuttle bay access.

Simen Agdestein stepped closer as Golovin disappeared. "Captain," he murmured, his voice low. "Is it wise to allow him to go planetside with the initial landing party?"

Maksim shrugged, a weary gesture. "Wise or not, Simen, it is happening. Golovin will do as he pleases regardless. At least this way," he added, a faint edge of bitterness entering his voice, "we will have a clearer picture of the *enthusiasm* he generates on the surface."

The shuttle bucked and shuddered, the swirling atmosphere of Samarqand buffeting the aged craft like a cosmic hand. Vladimir Golovin pressed a hand against his churning stomach, fighting back the bile that threatened to rise. Shuttle travel still unsettled him, the unpredictable turbulence a sharp affront to his sense of control. He glanced at the Marines arrayed impassively across from him, their faces stoic, untouched by the queasy motion. *Conscripts,* he thought with a curl of his lip. *But useful tools nonetheless.*

The jarring thump of landing gear touching duracrete jolted him. A hard landing. Inefficient. Typical Krasnaya engineering. Before he could dwell further on the inadequacies of their equipment, the shuttle hatch hissed open. Sublieutenant Popescu's voice, clipped and professional, cut through the recycled air. "Marines, deploy! Secure perimeter! Ratings, stand fast!"

Popescu moved like a machine, a precise, efficient instrument of force. Golovin, still fighting nausea, was held back by the Marine commander, a subtle but firm hand on his arm. Golovin bristled at the implied constraint, but Popescu was following protocol and orders. The Marines fanned out, weapons raised, their movements practiced and lethal. Only then did Popescu nod to Golovin. "All clear, Comrade Political Officer."

Golovin strode down the ramp, the two enlisted ratings trailing clumsily behind. The air was warm, humid, thick with the cloying sweetness of unfamiliar vegetation. He wrinkled his nose. Primitive. He scanned the immediate vicinity. The spaceport was indeed long derelict, cracked duracrete overgrown with tenacious weeds. Beyond the perimeter, a cluster of simple buildings huddled — Eastport, their charts had indicated. Villagers. Potential labor. Resources to be exploited.

Even as the thought formed, hesitant figures emerged from the village, their movements cautious, curious. They were… unremarkable.

14

Simply dressed, weathered faces etched with a mixture of apprehension and hope. *Pathetic,* Golovin thought, a flicker of disdain rising within him. Outwardly, he adopted a practiced bonhomie. He strode forward, past the watchful Marines, a wide, practiced smile plastered on his face. This was theatre now, the performance of benevolent liberator. Let them have their illusions, for now.

He extended a hand towards the nearest villager, a woman with dirt-stained hands and wide, questioning eyes. "Greetings, people of… Eastport, is it? I am Vladimir Golovin, Political Officer of the Krasnaya Rechka survey vessel **Vanquisher**. We have come a long way to reach you." He pumped her hand with forced enthusiasm, a politician on the campaign trail. "We are here to… reconnect! To offer assistance! To bring you back into the fold of civilization!"

Confusion flickered across the woman's face, then something brighter, something like nascent hope. A young boy darted forward from the edge of the group, his eyes wide with excitement. "Governor Bebe! I'll get Governor Bebe! They're here! From space!" He sprinted back towards the village, his excited shouts echoing in the humid air.

Within minutes, more villagers arrived, drawn by the commotion. An informal, boisterous gathering formed at the edge of the derelict spaceport. Food appeared as if by magic — rough-baked bread, chunks of dried meat, a fermented, cloudy drink offered in shared gourds. A makeshift feast erupted, a celebration of the unexpected, the unimaginable. The shuttle lifted back towards the **Vanquisher** for more crew and supplies, a tangible link to the heavens, a promise of salvation. The villagers chattered with excitement, their words tumbling over each other, a mixture of Russian dialect and something older, more guttural. Krasnaya Rechka! Mother Krasnaya! They remembered the old tales, the legends of a powerful, distant homeland. *Fools,* Golovin thought again, even as he laughed and clapped backs, basking in their naive gratitude.

Governor Bebe Borzhakova arrived, a woman of middle years, her face etched with a quiet strength. She greeted Golovin with a cautious but genuinely warm smile, her hand firm in his. They settled into rough-hewn chairs dragged from the village, seeking refuge from the strengthening sun beneath the meager shade of the shuttle's bulk. As the villagers buzzed around them, sharing food and drink with the bewildered Marines, Golovin began his subtle interrogation. Resources, infrastructure, industry… and then, the questions that truly interested him. Defenses. Weapons. How many villagers were capable of bearing arms? He framed them innocently, casually, as necessary for "mutual security." Bebe, caught up in the euphoric atmosphere and oblivious to the predatory glint in Golovin's eyes, answered without concern, unknowingly painting a picture of a community ripe for the taking.

Sunrise over Eastport. The humid air already thick with the promise of heat. Another feast awaited Golovin and his small contingent. Breakfast this time, laid out on rough tables near the village square: steaming bowls of root stew, sweet, sticky fruit, strong, bitter tea. The villagers, energized by the previous day's arrival, bustled around, their smiles wide, their hospitality overwhelming. Even Sublieutenant Popescu and his Marines, usually impassive, seemed to thaw in the face of such genuine warmth. *Sentimental fools,* Golovin thought again, even as he accepted a bowl of stew, forcing another practiced smile.

The shuttle descended again, the last load of **Vanquisher** personnel and equipment disgorging onto the spaceport – including Captain Bernatski and his Executive Officer. Maksim, Golovin noted with a flicker of annoyance, carried himself with his usual stiff-backed professionalism, his gaze cool and assessing. He was a stickler for order, for procedure, for *weakness.*

After breakfast, as the sun climbed higher, Golovin approached Governor Bebe. "Honored Governor," he began, his voice resonating with false sincerity. "The people of Eastport have shown us such… *unwavering* hospitality. It is time, I believe, for a formal announcement. To clarify our… beneficial presence here."

Bebe beamed. "Of course, Comrade Political Officer! Whatever you deem appropriate." She clapped her hands, calling out in her rapid dialect to the assembled villagers. Within minutes, most of Eastport had gathered in the village square, their faces expectant, their voices a low murmur of anticipation. The eight Marines, on Golovin's subtle command, arrayed themselves behind him, a silent, imposing presence.

Golovin stepped onto a low wooden crate, positioning himself to overlook the crowd. He cleared his throat, letting the murmur die down. He gestured expansively towards Bebe, standing slightly to his left. "Honored Governor Borzhakova, esteemed citizens of Eastport," he began, his voice ringing with practiced authority. "On behalf of Krasnaya Rechka and Komisar Pasnov, I thank you for your generous welcome. It is with great pleasure that I announce today a new chapter in the history of Samarqand. A chapter of… reunification." He paused for effect, letting the word hang in the air.

"Krasnaya Rechka," he continued, his voice rising in volume and fervor, "claims Samarqand as its rightful territory! From this day forward, you are under the protection and guidance of Mother Krasnaya!" He puffed out his chest, reveling in the dramatic pronouncement. "And I, Vladimir Golovin," he declared, pointing to himself with theatrical flourish, "am appointed as your *Глава колонии*! Your Head of Colony!" He waited for applause, for cheers, for validation.

Instead, a stunned silence. Then, a lone voice rose from the back of the crowd, laced with confusion and disbelief. "Governor Bebe is our governor!" the man shouted, his voice cracking with indignation. "We voted for her! We don't need a… a *Глава* from off-world!"

A Marine shouldered forward, and though his rifle lay slack against his chest, its muzzle found the space above the villager's head with practiced ease. The Marine's gaze was cold, devoid of emotion. The square fell silent, the humid air clotting, thick with fear. Golovin allowed the silence to stretch, to tighten, a physical manifestation of his newfound authority. Then, with a dismissive wave of his hand, he addressed the villagers again, his voice mild. "Details regarding the new administration," he announced, as if nothing had interrupted him, "and the responsibilities expected of you, will be announced this afternoon. Dismissed."

The stillness lasted a beat too long. When the crowd broke to leave, their movements were slow, reluctant; as if walking through a nightmare they couldn't quite process. The joyous atmosphere of the morning had evaporated, leaving behind a bitter taste of apprehension and dread.

The tropical sun dipped towards the horizon, casting long, encroaching shadows across the village square. The villagers had gathered again, compelled by Golovin's terse pronouncement, their faces now etched not with hope, but with wary resignation. Golovin paced before them, his movements agitated, his words rapid, sharp-edged. Maksim stood at the edge of the square, Simen beside him, watching the unfolding scene with a growing sense of dread. The air thrummed with unspoken tension.

Governor Bebe stepped forward, her shoulders squared, her voice steady despite the palpable fear emanating from the crowd. "Comrade *Глава*," she addressed Golovin, the new title laced with bitter irony. "Many of us… we do not understand. We welcomed you as… as guests. Not as… rulers."

Golovin stopped pacing, his gaze hardening, fixing on Bebe with something akin to predatory focus. He waved her closer, a curt, dismissive gesture. "Your… *concerns*?" he sneered. "Let's hear them. Publicly. In front of your… *citizens*." He emphasized the last word with dripping sarcasm.

Bebe walked towards him, stopping a few feet away, holding his gaze with unwavering dignity. "We are a self-governing community," she stated, her voice resonating across the hushed square. "We have chosen our leaders. We value democratic process. We do not understand why Krasnaya Rechka simply *claims* us without consultation, without…"

"Democracy. *Демократия*," Golovin spat the word like a curse, his lips curling in disgust. He scanned the faces in the crowd, a contemptuous sweep. Then, he nodded slowly, deliberately. "Krasnaya Rechka," he declared, his voice ringing with chilling finality, "is *not* a democracy."

Before anyone could react, before Maksim's mind could even register the flicker of movement, Golovin's hand blurred. A sidearm appeared as if from nowhere, a sleek, black pistol leveled at Bebe's head. A sharp, brutal crack echoed across the square. Bebe's eyes widened in shock, her face contorting for a fleeting instant before her body crumpled, collapsing onto the dusty ground. A strangled cry escaped from the crowd. A man behind Bebe stumbled, clutching his leg, a crimson stain blooming on his roughspun trousers. He fell, groaning, onto the ground at the front of the crowd.

A stunned silence descended, heavier than the humid air, thicker than the encroaching shadows. The villagers stood frozen, paralyzed by shock and horror. Even the Marines seemed taken aback, their professional masks faltering for a fraction of a second. Golovin holstered his weapon with a casual shrug, the acrid smell of gun smoke hanging in the air. He surveyed the motionless crowd, his gaze cold, challenging. "Anyone else wish to… *vote*?" he asked, his voice dangerously soft.

No one moved. No one spoke. Only the wounded man's whimpers broke the suffocating silence. A village healer rushed forward, kneeling beside the injured man, her movements trembling.

"Good." Golovin's voice cut through the stillness, brisk and businesslike. "Go home. Further instructions will be posted in the morning. Marines, secure the governor's… *office*." He gestured dismissively at Bebe's lifeless body with the toe of his boot.

The crowd began to disperse, shuffling away in stunned silence, leaving Bebe's body lying untouched on the dusty square. Golovin turned and strode towards one of the sturdier buildings, the Marines closing ranks around him.

Simen Agdestein beside Maksim shifted, a low growl rumbling in his throat. Maksim placed a hand firmly on his friend's arm, restraining him. *Not yet, Simen. Not yet.*

They stood motionless at the edge of the square, watching Golovin disappear into the deepening twilight, watching the villagers melt away like shadows, leaving only Governor Bebe's broken body and the cooling silence of a tropical night descending over a conquered village. The darkness felt absolute.

Occupation

Maksim Bernatski stood at the edge of the dusty village square, his boots crunching on the parched earth, and surveyed Pristan' Zorya. The name grated on his ears, forced and unnatural. Eastport, the simple, honest name the villagers had used, felt like a ghost now, lingering in the heavy silence that had descended with Krasnaya's arrival. The morning air, usually vibrant with the sounds of life, felt muted, stifled. The tropical humidity hung heavy, mirroring the oppressive weight settling upon the village.

He closed his eyes for a moment, breathing deeply. The air carried the usual scents of Samarqand: the sweet, cloying fragrance of unfamiliar blossoms, the damp earthiness of the jungle, but now, undertones of something else were present: the metallic tang of freshly worked steel from the prison construction, the faint acrid bite of smoke from distant brush fires, and beneath it all, a pervasive undercurrent of fear, sharp and metallic in his nostrils.

Golovin's voice, amplified by the crude loudspeakers the Marines had erected at the village's edges, shattered the fragile quiet. "Let it be known throughout Pristan' Zorya, by order of *Глава колонии* Vladimir Golovin! Any individual heard or observed using the former designation, 'Eastport,' will be subject to immediate punitive measures! Fines, reprimands, or more severe sanctions will be applied without exception! Compliance is mandatory! This is the official name! Pristan' Zorya! Pristan, for brevity!" The recorded announcement, harsh and grating in its repetition, abruptly cut off, leaving an echoing void filled with the buzzing of insects and the distant clang of hammers.

Maksim opened his eyes, his gaze drawn to the nascent symbols of Krasnaya's dominion. The open-cage prison, constructed of raw, roughly welded steel bars, cast long, skeletal shadows across the square. It was placed in the most public space, a constant, looming threat. The gallows frame beside it reached for the sky, a stark and brutal silhouette against the vibrant green of the jungle backdrop. Crude, yes, but undeniably effective in their message: *submit, or suffer.*

He watched a group of villagers, mostly women and older men, shuffling past the prison, carrying baskets laden with freshly harvested fruit. Their movements were subdued, heads bowed, eyes downcast. He noticed a young girl, no older than seven or eight, stumble slightly, dropping a few of the brightly colored fruits. Maksim moved to help, but stopped himself. He watched as the girl knelt, her small hands fumbling to gather the scattered fruit, her face pale with anxiety. No laughter, no chatter among them. Just the quiet scrape of their sandals on the dust, the rustle of their simple clothes, and the heavy, unspoken fear that permeated every interaction. His chest tightened. This wasn't control; it was suffocation.

Golovin, as if summoned by Maksim's dark thoughts, strode into view, his black uniform crisp and immaculate amidst the dust and disarray. He surveyed the mostly unchanged village with a dissatisfied frown. "Progress is insufficient, Captain Bernatski," he declared, his voice laced with its usual condescending tone. "I ordered proper buildings. Stone, timber. Something befitting Krasnaya's presence, not these shacks."

"Comrade Political Officer," Maksim replied, keeping his voice level and devoid of emotion. "Acquiring and processing building materials takes time. The villagers are unfamiliar with large-scale construction. We are working with limited resources and manpower."

Golovin scoffed. "Excuses, Captain. I need results, not excuses. And remember," he added, his gaze hardening, drifting towards the hazy horizon beyond the jungle, "we are not alone in this system. That Heimsee vessel is still out there, lurking. We must establish a defensible position, and quickly."

Golovin turned abruptly, pacing towards the administrative building: Bebe's former office, now Golovin's command center. He spun back, his eyes narrowed with an almost predatory gleam. "Have you promulgated the new levy yet, Captain? The twenty percent contribution? It's time these people understood their obligations."

"I have the announcements prepared," Maksim said, his jaw tightening. "Though, Comrade, I must reiterate my concern. Twenty percent of their production. It will be devastating for them. They operate on a very narrow margin as it is."

Golovin's lips curled into a sneer. "Sentimental nonsense, Captain. They will survive. They are survivors, aren't they? And Krasnaya provides protection. Protection from those 'Heimsee imperialists,' as we shall call them. A generous exchange, wouldn't you say?" He clapped Maksim on the shoulder with a jarring force, his grip uncomfortably tight. "Now, see to it that those announcements are posted. And perhaps," Golovin's voice dropped to a conspiratorial whisper, "you might want to emphasize the *consequences* of non-compliance. Fear, Captain Bernatski," he concluded, his eyes glinting with a disturbing intensity, "is a far more effective motivator than *gratitude*."

Golovin stalked away, leaving Maksim standing alone in the dusty square, the echoes of the political officer's words hanging in the humid air like a suffocating shroud. Maksim stared at the newly erected prison, at the skeletal gallows, at the bowed figures of the villagers laboring under the weight of their new reality. *Fear,* Golovin had said. And in Pristan' Zorya, fear was indeed becoming the only currency. And Maksim, trapped between his duty and his conscience, felt himself slowly drowning in it.

The **Covenant** hung in the inky blackness of Lagrangian Point 1, a silent, almost invisible observer perched on the gravitational edge of the Samarqand system. Captain Clement Hoffmann stood in the **Covenant**'s darkened observation dome, the panoramic viewport offering a breathtaking, yet unsettling vista. Samarqand, a swirling marble of green and blue, hung suspended in the void, bathed in the warm, orange-tinged light of the K2 subgiant, Ipak. The silence in the dome was absolute, broken only by the faint, rhythmic hum of the ship's life support systems and the almost imperceptible clicks and whispers of data streams flowing across nearby consoles. It was a silence conducive to thought, to observation, to waiting.

"Sensor readings remain stable, Captain," Astrid Cantara's voice, quiet yet firm, emanated from the comm panel beside him.

"**Vanquisher** remains in orbit around Samarqand. Shuttle activity continues to and from the surface, concentrated around the eastern edge of the large continent."

Hoffmann nodded, his gaze fixed on the mesmerizing swirl of clouds over Samarqand. From this distance, the planet seemed peaceful, idyllic, belying the brutal reality unfolding on its surface, a reality they could only infer from sensor readings and fragmented transmissions. He could almost feel the immense distance, the cold vacuum separating him from the unfolding drama below, a sense of frustrating detachment settling over him.

"Magnify sensor feed on shuttle landing zone, Astrid," he ordered, his voice a low murmur. "Let's get a closer look at their *operation*."

The image on the viewport shimmered, resolving into a tighter focus on a coastal plain dominated by secondary jungle and the stark, geometrical lines of a derelict spaceport. Shuttlecraft, clumsy and ungainly compared to the **Covenant**'s sleek lines, descended and ascended with rhythmic regularity, ants carrying burdens to and from the hive.

"Landing zone designated as 'Eastport' on outdated charts, Captain," Cantara reported, her voice laced with a hint of grim irony. "Though I doubt the Krasnayans are still using that designation."

Hoffmann allowed a ghost of a smile to touch his lips. "No, I imagine 'Eastport' is no longer politically palatable for their Komisar. They are likely renaming everything in sight." He paused, his gaze sharpening as he scrutinized the sensor feed. "Anything of note planet-side?"

"Increased construction activity around the landing zone, Captain. Basic structures being erected. No significant defensive emplacements detected, though their troop presence appears to be consolidating." Cantara's voice turned thoughtful. "And faint energy fluctuations, Captain. Intermittent, localized… possibly civilian distress signals, quickly suppressed."

Hoffmann's jaw tightened. Distress signals. Suppressed. The pieces were starting to fit together, painting a grim picture of Krasnaya's "survey expedition."

"Lagrange Point 1 is no longer optimal for observation, Captain," Cantara stated, breaking the silence again, her tone now crisp and professional. "For detailed planetary scans and closer monitoring of Krasnayan surface activities, we need to reposition."

"Agreed," Hoffmann affirmed, pushing himself away from the viewport. He turned to face Cantara square-on, his gaze decisive. "Chart a course for a stealth transit to orbit around Shard."

"Shard orbit plotted, Captain. Transit time approximately six hours, at point-five lightspeed, utilizing planetary gravity well for minimal drive signature."

"Execute," Hoffmann ordered. "Maximum stealth protocols, Astrid. I want to be a ghost in this system."

As the **Covenant** began its intricate dance through the system, maneuvering to keep Samarqand a concealing shield between itself and the **Vanquisher**, Clara Diamanda's voice broke through the tense quiet of the observation dome, her tone laced with excitement. "Captain! We're strengthening the encrypted transmission signals! Initial decryption attempts are showing… fragmented phrases… Standard Galactic… requesting assistance…"

Hoffmann turned sharply, his gaze locking onto Diamanda's console. "Standard, you say? Intriguing."

Diamanda nodded, her fingers flying across her console, refining the decryption algorithms. "Affirmative, Captain. The transmissions are faint, broken, but the message is becoming clearer. They are reaching out to *us*, Captain Hoffman. The people of Samarqand are asking for help."

Hoffmann stood in silence for a long moment, the weight of the unfolding situation settling heavily upon him. He stared back at the mesmerizing, indifferent beauty of Samarqand hanging in the viewport, now no longer serene, but a world in desperate need. He knew, with a growing certainty, that the **Covenant**'s mission was no longer simply observation. The race had become far more complex and dangerous.

The jungle's edge, a riot of emerald and jade, pressed close against the haphazard edge of Pristan Zorya, a constant, silent reminder of the world beyond Golovin's imposed order. The political officer, his Periblue-enhanced orange skin stark against the deep greens, gestured impatiently at the dense foliage, his voice sharp and insistent. "Clear this. All of it. Back to the tree line." He swept his arm wide, encompassing a swathe of vibrant vegetation that pulsed with unseen life. "I want open space. Sunlight. Room to breathe, and room to build."

Maksim stood beside him, the humid air clinging to his uniform like a damp cloth. He could hear the jungle itself — a symphony of chirps, rustles, and unseen movements, a chorus of life about to be disrupted. Beside them, Sublieutenant Popescu barked orders at a squad of **Vanquisher** crew, armed with crude machetes and powered brush cutters scavenged from the shuttle's stores. The whine of the cutters sliced through the morning air, a harsh, discordant note in the jungle's natural music.

A small group of villagers stood at the edge of the village square, their faces etched with concern. One of the older men, his face deeply lined and weathered like ancient bark, stepped forward, his voice low but clear. "Comrade *Глава*," he began, addressing Golovin with forced deference, "with respect, this jungle, it is not cleared quickly. Not without care."

Golovin rounded on him, his Periblue-enhanced eyes unnervingly bright. "Care? We need space, old man, not lectures. Clear it. Burn it. Make it *civilized*."

Another villager, a woman with *тревога* etched in her eyes, added her hesitant voice. "The plants, they have sap. Aromas. They can make people sick. Burning them releases toxins."

Golovin laughed, a harsh, dismissive sound that echoed in the humid air. "Toxins? Superstition! Krasnaya citizens are not swayed by

25

primitive fears. Get to work. All of you." He gestured dismissively at both the crew and the villagers. "Clearing begins now."

The **Vanquisher** crew, under Popescu's direction, plunged into the jungle, hacking and sawing at the dense undergrowth. The initial sounds of the jungle clearing were energetic at first: the rhythmic chop of machetes, the high-pitched whine of plasma cutters, the crashing fall of smaller trees. The air filled with the green, sappy scent of fresh-cut vegetation, a smell almost invigorating, but soon becoming cloying and oppressive. Mixed with it was the rising, acrid tang of smoke as piles of brush were ignited, the flames leaping like dancers, consuming the verdant life.

As hours passed, the initial energy waned. Maksim observed his crew with growing concern from the edge of the clearing. Their movements were becoming sluggish, their faces pale beneath the grime and sweat. He saw Ensign Petrov stumble, his hand flying to his head, muttering about "shadows flicking at the edge of his vision." Corporal Volkov, a picture of stoic efficiency before, swayed on his feet, his muscles twitching in his arms and legs as he struggled to wield his machete. Whispers of "fatigue," "dizziness," and "strange visions" circulated among the weary workers.

Golovin remained oblivious, willfully ignorant of the changes and risks. He paced along the cleared perimeter, his Periblue-enhanced stamina inexhaustible, his voice booming with relentless demands for faster progress. "Faster! Move faster! Are you Krasnaya citizens, or pampered Sol League layabouts?!"

Then, Golovin, in a grotesque display of "leadership from the front," grabbed a discarded cutter from a faltering crew member. He waded deeper into the jungle, hacking at the thick vines with manic energy, his breath coming in ragged gasps, his orange skin glistening with sweat, attracting biting insects that buzzed angrily around him. Maksim watched, a cold dread settling in his stomach. This recklessness; it was beyond foolishness; it verged on self-destruction.

Hours later, as the afternoon sun began to dip below the horizon, painting the smoke-filled sky in hues of bruised purple and angry orange, a frantic call crackled over Maksim's comm unit. It was

Sublieutenant Popescu, his voice tight with urgency. "Captain! Comrade Political Officer, he's gone! We can't find him! He was working deeper in the jungle, and now…"

Maksim's heart plummeted. He swore under his breath. "Organize search parties, Sublieutenant. Now! Marines first, then able-bodied crew. Searchlight teams. And, and send for Chaka. Now." He barked orders, his voice sharp with command, masking the icy dread that gripped him. He knew, with a chilling certainty, what they would find.

It took almost two hours of frantic searching, the jungle echoing with shouted calls and the harsh glare of searchlights cutting through the deepening twilight. It was Corporal Volkov who stumbled upon him, deep within the unyielding vegetation, a mile from the clearing perimeter. Golovin was collapsed at the base of a giant tree, his brush cutter lying tangled in vines beside him. He was unconscious, his face ashen beneath the unnatural orange hue, his breathing shallow and ragged.

They carried him back to Pristan on a makeshift stretcher, his limp form a stark testament to his hubris. Chaka examined him in the infirmary, her expression grim. "The toxins, they have overwhelmed him. His system is reacting violently."

Maksim stood beside Golovin's cot, watching the political officer's feverish, restless sleep, the jerky twitches that spasmed through his limbs. The air in the infirmary, despite Chaka's efforts, still carried the faint, sickly sweet aroma of the jungle's distress, a scent of warning ignored. He met Chaka's gaze across the cot. Her eyes held a mixture of weariness and something akin to pity.

"He was warned," she said, her voice a whisper.

Maksim nodded, his own weariness bone-deep. "He never listens." He looked down at Golovin's unconscious figure again, a complex swirl of emotions within him: frustration, anger, a flicker of something almost like… pity, quickly suppressed. He sighed, turning away. The jungle clearing had become yet another disaster born of Golovin's arrogance. The occupation of Samarqand was spiraling into chaos.

✧ ¤ ✧ ¤ ✧

Chaka bin Decaro stood in her small, cluttered clinic, her hands deftly organizing herbs and tinctures. The smell of medicinal plants filled the air, a calming balm to the chaos outside. The door swung open with a crash and Golovin strode in, his skin a strange hue of orange from the Periblue flowers' extract. His bloodshot eyes locked onto Chaka.

"Speak," he demanded, his voice a harsh rasp. "Tell me about these plants, drugs, whatever witchcraft you practice. Especially about this synbergris. What is it?"

Chaka regarded him with calm aplomb, though inwardly she recoiled. "Synbergris is a complex biochemical compound produced by the Mesenga Strangler vine, in conjunction with the Elven Parasol tree. It's highly potent, both as a psychoactive and a mild aphrodisiac. But it's also very addictive and can cause wild mood swings in certain individuals."

Golovin's eyes narrowed. "And where can I find this synbergris?"

Chaka hesitated. "It is not easily harvested. The process is slow, and the vine is rare. Production takes years."

"Enough with your scientific mumbo-jumbo," Golovin snapped impatiently. "What about something else to increase stamina and focus? Something that doesn't change the color of my skin. I need to be at my peak, not bedridden like a weakling."

Chaka nodded. "There is a preparation I can make from a small herb. It increases stamina and focus but comes with significant risk. The side effects can be unpredictable, affecting nerves and thinking.

Golovin waved her off. "Do it. I don't care about side effects. I need results."

Chaka sent a young girl to gather the necessary plants and began her preparations, her movements precise and deliberate. She couldn't suppress a shiver of dread as she completed the concoction. Handing the drink to Golovin, she watched as he swallowed it in one gulp, grimacing at the bitter taste.

Almost immediately, his posture straightened, his gaze sharpening. "Excellent," he hissed. But within minutes, his skin took on an even

28

deeper orange hue. He looked at his hands, his eyes widening in disbelief. "What is this?" he roared.

"You asked for increased stamina and focus," Chaka replied evenly. "You did not inquire about the side effects in detail."

Golovin's face contorted with rage, but he knew there was no turning back. "Next time," he growled, "you will disclose everything. Otherwise, there will be consequences."

Chaka nodded, her heart pounding. "Of course, Comrade Golovin. I understand."

He released her with a curt nod, and she slipped out of the clinic, her mind racing. The political officer's desperation was palpable, as was his growing instability. Chaka knew she had to tread with care, for her sake and for the safety of her people. As she made her way back to the village square, she offered a silent prayer for guidance and strength.

Defiance

The darkness in Pristan' Zorya had become a shroud, thick and suffocating. It wasn't just the absence of light; it was the absence of hope, a palpable dread that clung to the humid night air. Maksim stood near the gallows, a stark silhouette against the faint starlight filtering through the jungle canopy. He listened. The usual night sounds of Samarqand — the chirping insects, the distant calls of nocturnal creatures — were overlaid with a new, unsettling quiet. The quiet of fear. And, more recently, the quiet of departure.

Whispers had reached him through Simen, who maintained discreet channels with some of the less fanatical **Vanquisher** crew. People were slipping away under the cover of darkness. Mostly men. Often, men who owned hunting rifles or makeshift weapons. They were melting back into the jungle that Golovin sought to tame, seeking refuge, perhaps seeking allies. Defiance, silent but potent, was taking root.

Golovin, predictably, reacted with brute force. His voice, amplified and distorted by the village loudspeakers the next morning, carried a new, chilling edict. "Let it be known! Any man abandoning his duties in Pristan' Zorya will be declared a traitor! His family remaining here will face the consequences! Their lives are forfeit if the deserter does not return! There is nowhere to hide from Krasnaya justice!"

The threat hung heavy in the air, a poison seeping into the already fractured community. To enforce it, Golovin ordered Sublieutenant Popescu and a team of Marines, accompanied by reluctant administrative techs, to conduct a full census. Every man, woman, and child was to be counted, registered. Daily headcounts of adult males were instituted. Pristan' Zorya was becoming an open-air prison, its invisible walls built of fear and intimidation.

Maksim was conferring with Simen near the makeshift command post later that day, discussing dwindling ration supplies, when a sharp *crack* echoed through the village, followed by the high-pitched whine of a projectile ricocheting off the metal roof above Golovin's office doorway. Golovin himself stumbled out, his orange face contorted in fury, clutching his shoulder where a sliver of metal had grazed him.

"SNIPER!" Popescu roared, Marines scrambling for cover, weapons raised, scanning the jungle edge.

Golovin, however, didn't seek cover. He stood exposed, trembling with rage. His eyes, wild and bloodshot from the Periblue concoction, scanned the terrified faces of the villagers who had frozen nearby. His gaze landed on Chaka, the healer, who was tending to a child's scraped knee near her clinic.

"SEIZE HER!" Golovin screamed, pointing a shaking finger. "That witch! She conspires against me! Lock her in the cage! She'll stand trial for treason!"

Marines dragged the bewildered Chaka away, ignoring her protests. Maksim stepped forward, his voice tight with controlled anger. "Comrade Political Officer, this is irrational! Chaka had nothing to do with this! And," he added, forcing a pragmatic tone, "jailing the only skilled healer in the village is tactically foolish. Injuries, illnesses... the jungle is dangerous. We *need* her."

Golovin whirled on him. "Need her? We need loyalty, Captain! Compliance! Fear! She'll serve as an example!"

Before Maksim could argue further, Popescu approached, his face grim. "Comrade Глава, the morning headcount... two men missing. From the Borzhakov and Kubaska families."

Golovin's face purpled beneath the orange tinge. "Find their families! Bring them to the square! Now! They will pay the price for this treachery!"

As Marines roughly rounded up the terrified women and children, Simen stepped beside Maksim, his voice low but firm enough for Golovin to overhear. "Comrade Political Officer, subsistence living requires hunting. They are likely gathering food, nothing more. Give them time to return."

Golovin hesitated, his drug-addled mind struggling. He glared at the weeping families, then back at Simen. "Five days," he spat. "If those men are not back in five days, I will carry out the sentence myself.

31

Ensure they understand." He stormed back into his office, leaving Maksim and Simen standing amidst the quiet despair of the threatened families. The defiance had begun, but the cost, Maksim feared, would be unbearably high.

Captain Clement Hoffmann entered the **Covenant**'s bridge, the familiar scent of recycled air and brewed coffee greeting him. He found Executive Officer Astrid Cantara and Comms Tech Bryani Sacarello huddled over the main communications console, their faces illuminated by the soft glow of the holographic displays. Despite the lines of fatigue etched around their eyes, their expressions held a spark of triumphant excitement.

"Captain," Cantara began, straightening up, "Bryani has made significant progress overnight."

Sacarello, a young woman with bright, intelligent eyes, turned to Hoffmann, a weary but proud smile touching her lips. "Sir, we've managed to decrypt more of those fragmented transmissions. They weren't just random distress calls. They were targeted, coded attempts to establish contact."

Hoffmann leaned closer, his interest piqued. "And? Did they succeed?"

"Affirmative, Captain," Sacarello confirmed, tapping commands into her console. "The signals originate from a smaller settlement nearby, Kifaru Rotko. 'Kifaru' they call it. Apparently, they still have a functional long-range communicator salvaged from before the Collapse. They've formed a resistance movement, led by —" she checked her notes, "Kaliq Leot Borzhakov."

Hoffmann frowned. "Borzhakov? Any relation to the murdered governor?"

Cantara nodded, her lips a grim slash. "Her son, Captain. He's requesting direct communication with the commander of the Heimsee vessel."

A wave of conflicting emotions washed over Hoffmann: satisfaction at the breakthrough, grim determination, and a heavy sense of responsibility. "Establish contact, Bryani. Standard Heimsee protocols, secure channel if possible."

"Working on it, sir. Their equipment is old. Matching protocols is proving tricky." Bryani's fingers flew across the console. It took another hour, a frustrating delay as the **Covenant** orbited away from the optimal transmission window over Kifaru. Hoffmann paced the bridge, maintaining a calm exterior for his crew, but internally chafing at the enforced wait. Night had fallen over Samarqand again by the time Bryani announced, "Channel established, Captain! Connection is noisy, unstable, but it's holding."

Hoffmann settled into the command chair, taking a deep breath. "On screen. Audio only for now." He spoke with intensity into the pickup. "Kaliq Borzhakov, this is Captain Clement Hoffmann of the Bad Alpenheimsee Naval Survey ship **Covenant**. We are receiving your transmissions. Please confirm your situation."

A voice crackled back, distorted by static but filled with urgency. *"Captain Hoffmann... thank the stars! Yes... it is Kaliq Borzhakov. The Krasnayans... they control Eastport – Pristan' Zorya, they call it now. They are... brutal. They murdered my mother... Governor Bebe... executed her in the square..."* The voice broke with grief and rage.

Hoffmann felt a pang of sympathy. "Mr. Borzhakov, on behalf of the **Covenant** and Heimsee, I extend my deepest condolences for your loss. Your mother's death is an outrage. How can we assist you?"

"Captain, we need..." The signal dissolved into a burst of static as the **Covenant** slipped below Kifaru's horizon.

"Connection lost, sir," Bryani reported.

Another agonizing wait — 107 minutes until the next orbital pass. When the connection was re-established, Kaliq's voice was clearer, more determined. *"Captain Hoffmann, we are gathering fighters from Kifaru and other villages. We intend to retake Pristan. To drive the Krasnayans out. But we lack resources. We need weapons, medical supplies, equipment... anything you can spare."*

Hoffmann considered the desperate plea. His orders were clear: observation, avoid interference. Direct military aid was strictly forbidden. Yet… "Mr. Borzhakov, I understand your request. Give me one orbit to confer with my officers. We will have an answer for you on our next pass." He cut the connection.

"Astrid," Hoffmann said, turning to his XO. "Call Sergeant Figueredo. My ready room. Now."

Minutes later, the three officers stood around the small table in Hoffmann's private quarters. Sergeant Alfons Ikaia Figueredo, the **Covenant**'s Marine detachment commander, listened, his expression unreadable.

"First," Hoffmann began, looking directly at Cantara, "commendations are in order. For yourself and Ensign Sacarello. Outstanding work establishing that link under difficult circumstances."

Cantara flushed. "Thank you, Captain. Bryani deserves the lion's share of the credit. She cracked the encryption. I'll write hers."

"Noted," Hoffmann smiled. He'd write Cantara's commendation himself later. "Now, the critical issue. Assisting the Samarqand resistance." He outlined Kaliq's request.

Figueredo frowned. "Sir, we have limited surplus weaponry. Standard sidearms, some pulse rifles… enough for maybe a dozen fighters. Delivering them covertly would be extremely high-risk."

"And politically disastrous if discovered," Cantara added. "Rules of Engagement strictly prohibit direct intervention or supplying arms to non-aligned forces without explicit authorization from High Command."

Hoffmann leaned forward, his voice low. "Which brings me to my question, Astrid. Are there *any* exceptions? Any legal precedents, emergency clauses, interpretations of interstellar law that might give us latitude? A lost colony facing hostile takeover by a non-League power. Surely there's something?"

Cantara met his gaze, understanding dawning in her eyes. "I can search the legal databases, Captain. Look for loopholes related to

34

humanitarian crises, protection of pre-Collapse populations, unsanctioned military actions by aggressor states…"

"Do it," Hoffmann ordered. "Find me something, Astrid. Anything. Because if you can't… I may be about to authorize actions that could end all our careers." The weight of command settled on him, pressing his shoulders down. He sailed into uncharted waters with his desire to help, guided only by his conscience and the desperate pleas from the world below.

The jungle pressed close, a wall of vibrant, suffocating green. Xevera Coffi, barely sixteen summers old, pushed a damp strand of dark hair from her forehead, her fingers sticky with the sap of the broad leaves she'd been gathering. Beside her, Sidonie, younger by a year, giggled, pointing at a brightly colored beetle crawling up a thick vine.

"Stay close, you two!" The harsh voice belonged to Artem Bondar, the young Krasnaya Marine assigned to escort them. He stood as straight as a ramrod, his pulse rifle held at the ready, his eyes scanning the dense undergrowth with a nervousness that seemed comical to the girls who had known this jungle their entire lives. He looked out of place in his drab uniform, sweating in the humid air, swatting in irritation at buzzing insects. His helmet hung at his belt, removed to allow him to breathe in the gelatinous air.

"It's just a gathering place, Marine," Sidonie said cheekily. "Periblue Flowers like the shade near the creek." They moved deeper into the foliage, their bare feet making little sound on the damp earth, easily finding the clusters of vivid blue blossoms Chaka needed.

Artem grumbled, crashing through the brush behind them, his movements loud and clumsy. "Just get the plants and let's go. This place gives me the creeps." He swore in Russian under his breath, then remembered he was watching over children.

Without warning, a distinct rustling sound came from a thicket of ferns just ahead. Artem tensed, swinging his rifle towards the noise. "What was that?"

35

Xevera glanced at Sidonie, a shared, knowing look passing between them. "Striped lizard, maybe," Xevera said, dismissing his concern. "Big ones, but harmless. Sleepy in the heat."

Artem wasn't convinced. His face pale beneath his tan, he gestured with a sharp wave. "Stay here. Don't move." He crept forward, rifle raised, peering into the ferns.

Xevera held her breath. She saw a flicker of movement within the green depths, darker than a lizard. Then, Artem gave a choked cry of surprise. Xevera saw a shape emerge — Kaong Kubaska, his face grim, his eyes hard. Kaong's son was one of the men who had disappeared into the jungle days earlier. Before Artem could bring his rifle to bear, Kaong lunged, swinging a heavy, knotted club. The sickening thud echoed in the sudden silence. Artem crumpled to the ground, his rifle clattering beside him.

Xevera gasped, her hand flying to her mouth. Sidonie whimpered, pressing close to her. Kaong knelt beside the stunned Marine. He drew a long, wickedly sharpened stick, fire-hardened wood, from his belt. "For Bebe." With brutal efficiency that made Xevera's stomach clench, Kaong drove the point under the edge of Artem's chest armor, angling it sharply upwards. Artem's body convulsed once, then lay still.

Kaong rose, wiping his hands on the Marine's armored trousers. He looked at the two terrified girls, his expression unreadable. "He fell," Kaong said, his voice low and rough. "He was clumsy. Not smart in the jungle. The stick, it pierced him when he fell." He gestured towards the path back to Pristan. "Go. Tell the Глава what happened. Tell him Artem Bondar was careless." He met Xevera's eyes, his gaze intense. "Say nothing else."

Xevera gave a tense nod. Kaong glanced longingly at the soldier's rifle. He knew he must leave it or the 'accident' story would die.

As quickly as he had appeared, Kaong Kubaska melted back into the jungle, leaving Xevera and Sidonie alone with the dead Marine and the heavy, suffocating silence of the forest. Trembling, clutching their baskets of gathered plants, the two girls fled back towards Pristan' Zorya.

✧ ☐ ✧ ☐ ✧

Golovin's roar of fury echoed across the village square, startling roosting birds from the eaves of the buildings. His face, still tinged an unhealthy orange, was contorted with rage, veins standing out on his temples. "Dead? One of my Marines? Dead? How?"

Sublieutenant Popescu stood stiffly before him, flanked by two grim-faced Marines carrying the makeshift stretcher bearing Artem Bondar's body. Xevera and Sidonie huddled nearby, guarded by another Marine, both girls pale and trembling, avoiding Golovin's terrifying gaze.

"The girls report he fell, Comrade *Глава*," Popescu stated with formal precision. "An accident. Impaled on a sharpened branch."

"Accident?" Golovin shrieked, his voice cracking. He stalked towards the trembling girls, his fists clenched. "Lies! They did this! These treacherous village scum! They lured him into a trap!" He raised a hand as if to strike Xevera.

Maksim stepped between Golovin and the girls, positioning himself as a protective wall. "Comrade Political Officer," Maksim said, his voice low but firm, cutting through Golovin's tirade. "Look at them. They are children. Scared children. Accusing them of killing a trained Marine is… illogical." He deliberately avoided using the word 'stupid,' though it screamed in his mind. Golovin's drug-fueled paranoia was making him dangerously irrational. The lingering orange tint to his skin fueled his embarrassment and anger.

Simen Agdestein moved to stand beside Maksim, adding his silent presence to the buffer between Golovin and the girls. "Let us examine the body, Comrade," Simen suggested in an even, calm voice.

Golovin glared, but reluctantly gestured towards the stretcher. Maksim, Simen, and Golovin leaned over the body. Artem Bondar lay still, his eyes wide and unseeing. Protruding from beneath his chest plate, angled sharply upwards, was a crude, wooden limb. Maksim exchanged a quick, meaningful glance with Simen.

"As the girls reported, Comrade," Maksim said carefully. "A tragic accident. He must have stumbled while investigating something, falling

37

onto this dead wood hidden in the undergrowth. A terrible misfortune, but plausible. He lacked jungle experience."

Simen nodded. "Indeed. The angle is consistent with a fall. A cruel trick of fate."

"It *must* be murder!" Golovin screamed.

"Then why was he found with all his gear and weapons?" Simen said. "Surely a local murderer would have taken something."

Golovin stared at the wound, then at the girls, then back at the body. His breathing came in ragged gulps. He clearly *wanted* it to be murder, wanted someone to punish, but even in his drug-addled state, the 'accident' narrative offered a way to save face, to avoid admitting his forces were vulnerable. Finally, grudgingly, he nodded. "Yes… an accident. A heroic sacrifice nonetheless!" He straightened up, puffing out his chest, his tone shifting without warning to grandiose pronouncement.

"Marine Artem Bondar!" Golovin declared at full volume, addressing the assembled villagers and crew who had gathered in nervous anticipation. "The first hero of Pristan' Zorya! The first to give his life on Samarqand for the glory of Mother Krasnaya! His sacrifice will not be forgotten! He died securing this world for the righteous!" He seemed to swell with importance, basking in the melodrama. "Sublieutenant Popescu! Bury him with full honors! Beyond the village perimeter! Let his grave serve as a reminder of our noble cause!"

As the Marine detachment carried Artem's body away, Maksim watched Golovin. The political officer's initial fury seemed to be fading, replaced by a restless agitation. The Periblue high was wearing off. Golovin rubbed his temples, his gaze darting around nervously. He spotted Chaka, recently released from the cage after Maksim's persistent and pragmatic arguments about needing her skills, standing near her clinic.

Golovin strode towards her. "Healer! Prepare another dose. Now."

Chaka recoiled slightly. "Comrade *Глава*, I advised against frequent use. The preparation… it affects the mind. Continued use can lead to… instability. Madness, in some."

38

Golovin laughed, a harsh, grating sound. "Madness? I am too strong for such weakness! Krasnaya steel runs in my veins! Prepare it!" He snatched the cup Chaka reluctantly offered and downed the bitter liquid in one gulp, his eyes already gleaming with renewed, unnatural intensity. Maksim watched him, a cold knot forming in his stomach. Golovin wasn't merely unstable; he was actively poisoning himself, dragging them all closer to the precipice.

Exposure

Captain Clement Hoffmann stood before the main holographic display on the **Covenant**'s bridge, the swirling blue-green marble of Samarqand dominating the view. The ship felt unnaturally quiet, the usual hum of activity subdued by the weight of their recent discovery and the decision that now loomed before them. Astrid Cantara stood beside him, fatigue evident in the slight shadows beneath her eyes, but her posture radiated a focused intensity.

"I've completed the legal review, Captain," Cantara reported, her voice low but clear. She gestured towards a data slate she held. "As expected, the standard Rules of Engagement offer no justification for direct intervention. However, I found two potential precedents that might offer… *interpretive* latitude."

Hoffmann turned from the mesmerizing view of the planet, focusing on his Executive Officer. "Interpretive latitude. I see. Go on, Astrid."

"The first involves invoking the 'Unforeseen Humanitarian Crisis' clause, citing the potential for genocide or mass enslavement of a pre-Collapse population. It's flimsy, Captain. Open to significant legal challenge, relies heavily on assumptions we can't fully verify from orbit."

Hoffmann nodded. Flimsy wasn't good enough when careers and lives were on the line. "And the second option?"

A faint, almost imperceptible smile touched Cantara's lips. "The second hinges on self-defense and the established principle of responding to unprovoked attack. It helps immensely, Captain, that the Krasnayans were foolish enough to fire upon us without provocation during our initial approach." She paused, adding, "I took the liberty of directing Ensign Sacarello to archive all sensor logs and bridge recordings from that encounter. Triple redundancy, locked down under my command codes."

Hoffmann felt a surge of gratitude for his XO's foresight. "Excellent, Astrid. Continue."

"The precedent," Cantara explained, calling up a historical file on her slate, "dates back nearly a century before the Great Collapse, during Bad Alpenheimsee's early colonial period. Two warships from Roma Secundus, the cruiser **Ursa** and destroyer **Strike**, arrived in orbit and demanded Heimsee's immediate surrender. Our fledgling fleet, just three ships, had strict ROEs against direct engagement without authorization. However, the **Ursa** fired upon the Heimsee destroyer **Volpe**, led by Commander Gustav Fischer."

Hoffmann leaned in, captivated.

"Fischer," Cantara continued, her voice resonating with the historical weight of the event, "without authorization, engaged both Roma vessels. He disabled the **Ursa**, damaged it beyond repair. But the **Volpe** took heavy damage in the exchange, losing most maneuvering control. As the Roma destroyer **Strike** moved in for the kill, Fischer rammed it. Total loss of both ships." Cantara looked up from the slate, meeting Hoffmann's gaze, unblinking. "Commander Fischer was posthumously cleared of all charges. His actions were deemed justified self-defense in the face of unprovoked aggression, upholding Heimsee sovereignty."

The 'Fischer Precedent'. Hoffmann let the name settle. Self-defense. Response to aggression. It was thin, perhaps, applying it to aiding a third party, but it was *something*. A shield, however precarious, against the inevitable court-martial. A wry smile touched his lips. "Let's hope achieving absolution doesn't require ramming the **Vanquisher**, Astrid."

He straightened, his decision made. The weight on his shoulders didn't lessen, but it shifted, solidifying into resolve. "Sergeant Figueredo," he said over the bridge comm, "prepare your Marines. Full combat loadout. Deployment imminent."

"Aye, Captain," Figueredo's calm voice responded instantly.

"Executive Office Astrid Cantara, from this point forward, all our actions are to be recorded and securely archived under heading 'Fischer Precedent' pending official review and possible courts-martial at Bad

Alpenheimsee. Authorization Enfield-Lamed-Six-Four. Do you understand?"

Cantara stared, then nodded. "Received and understood." She turned to face Comms. "Sacarello, enable continuous recording and double archiving of all sensors, cameras and microphones on **Covenant** from this point forward, including the previous ten minutes, until the Captain orders otherwise. Authorization Camden-Alpha-Niner-Seven." She watched as Sacarello completed her task.

"Recording and archiving complete, Commander," Sacarello said, leaning back in her chair.

Hoffmann turned to the navigation console where Ensign Lazar Woelke sat, alert and waiting. "Ensign Woelke, adjust our orbit. Bring us low, ahead of our current position. I want a sensor lock on the **Vanquisher** just as it crests the horizon."

"Aye, Captain. Adjusting orbit." The **Covenant** responded with its usual smooth motions, altering trajectory. Minutes later, the angular, slightly menacing silhouette of the Krasnaya vessel appeared on the tactical display.

"Hold position," Hoffmann ordered. "Astrid, sensor sweep. Life signs aboard the **Vanquisher**?"

Cantara anticipated the command, her fingers already flying across her console. "Scanning. Minimal life signs detected, Captain. Estimate two individuals. Possibly a skeleton bridge crew."

Two. Just two. Hoffmann nodded slowly, a crucial piece of information clicking into place. "Thank you, Astrid. Ensign Woelke, resume previous orbit. Return us to stealth position behind Samarqand."

As the **Vanquisher** slipped back below the horizon and the **Covenant** melted into orbital obscurity, Cantara turned to him, a question in her eyes. "Captain? Why confirm the crew count?"

Hoffmann met her gaze, his expression grim but resolute. "Because, Number One," he said, his voice low but carrying across the silent bridge, "I needed to be certain there weren't enough hands aboard her to effectively engage us."

A collective intake of breath rippled through the bridge crew. Cantara looked startled. "Sir, you intend to engage the **Vanquisher**?"

"No, Astrid," Hoffmann clarified, shaking his head. "I have no intention of firing the first shot this time. But I *will not* have them shooting us in the back while we attempt to land Marines and supplies on Samarqand. Knowing they're undermanned gives us a crucial tactical advantage during the descent."

Understanding dawned on Cantara's face, mirrored by easing tension in the postures of the bridge crew. It wasn't an attack order, but a calculated risk assessment. Hoffmann gripped the cool metal armrest of his command chair, grounding himself. The choice was made. The **Covenant** was committed. Support for the Resistance was on its way.

Sleep offered little respite in Pristan' Zorya. Maksim drifted through a shallow, uneasy doze, his senses perpetually on edge. The faint click of the latch on his quarters' outer door jolted him awake, adrenaline surging through his veins. He remained motionless, forcing his breathing into a slow, even rhythm, feigning sleep while his mind raced. *Golovin? Has he finally sent someone? An assassin in the night?* He cracked his eyelids just enough to see through the gloom filtering from the corridor.

A figure slipped into the outer room, making no sound, small and indistinct in the shadows. Not a Marine. Not one of the crew. A local. The figure moved with a quiet deliberation that spoke of familiarity with stealth, pausing just outside the doorway to Maksim's sleeping chamber. Maksim waited, his muscles tensed, ready to react.

A low whisper broke the silence, barely audible above the thrumming of his own pulse. "Captain Bernatski?" The voice was rough, aged. "I know you are awake. Your breathing gives you away."

Maksim pushed himself up, swinging his legs over the side of the cot. He peered into the darkness, trying to make out the intruder's features. "Who are you? What do you want?"

43

"No lights, please," the figure whispered back, stepping into the doorway. Maksim could now discern a short, wiry man, dressed in rough, homespun clothing. His face remained obscured by shadow, but Maksim saw the glint of watchful eyes and, clutched tightly in one hand, a short, heavy club. "The children call me Kong. My given name is Kaong Kubaska."

Maksim's gaze fixed on the club. "Why come armed into my quarters?"

Kong shifted slightly. "Needed it. For the guard outside your door."

A cold knot formed in Maksim's stomach. "Is he…?"

"No," Kong interrupted. "Just sleeping. Unlike the soldier I met in the jungle." The admission hung in the air, heavy and chilling. "I killed him. I know my life is forfeit if your *Глава* catches me. But," he added, a note of fatalistic resignation in his voice, "it is forfeit soon anyway. Chaka says the jungle sickness gives me a few months left on my path."

Maksim processed this grim confession. The dead Marine, Artem Bondar. This man, Kong, was the killer. Yet he stood here, risking everything. "Why are you here, Kong?"

"A message," Kong replied. "From Kaliq Borzhakov. Son of the governor your *Глава* murdered." The name resonated with Maksim: the resistance leader Hoffmann had contacted. "Kaliq builds an army in the bush. Men gather. He wants vengeance, yes. But more, they want Samarqand free. You Krasnayans, you brutes." Kong paused to take a breath, then spat on the floor. "You must be driven out. Or killed."

Maksim remained silent for a long moment, choosing his words carefully. "Not all of us are brutes, Kong. Some of us disagree with Golovin's methods." He paused, letting the implication hang in the air. "I bide my time. Waiting for an opportunity."

A barely perceptible nod from the shadowy figure. "I was told you might be different. That you could be a man of conscience trapped in a bad uniform."

"Is that all of your message?" Maksim asked, his heart pounding with a mixture of fear and burgeoning hope.

"No." Kong stepped a fraction closer, his whisper intense. "Be ready, Captain. If you truly seek an opening, Kaliq and his fighters will make one for you. Soon."

Before Maksim could respond, the outer door to his quarters burst inward with explosive force, crashing off its hinges. Harsh beams from tactical lights flooded the room, blinding him. Chaos erupted. Two burly Marines lunged, seizing Kong, slamming him roughly against the wall.

Vladimir Golovin strolled into the room, his orange-tinged face alight with triumphant malice. He surveyed the scene: Maksim sitting on his cot, the captured local pinned against the wall. "Well, well, Captain Bernatski. Entertaining visitors in the dead of night? A secret rendezvous with the Resistance, perhaps?"

One of the Marines twisted Kong's arm behind his back, forcing a pained grunt from the villager. "Is that true, old man?" Golovin purred. "Were you delivering messages to this traitor captain?"

Kong spat towards Golovin, his eyes blazing defiance despite the pain. "NO! I came to kill him! To kill you all! Death to Krasnaya invaders!"

Golovin signaled the Marine with a flick of his wrist. The Marine applied pitiless pressure. A horrific, sickening *snap* echoed through the small room, followed by Kong's raw, agonized scream. Maksim flinched, bile rising in his throat. He clamped his jaw shut, fighting the urge to cry out, to intervene, knowing it would be suicide.

When Kong's screams subsided into ragged gasps, Golovin leaned closer. "Now, tell me again. Were you conspiring with our beloved Captain?"

Kong, cradling his shattered arm, his face pale and beaded with sweat, lifted his head and met Golovin's gaze. "I came to kill you," he choked out, his voice thick with pain but unwavering in its hatred. Then he spat, the glob hanging off of Golovin's chin.

Golovin stared at Kong for a long moment, then wiped the mess away. He waved dismissively at the Marines. "Take him to the cage. He might be more cooperative later." The Marines dragged the injured, semi-conscious Kong away.

"Do we bring the healer?"

"No. Patching up a dead man is such a waste."

Golovin turned back to Maksim, his eyes narrowed, scrutinizing. "You seemed remarkably calm, Captain, for a man facing a potential assassin in his own quarters."

Maksim could only stare back, the image of Kong's arm breaking, the sound of his scream, replaying in his mind. The brutality, the casual cruelty left him speechless, numb with horror.

Golovin frowned at Maksim's silence. "You didn't call for help. Why?" The question hung in the air, heavy with suspicion. Without waiting for an answer Maksim couldn't give, Golovin turned and left, leaving Maksim alone in the harsh glare of the lights, the silence broken only by the frantic pounding of his own heart and the lingering echo of Kong's pain. He was exposed. Golovin suspected him. And for Golovin, from suspicion to certainty was a small leap. The time for biding was running out.

The **Covenant** bucked and groaned, fighting its way through Samarqand's turbulent atmosphere. Rain lashed against the hull, driven by winds that howled like banshees. On the main screen, sensor overlays depicted swirling storm cells, angry red and yellow vortices engulfing their projected landing zone near Kifaru Rotko. Hoffmann gripped the arms of his command chair, his knuckles white, feeling every shudder, every jarring drop as the ship plunged through the tempest. This was controlled chaos, a high-stakes gamble using the storm as cover.

"Altitude five thousand meters," Ensign Woelke reported from Navigation, his voice tight but steady. "Severe wind shear detected, port side."

"Compensate, Ensign," Cantara ordered from the XO station, her eyes scanning the readouts. "Maintain descent profile."

Impact alarms blared sporadically, false positives triggered by extreme turbulence or hail striking the ship. Each shrill warning sent a jolt of involuntary adrenaline through Hoffmann despite his practiced calm. They were committed now, descending into the unknown, shielded only by the fury of the storm and the hope that the **Vanquisher**, undermanned and likely focused on Pristan, wouldn't detect their plunge.

The violent shaking eased as they dove into a pocket of smooth air. The roar of the wind lessened. They broke through the storm front into a pocket of eerily smooth air, the ground rushing up to meet them, visible now through the rain-streaked side port — a rough, uneven clearing hacked in haste from the jungle's edge.

"Altitude five hundred meters," Woelke called out. "Landing sequence initiated."

Hoffmann met Cantara's gaze across the bridge. He saw the tension, the shared understanding of the irrevocable step they were taking. "Last chance, Number One," he said quietly, his voice barely audible above the hum of the descending ship. "We can still abort. Punch back through the storm, return to orbit. Avoid a court, the legal quagmire."

Astrid Cantara looked back at him, not with hesitation, but with a fierce, steady resolve shining in her eyes. A small smile touched her lips. "Sir, these people have been invaded. Their leader murdered. We were fired upon without provocation. Standing by is not an option. We act."

Hoffmann nodded, a surge of pride and relief washing over him. He had the best XO in the fleet, by damn. "As you were, Number One. Get us down in one piece, please."

The landing was textbook, Cantara orchestrating the final moments like a symphony conductor, easing the **Covenant** onto the soggy ground without a perceptible jolt. The engines whined down silence.

"Power down complete. All systems nominal," Engines reported.

Hoffmann unstrapped himself the moment the confirmation came. "Astrid, you have the bridge. Maintain Level Two readiness. Sensor sweeps active." He moved quickly, almost running, towards the aft loading bay.

He found Sergeant Figueredo waiting, clad in sleek, dark green battle armor that seemed impervious to the chaos outside. Figueredo stood relaxed amidst his short squad of four Marines, who snapped rigidly to attention as Hoffmann entered the bay.

"As you were." Hoffmann waved them off. He pulled on a clear plastic slicker handed to him by a crewman, flipping the hood up against the deluge he could hear pounding on the hull. "Sergeant, are we ready?"

"Ready on your command, sir," Figueredo replied, his voice calm and resonant within his helmet.

"Then let's go meet our hosts." Hoffmann nodded.

Figueredo hit the ramp control. It lowered with a hydraulic hiss, revealing a dark world awash in driving rain and swirling mist. The air that rushed in brought the smell of wet earth, ozone, and the heavy perfume of the alien jungle. Hoffmann stepped onto the ramp, Figueredo and his Marines fanning out as their training required, weapons held ready, scanning the perimeter.

Figures emerged from the tree line, indistinct shapes in the downpour. One stepped forward — a young man, drenched but standing tall, his face set with grim determination. Kaliq Borzhakov. Hoffmann strode confidently across the muddy clearing, extending a hand.

"Mr. Borzhakov, I presume? Captain Hoffmann."

Kaliq gripped his hand with a firm shake. "Captain. Thank you for coming. Your timing. The *гроза* is good cover." He gestured towards a makeshift shelter beneath a heavy tarp strung between several large trees. "This way, out of the worst of it."

Under the relative dryness of the tarp, Hoffmann found himself face-to-face with Kaliq and two other men, their expressions a mixture of hope and desperation. The Marines maintained a protective perimeter, their helmeted faces showing only reflections.

"Your people contacted us," Kaliq began, his voice urgent. "You offer aid?"

Hoffmann nodded. "We offer what we can. Sergeant Figueredo, outline the available support."

Figueredo stepped forward, detailing the limited number of pulse rifles, sidearms, medical kits, communicators, and ration packs they could spare. Disappointment flickered across the faces of Kaliq and his men.

"We hoped for more," Kaliq admitted, his voice strained. "Troops. Weapons."

"Mr. Borzhakov," Hoffmann interrupted gently, "The **Covenant** is a survey vessel. We have a small Marine detachment for security, not an invasion force. My orders prohibit direct military intervention. What we are doing now, providing you material support, is already a severe breach of protocol. I am risking my ship, my crew, and my career to offer this assistance."

He saw understanding, mixed with fading disappointment, dawn in Kaliq's eyes. Hoffmann turned to Figueredo. "Sergeant. A demonstration, if you please."

Figueredo raised his pulse rifle in a fast, smooth swing. He sighted on a thick branch high in a nearby tree, nearly obscured by the rain. He squeezed the trigger. A brief, blinding flash of blue-white energy, a sharp *crack* that momentarily overpowered the storm's roar, and the heavy branch ceased to exist at its connection point, showering the ground with vaporized wood and steaming leaves.

A glimmer of excitement sparked in Kaliq's eyes. Hoffmann pressed his advantage. "Our weapons are effective. But our presence here makes the **Covenant** vulnerable. The **Vanquisher** remains in orbit. Your people must ensure this ship disappears before dawn and that storm breaks."

Kaliq whispered urgently to one of his companions, who nodded once and melted back into the rain-swept jungle. "Consider it done, Captain," Kaliq assured him, turning back with renewed determination. "We have ways. Your ship will be hidden. We are grateful for whatever aid you provide."

Hoffmann nodded. "Very well. We will return to the **Covenant** and prepare the supplies for transfer." He offered his hand again. Kaliq gripped it tightly. A silent understanding passed between them — two leaders, bound by circumstance and a shared enemy, taking a desperate gamble in the heart of a storm. As Hoffmann turned back towards the waiting ship, Kaliq and his men vanished back into the jungle, leaving the pounding rain and the heavy scent of wet earth behind. The die was cast.

Escalation

The air in the cramped storage locker behind the main barracks tasted stale, thick with the scent of dust and mildewed canvas. Simen Agdestein kept his breathing shallow, listening intently. Outside, only the rhythmic chirping of nocturnal insects and the distant, unsettling scrape of Marine boots on packed earth broke through Golovin's oppressively silent curfew. He shifted his weight, the rough wooden crate he sat on digging into his thigh. Waiting.

Simen sensed the faintest whisper of movement at the door. Simen tensed, his hand moving towards the sidearm holstered beneath his tunic. The door creaked open a fraction, revealing Maksim Bernatski's familiar silhouette against the dim starlight filtering through a high, grimy window. Maksim slipped inside, sealing the door behind him with practiced silence.

"Clear?" Simen whispered, his voice barely audible.

Maksim nodded, his face drawn and weary in the near-darkness. "The patrol passed two minutes ago. Golovin is occupied. Ranting about inadequate lighting near the gallows." He sank onto an overturned bucket opposite Simen, running a hand over his tired eyes. "This is getting dangerous, Simen. Meeting like this."

"Everything is dangerous now, Max," Simen countered, keeping his voice low but intense. "Staying silent is dangerous. Doing nothing is dangerous. Golovin is unraveling."

Maksim sighed, a sound heavy with frustration. "I know. The drugs Chaka gives him. They make him erratic. Stronger for a time, yes, but the paranoia, it's getting worse. The sniper shot yesterday? Missed his head by centimeters while he was inspecting the cage."

"I know," Simen confirmed. "And the firebomb near the supply depot last night? Minor damage, but it spooked the crew. The resistance isn't just hiding anymore, Max. They're pushing back. That messenger, Kong. He wasn't bluffing."

Maksim nodded slowly. "Kong came to warn me. To offer an opportunity, if I was willing to take it. Then Golovin burst in." He recounted the brutal interrogation, the casual breaking of Kong's arm, the political officer's simmering suspicion. "He thinks I'm conspiring, Simen. He watches my every move."

A cold anger settled in Simen's gut. Golovin's brutality wasn't just tactical; it was sadistic. "He's a rabid dog, Max. You can't reason with him. Your strategy, 'biding your time,' it's going to get you killed. Or worse."

"And what do you suggest?" Maksim challenged, though his voice lacked its usual authority. "Open rebellion? Golovin has the Marines. Popescu follows his orders without question. We'd be cut down before we reached the command post."

"No," Simen conceded. "Not open rebellion. Not yet. But we need allies. We need contact with this Kaliq Borzhakov." He leaned forward, his gaze locking with Maksim's in the dim light. "Let me do it, Max."

Maksim looked startled. "You? Simen, if Golovin suspects *me*, he'll tear the ship apart looking for any connection *you* might have. It's too risky."

"It's riskier *not* to," Simen argued, his passion clear. "Golovin watches *you*. He expects *you* to be the weak link, the sympathizer. Me? I'm just the loyal XO, following orders, keeping my head down. I can slip away easily. Find a way to get a message to Kifaru, arrange a meeting." He saw the conflict in Maksim's eyes, the ingrained caution warring with the dawning realization that their situation was desperate.

"This Kaliq Borzhakov, he's the key," Simen pressed. "If the resistance is real, if they have strength, maybe, just maybe together we can find a way to neutralize Golovin. To regain control. Restore some sanity."

Maksim remained silent for a long moment, the weight of decision heavy in the small, dark space. The sounds of the jungle seemed to press closer, whispering warnings. After long moments, he nodded, a barely perceptible movement. "Alright, Simen. Alright. Find a way. But be careful. For God's sake, be careful. If anything happens to you…" His voice trailed off, the unspoken fear hanging between them.

"I will be careful, my friend," Simen promised, clapping a hand briefly on Maksim's shoulder. "Someone has to take the chance. And it's better me than you right now." He rose from the crate. "I'll find a way. Just. Stay alive until I do." He slipped back out into the oppressive darkness, leaving Maksim alone with his thoughts and the suffocating silence of Pristan' Zorya.

The tension in Pristan' Zorya had become a physical entity, a suffocating blanket woven from fear, resentment, and the cloying humidity of the Samarqand jungle. Days bled into weeks under Golovin's increasingly erratic rule, each sunrise bringing fresh anxieties. The resistance, once a murmured rumor, was now a palpable force, striking with unnerving precision and melting back into the green labyrinth that bordered the village.

Maksim stood near the perimeter fence, another of Golovin's recent additions. Flimsy wire hastily strung between rough-hewn posts. He watched villagers trudge towards the recently cleared fields under the watchful eyes of tense Marines. Another sniper shot had cracked through the morning air two days prior, kicking up dust near Sublieutenant Popescu as he inspected the guard rotation. No one was hit, but the message was clear: no Krasnayan was safe. The previous night, a well-aimed firebomb, likely hurled from the darkness beyond the fence, had engulfed a storage shed containing tools and replacement parts for the atmospheric processor. The fire had been extinguished in minutes, but the attack frayed nerves further, casting flickering shadows of doubt and fear amongst the crew.

Maksim never knew which Golovin would surface: the cold strategist or the rabid beast. Both versions made his blood freeze. Golovin's rages became volcanic, fueled by the Periblue concoction and his mounting paranoia. He doubled patrols, imposed stricter curfews, and delivered furious, rambling speeches over the loudspeakers, threatening collective punishment and decrying the villagers' 'treacherous ingratitude'. His orange skin seemed to glow with an unhealthy intensity, his eyes darting constantly, seeing conspiracy in every shadow, betrayal in every averted gaze.

The situation reached a new boiling point when the morning headcount revealed six **Vanquisher** crew members missing: two engineers, three technicians, and a young navigator's mate. They hadn't simply vanished; their bunks were empty, personal effects gone. They had defected, slipped away in the night, presumably to join Kaliq Borzhakov's growing band.

Golovin stormed into the command post, his face a mask of fury, and slammed his fist onto the makeshift desk, rattling the comm unit. Maksim, who had been reviewing dwindling water purification reports, looked up.

"Six of them!" Golovin spat, his voice hoarse. "Six *предатели*, traitors! Gone! Crawled off into the jungle to join the terrorists!" He rounded on Maksim, his eyes blazing with suspicion. "And you, Captain? Did you know about this? Did your 'conscience' compel you to look the other way? Perhaps even *assist* them?"

"Comrade Political Officer," Maksim began, keeping his voice calm, betraying none of the turmoil churning within him. "I assure you, I had no knowledge of any planned desertions. Crew morale is low, that is true. Your methods have created significant unrest."

"My methods?" Golovin sneered. "*My* methods are necessary to maintain order! To secure this planet for Krasnaya! It is *your* weakness, your constant questioning, your *sympathy* for these primitives that encourages such treason!" He leaned closer, his breath hot and smelling faintly of the bitter Periblue drink. "They wouldn't dare defy *me* unless they felt they had support from within. From *you*, Captain!"

"That is an unfounded accusation, Comrade," Maksim replied, meeting Golovin's glare without flinching, though his heart hammered against his ribs. He knew Simen was trying to make contact, knew that his own encounter with Kong had increased Golovin's paranoia. He was walking a razor's edge.

"Unfounded?" Golovin laughed, a harsh, grating sound devoid of humor. "We shall see, Captain. We shall see." He turned abruptly, pacing the small office like a caged predator. "Increase surveillance on all remaining crew. Confine anyone expressing discontent to quarters. I'll find someone and make them *pay*."

Maksim felt a chill despite the oppressive heat. More threats, more fear. This cycle of violence and reprisal couldn't continue. It would destroy them all. He had to try something, anything, to break it, before Golovin's madness consumed them.

The air in Golovin's cramped office crackled with tension. Outside, the midday sun beat down relentlessly, but inside, a cold dread held sway. Golovin sat hunched behind the desk that had once belonged to Governor Bebe, his fingers drumming a chaotic rhythm on the scarred wooden surface. His orange skin had faded slightly, but his eyes held a feverish, hunted look. The Periblue's effects seemed to be waning, leaving him raw-nerved and dangerously volatile. Another report had just come in: a patrol ambushed near the river, two Marines wounded, the attackers vanishing without a trace.

Maksim stood before the desk, feeling the weight of the political officer's suspicion like a physical pressure. He knew his time was running out. Simen hadn't reported any success in contacting the resistance yet, and Golovin's paranoia was escalating with every incident. He had to try to divert this disaster, even if the attempt was futile.

"Comrade Political Officer," Maksim began, choosing his words with extreme care. "These constant attacks, the desertions. This strategy of pure suppression isn't working. It's breeding more resentment, strengthening the resistance."

Golovin looked up, his eyes narrowing. "Are you questioning Krasnaya doctrine, Captain? Are you suggesting weakness?"

"I am suggesting pragmatism, Comrade," Maksim countered, forcing himself to hold Golovin's unstable gaze. "We are bleeding resources, losing personnel. The crew is terrified. Perhaps, perhaps there is another way. A temporary solution, at least."

"Another way?" Golovin echoed, leaning forward, dangerous curiosity flickering in his eyes. "Enlighten me, Captain."

Maksim took a deep breath. This was the precipice. "The resistance is led by Kaliq Borzhakov. He is fighting for his home, for vengeance, perhaps. But he may also be rational. Maybe we could arrange a parley."

The word hung in the air, heavy and explosive.

"A *parley*?" Golovin whispered, his voice soft, almost silky, which was far more terrifying than his usual shouting. "You want to, to *talk* to these terrorists? To the murderers who killed Marine Bondar? To the traitors who ambush our patrols?"

"If we could understand their demands, perhaps find some common ground, negotiate a ceasefire —" Maksim started, but Golovin cut him off, surging to his feet, his face contorting into a mask of absolute fury.

"*NEGOTIATE*?!" he roared, slamming both fists down on the desk, sending datapads skittering. "You want to *negotiate* with vermin who defy the will of Krasnaya?! You truly are rotten to the core, Bernatski!" His voice rose to a near-scream. "This proves it! Your constant undermining, your bleeding-heart sympathies, your reluctance to enforce discipline! It isn't just weakness! It *is* collusion! Treason!"

He stabbed a trembling finger towards Maksim. "Suggesting we talk to them." Spittle flew from Golovin's lips, spraying Maksim's uniform blouse. "That is the final straw. That is blatant ideological deviation! You actively seek to compromise our mission, to betray Mother Krasnaya!"

He spun towards the door, bellowing, "Popescu! Marines! To the command post! Now!"

Sublieutenant Popescu and two armed Marines burst into the office moments later, their expressions grim.

"Captain Maksim Bernatski," Golovin declared, his voice ringing with venomous triumph, "is hereby placed under arrest! Charge: Ideological deviation and suspected collusion with enemy forces!" He savored the words, his eyes glittering with manic satisfaction. "Confine him to his quarters under maximum security until further notice!"

Popescu hesitated for only a fraction of a second, perhaps a flicker of surprise or doubt crossing his stony face, before his training took over. "Sir, yes, sir." He gestured to the Marines. "Captain, you will come with us."

As the Marines stepped forward, Popescu glanced around the flimsy structure of the command post, then back at Golovin. "Comrade *Глава*," he interjected, his voice practical, "with respect, the Captain's quarters offer minimal security. Simple wood construction, easily breached —"

Golovin paused, his furious expression shifting as a new, crueler idea sparked in his eyes. He looked from Popescu back towards the village square, where the steel cage stood starkly under the unforgiving sun. A slow, malicious smile spread across his orange-tinged face.

"You are quite right, Sublieutenant," Golovin purred, the earlier rage replaced by a chilling satisfaction. "His quarters *are* inadequate for such a traitor." He waved a dismissive hand towards the door. "Take him to the cage. That's even better! Let the entire village see the fate of *anyone* who dares betray Krasnaya. He can rot in there with that worthless local Kong. Perhaps they can conspire more effectively behind bars."

Popescu's face remained impassive, betraying nothing. "As you command, Comrade *Глава*." He turned back to the Marines. "Escort the prisoner to the detention cage."

Maksim stood rooted in place, blood draining from his face. He had tried to reason, to find a path away from the abyss, and instead, he had leaped directly into it. His suggestion of a parley, meant as a desperate attempt to de-escalate, had been twisted by Golovin's paranoia into the ultimate proof of betrayal. Confinement was expected, but the cage: public humiliation, exposed to the elements and the scorn Golovin intended to incite. There was no reasoning with this madness. As the Marines moved towards him, their grips firm on his arms, Maksim knew his command was over. His fate, and the fate of the **Vanquisher** crew still loyal to him, now rested entirely on Simen, and the desperate gamble they had set in motion. He offered no resistance as they

57

marched him out of the office and towards the village square, towards the waiting cage, the political officer's triumphant glare burning into his back.

Despair

The Samarqand sun beat down relentlessly on the dusty village square, reflecting in harsh glints off the steel bars of the cage where Captain Maksim Bernatski now stood beside the defiant local, Kong. Simen Agdestein stood near the makeshift platform Golovin used for pronouncements, the oppressive heat pressing in on him, mirroring the suffocating weight of injustice that choked the air of Pristan' Zorya. He kept his face impassive, a mask of dutiful attention he had perfected over the past weeks, while inside, a cold fury mingled with gnawing helplessness.

The villagers were assembled, forced from their work, their faces a mixture of fear and dull resignation. Marines stood at intervals around the square, their weapons held ready, their presence a constant, menacing reminder of Golovin's absolute control. Golovin himself presided from a high-backed chair dragged from Bebe Borzhakova's former office, his orange-tinged skin glistening with sweat, his eyes alight with cruel satisfaction. This wasn't justice; it was theatre, a brutal performance designed to crush any lingering hope.

First came Kong. The old man was dragged from the cage, his broken arm bound crudely against his chest, his face pale but his eyes still burning with defiance. Golovin read the charges: murder of Marine Artem Bondar, resisting Krasnaya authority, conspiracy. The trial was a farce. Kong was offered no defense, no chance to speak beyond spitting curses at Golovin when prompted for a plea. Golovin acted as prosecutor, judge, and jury, his voice dripping with mock solemnity as he recounted Kong's 'crimes'.

"Kaong Kubaska, "Golovin declared, rising from his chair to address the silent crowd, "this tribunal finds you guilty on all counts. Your defiance ends here. Your sentence is death by hanging. To be carried out at dawn." He waved dismissively, and Marines hauled the struggling Kong back towards the cage, his defiant shouts quickly muffled.

Simen's gut clenched. He forced himself to remain still, betraying nothing. Then it was Maksim's turn.

Captain Bernatski was escorted from the cage, his sweat-soaked uniform dusty and torn, his bearing still retaining a shred of command dignity despite the humiliation. He stood straight, his gaze sweeping over the assembled crew and villagers, coming to rest for a moment on Simen. Simen could only offer a fractional, almost imperceptible nod, hoping Maksim understood it wasn't abandonment, but caution.

Golovin launched into the charges against Maksim: ideological deviation, dereliction of duty, failure to uphold Krasnaya principles, and suspected collusion with enemy forces. The evidence presented was laughable – Maksim's questioning of the food levy, his concern for the healer Chaka, his attempt to buffer Golovin's rage against the villagers, and finally, the damning suggestion of a parley.

"Captain Bernatski," Golovin sneered, pacing before Maksim. "You had command. You had the trust of Mother Krasnaya. And you betrayed it. You sympathized with terrorists, questioned lawful orders, and advocated for surrender through your cowardly suggestion of 'negotiation'." He spat the word out like poison. "Do you deny these charges?"

Maksim's voice, when he finally spoke, was quiet but steady, carrying across the hushed square. "I deny betraying Krasnaya. I sought only to protect my crew and fulfill our mission objectives without unnecessary bloodshed. Your methods, Comrade Political Officer, have undermined both."

Golovin laughed, a harsh, grating sound. "Protect the crew? By consorting with the enemy? By advocating weakness? Your definition of protection is treason, Captain!" He turned back to the assembled crowd, his voice ringing with theatrical finality. "This tribunal finds Captain Maksim Dimitrovich Bernatski guilty as charged! His ideological corruption is a cancer that must be excised. His sentence is death by hanging. To be carried out alongside the local terrorist at dawn tomorrow."

A collective gasp, quickly suppressed, rippled through the villagers. Some of the **Vanquisher** crew shifted uncomfortably. Simen felt a wave

60

of cold dread wash over him. He had expected this, yet hearing the sentence pronounced, seeing Maksim standing there condemned, was like a physical blow. Maksim was led back to the cage, his face grim but resolute. Golovin surveyed the square, his gaze lingering on the gallows nearby, a satisfied smirk playing on his lips. The performance was complete. Fear had been reinforced. Despair deepened its roots in Pristan' Zorya.

Later that afternoon, Simen sought out Golovin in the command post. The air inside was thick with the cloying scent of the Periblue concoction Golovin favored. The political officer was hunched over maps, plotting defensive positions, his movements jerky and agitated. The trials seemed to have energized him, feeding his paranoia rather than sating it.

Before Simen could speak, Golovin looked up, his eyes burning with a manic gleam. "Excellent news, Comrade Executive Officer! We have apprehended more traitors!"

Simen kept his expression neutral. "Sir?"

"Those two girls!" Golovin declared triumphantly. "The ones who were with Bondar when he 'fell'. Xevera Coffi and Sidonie Tolar. Accessories! They knew that murderer Kong was hiding! They conspired through their silence!" He slammed his fist on the map. "I've had them arrested. Taken from their families."

Simen felt a sickening lurch in his stomach. The girls? They were children, terrified witnesses forced into silence by a killer. "Comrade Глава," Simen began, choosing his words like navigating a minefield. "Will you be holding a trial for them as well?"

Golovin waved a dismissive hand, scoffing. "A trial? For children? Don't be absurd, Agdestein. That would be unnecessarily cruel." The statement hung in the air, thick with grotesque irony. "No, no trial. Their guilt is obvious. Accessories to the murder of a Krasnaya hero. Their sentence is the same as the others. Death."

Simen stared, speechless at the casual ruthlessness, the utter disregard for any semblance of justice. "You intend to hang two teenage girls?" he asked, his voice barely a whisper, struggling to keep the horror from it.

Golovin frowned, studying Simen's face intently, suspicion flickering in his eyes. "Do I detect a note of dissent, Comrade XO? Have you perhaps spent too much time listening to Bernatski's sentimental drivel? Has his weakness infected you too?"

Simen composed himself, forcing a blandly inquisitive expression. "Not at all, Comrade Глава. I merely wish to understand the full scope of the situation. To ensure all protocols are followed correctly, as befits Krasnaya discipline." It was a weak deflection, but the best he could manage.

Golovin seemed momentarily placated, though his eyes remained narrowed. "There are no protocols for dealing with treacherous vermin beyond swift extermination, Agdestein. They hang with the others. At dawn." He turned back to his maps. "I've had the execution order posted in the square. Attendance is mandatory. For *everyone*. Crew and villagers alike. Let them all witness the price of defiance."

Simen nodded. "Understood, Comrade." He backed out of the office, his mind reeling. Maksim, Kong, and now two young girls condemned to die. Golovin's madness was accelerating, consuming everything in its path. Dawn was only hours away. His own secret efforts to contact the resistance felt desperately inadequate, a flickering candle against a hurricane. The despair he had felt earlier deepened, threatening to extinguish that small flame for all time. He had to maintain his cover, had to keep searching for an opening, but the thought of standing by and watching those executions; it was almost unbearable.

Dusk painted the Samarqand sky in bruised shades of purple and orange as Simen stood near the western perimeter fence, observing the uneasy quiet. The humid air was unnaturally still, the usual evening chorus of the jungle muted. Tension coiled in the pit of his stomach. The executions were scheduled for sunrise, mere hours away. Hope felt like a fragile, foolish thing.

Chaos erupted at the edge of the jungle.

A series of sharp cracks echoed from the jungle: pulse rifle fire, but not Krasnaya issue, which always warbled a bit. Figures burst from the tree line, low and fast, firing sporadically towards the Marine positions along the fence. The resistance. Kaliq Borzhakov was making his move. Simen's heart leaped, a wild surge of hope warring with immediate fear for the attackers. They were charging into a prepared defense.

Alarms blared across Pristan' Zorya. Marines, already on high alert, returned fire with disciplined volleys. Searchlights flared to life, pinning the attackers in their harsh glare. Simen saw flashes of return fire, heard the desperate shouts of the resistance fighters, but they were outnumbered and outgunned. Ratings and off-duty crew, armed with sidearms and makeshift weapons, rushed to reinforce the perimeter under Popescu's bellowed commands.

The firefight was brief and brutal. The resistance fighters, likely villagers armed with a motley collection of hunting rifles and perhaps a few weapons supplied by the **Covenant**, pressed their attack bravely but against the trained Marines and superior firepower, they had no chance. Simen watched helplessly as several attackers fell, caught in crossfire. Within minutes, the assault faltered. The surviving resistance fighters broke contact, melting back into the deepening shadows of the jungle as quickly as they had appeared, leaving behind the chilling silence and the bodies of their fallen comrades sprawled near the fence line.

A triumphant roar went up from Golovin, who had emerged from the command post to observe the final moments of the firefight. "Victory!" he bellowed, striding towards the perimeter, his orange face flushed with manic energy. "We have crushed them! The terrorists are broken!"

He clapped Popescu on the back, showering praise on the Marines and the ratings who had joined the fight. "Commendations! Commendations for all who fought! You have defended Mother

Krasnaya with honor!" He seemed almost giddy, high on the adrenaline of the brief battle.

Golovin ran to where Popescu examined a fallen attacker. A colonial, with a crude rifle. "Do we bury them, sir? Give them to the locals?"

Golovin's answer came immediately. "No, they are ours. Burn them on the square. Let the town see, let the captives suffer their smoke." He turned toward his office.

Later, however, as Simen passed the command post, he overheard Golovin talking in great agitation to Popescu inside. The earlier elation had faded, replaced by a restless suspicion. "...too easy, Popescu," Golovin was saying, his voice tight with paranoia. "Why attack now? So close to the executions? Was it a real attempt? Or just a test? Probing our defenses?"

Simen lingered in the shadows, listening.

"Double the patrols tonight!" Golovin ordered. "Maximum alert. No one sleeps soundly until those traitors are swinging from the gallows!" There was a pause, then Golovin's voice dropped, becoming demanding. "And find that healer! Chaka! Tell her I require another dose. Immediately! I need to be sharp tonight. I must stay awake."

Simen slipped away before he could be seen, a cold dread settling over him. The resistance attack had failed, their desperate gamble unsuccessful. Maksim, Kong, and the two girls remained condemned. And Golovin, far from being satisfied by his victory, was retreating further into paranoia and drug dependency, demanding more of the substance that was clearly driving his madness. The night ahead stretched before Simen, long and dark, filled with the certainty of the dawn's horror and the crushing weight of failure. Despair, cold and absolute, tightened its grip.

Uprising

The humid night air in the Kifaru Rotko encampment hung thick with the scent of woodsmoke, damp earth, and unwashed bodies. Lantern light cast flickering, uncertain shadows across the rough-hewn shelters and the tense faces gathered beneath a large canvas awning stretched between towering jungle trees. Captain Clement Hoffmann stood beside Kaliq Borzhakov, the young resistance leader whose face seemed permanently etched with a mixture of grief and fierce determination. They were waiting.

A rustle in the undergrowth at the edge of the clearing signaled an arrival. Two of Kaliq's sentries emerged, escorting a figure dressed in the drab grey duty uniform of a Krasnaya Rechka starship officer. Simen Agdestein, Executive Officer of the **KRSS Vanquisher**. He looked exhausted, his face pale and strained in the lantern light, but his eyes held a desperate urgency.

"Captain Hoffmann. Mr. Borzhakov," Agdestein greeted them, his voice low and hoarse. He didn't waste time on pleasantries. "I apologize for the intrusion, but I had to come. Golovin, he held trials today. Farces, both of them."

Hoffmann felt a cold knot tighten in his stomach. "The prisoners? Kong and Captain Bernatski?"

Agdestein nodded. "Sentenced to death. Both of them. By hanging. Along with two young village girls, Xevera Coffi and Sidonie Tolar, accused as accessories to the Marine's death. Golovin plans to execute all four at dawn tomorrow. Publicly. Attendance mandatory."

A wave of murmurs swept through the resistance fighters gathered nearby. Kaliq swore viciously under his breath, his knuckles white where he gripped the edge of the crude wooden table between them. Hoffmann exchanged a quick, grim look with Sergeant Figueredo, who stood impassively nearby, his hand never far from his sidearm.

Kaliq turned narrowed eyes on Agdestein. "How do we know this isn't a trap? How do we know *you* aren't Golovin's spy, sent to feed us false information, lure us into an ambush?" The suspicion in his voice was palpable, understandable.

Agdestein stared back into Kaliq's hostile gaze. "Because I served with Maksim Bernatski for ten years. He is a good man, caught in an impossible situation. Golovin is a paranoid madman destroying his own command. And because," his voice dropped, filled with raw disgust, "I will not stand by and watch him hang children."

Hoffmann studied the Krasnaya officer. Agdestein's sincerity felt genuine, born of desperation. But trust, especially now, was a dangerously rare commodity. He needed verification.

"Mr. Borzhakov raises a valid point, Commander Agdestein," Hoffmann said. "Trust must be earned." He turned slightly. "Sergeant Figueredo, if you would."

Figueredo nodded once and spoke into his helmet comm. Moments later, two figures were escorted into the firelight by **Covenant** Marines. They wore ragged civilian clothes though they carried themselves with the unmistakable bearing of former military personnel. Their faces were thin, haunted, but relief flickered in their eyes as they saw Agdestein.

"These men," Hoffmann explained, gesturing to the newcomers, "are Engineers Voronov and Petrov. Formerly of the **KRSS Vanquisher**. They sought refuge with us two days ago after deserting Golovin's command." He looked at the two engineers. "Do you know this officer?"

Both men snapped to attention, surprise and recognition clear on their faces. "Commander Agdestein! Sir!" Voronov exclaimed.

"At ease," Agdestein said, looking equally surprised to see them.

"Mr. Borzhakov," Hoffmann suggested, "perhaps you would care to question one of these men? I will speak with the other. Then we can compare notes."

Kaliq nodded, his suspicion still evident but slightly tempered. He drew Engineer Petrov aside, speaking to him in low, intense tones. Hoffmann stepped away with Voronov, Figueredo standing nearby.

"Engineer Voronov," Hoffmann began quietly. "Tell me about Commander Agdestein. What kind of officer is he? Is he loyal to Golovin?"

Voronov glanced nervously towards Agdestein, then back at Hoffmann, licking his dry lips. "The Commander, Sir Agdestein. He is a correct professional. Follows regulations. Not like," Voronov swallowed. "Not like the Political Officer." He shuddered. "Golovin is *mad*, Captain Sir. The drugs, the paranoia, he sees enemies everywhere. Commander Agdestein has tried to moderate him. Tried to protect the crew from the worst of it, quietly. Always looked out for the Captain Bernatski, I mean. They were close."

"Did he ever express sympathy for the locals? Or opposition to Golovin's actions?" Hoffmann pressed.

Voronov hesitated. "Not openly, sir. That would be suicide. But you could see it. In his eyes sometimes. He disagreed. Strongly. Especially after, after they arrested Captain Bernatski."

Hoffmann thanked the engineer and rejoined Kaliq, who had finished his own intense interrogation of Petrov. They stepped away from the others.

"Well?" Hoffmann asked in flat tones.

Kaliq's expression was still grim, but the overt suspicion had faded. "Petrov says much the same. Agdestein is respected by the crew, unlike Golovin. He tried to maintain order, protect his captain. He believes Agdestein despises Golovin but was trapped by his position. Petrov saw him arguing with Golovin shortly before Captain Bernatski was arrested." He looked towards Agdestein, who stood waiting patiently, his face etched with anxiety. "He took a great risk coming here."

Hoffmann nodded. The stories corroborated. The risk Agdestein had taken was undeniable. "It seems, Mr. Borzhakov," Hoffmann said, making the decision, "that we have found an unlikely ally. We have less than twelve hours until dawn. We must trust him."

Kaliq stared at Agdestein for a long moment, then gave a curt nod. "Agreed. Commander Agdestein," he called out, his voice firm. "Tell us everything you know about Golovin's defenses in Pristan'." The uprising had found its inside man.

The air under the canvas awning grew thick with tension and the low murmur of strategic discussion. Crude maps of Pristan' Zorya, sketched by villagers familiar with every hut and pathway and augmented by Simen Agdestein's detailed knowledge of Marine patrols and weapon emplacements, were spread across the rough wooden table. Hoffmann, Kaliq, Agdestein, and Sergeant Figueredo huddled around the maps, the flickering lantern light casting their faces in sharp relief. Outside, the sounds of the resistance camp preparing for battle, the quiet clink of weapons being checked, the hushed commands, the shuffling of feet, formed a backdrop to their urgent planning.

Time was their enemy. Dawn, and the scheduled executions, were only hours away.

"Golovin has concentrated his main force around the square and the command post," Agdestein explained, tracing lines on the map with a finger. "Two heavy pulse cannons salvaged from the shuttle cover the main approach from the west. Marine patrols are doubled, especially along the southern perimeter after last night's attack. The cage and the gallows area," his voice tightened a slight bit, "will be heavily guarded."

"Our best approach is multi-pronged," Figueredo stated, his voice calm and professional as he pointed to the eastern edge of the village, near the derelict processing sheds. "A diversionary attack here," he tapped the western fence line, "to draw their attention. My squad, supported by Mr. Borzhakov's best fighters, will infiltrate from the east, bypass the main defenses, and hit the command post and the square simultaneously. Priority one: neutralize Golovin and Popescu. Priority two: secure the prisoners."

Kaliq nodded, his eyes gleaming with fierce intensity. "My fighters know the eastern jungle paths like their own hands. We can guide your Marines, bypass the patrols Agdestein mentioned. We'll hit them hard, fast."

"Speed and surprise are indeed critical," Hoffmann emphasized. "The attack must commence precisely as the first light touches the square. The moment Golovin intends for the executions. Maximum confusion." He looked at Agdestein. "Your information on patrol routes and communication codes is invaluable, Commander. It gives us a fighting chance."

"I've told you everything I know," Agdestein said, rubbing his temples, his fatigue evident. "Weapon stores locations, comm frequencies Golovin uses, Popescu's likely tactical responses." He straightened up, his expression resolute despite his exhaustion. "I must get back. If I'm not there when the sun rises, Golovin's suspicion will turn to certainty. I might be able to create a diversion from inside, disable a key system if the opportunity arises."

Hoffmann met his gaze. "It's a big risk, Commander."

"Less risk than letting those executions proceed," Agdestein countered. He offered a hand first to Hoffmann, then to Kaliq. "Good luck. Good hunting."

"And to you, Commander," Hoffmann replied, gripping his hand firmly. "And thanks."

Kaliq echoed the sentiment with a curt nod. Agdestein gave a final nod to Figueredo and slipped back into the darkness, escorted by two of Kaliq's scouts who would guide him close to Pristan'.

Hoffmann watched him go, feeling a mix of admiration and apprehension. They were relying heavily on the Krasnaya officer. He turned back to the map, the urgency returning full force. "Alright. Let's finalize assignments. Sergeant, coordinate with Kaliq's section leaders. synchronize timing. We move out in one hour."

Figueredo nodded. "Aye, Captain."

Kaliq began issuing quiet, rapid commands to his waiting fighters. The low murmur of the camp intensified, shifting from preparation to deployment. Weapons were hoisted, faces grim with determination. The resistance fighters, armed with a mix of scavenged Krasnaya weapons, Heimsee pulse rifles, and their own determination, began to melt into the jungle, moving towards their designated attack positions around the besieged village. The plan was set. The fuse was lit. All that remained was the dawn.

The first hint of grey began to dilute the oppressive blackness of the Samarqand night as Simen Agdestein slipped through the poorly maintained perimeter fence back into Pristan' Zorya. His heart hammered against his ribs, a frantic drumbeat against the pre-dawn stillness. Every shadow seemed to hold a threat, every rustle of leaves sounded like an approaching patrol. He hugged the jungle's edge, where shadows pooled deepest, and picked his path back toward the barracks. He had made it back undetected.

Or so he thought.

As he rounded a cluster of storage sheds, a harsh voice cut through the gloom. "Commander Agdestein! Taking an early morning stroll?"

Simen froze, turning slowly. Vladimir Golovin stood silhouetted against the faintly lightening eastern sky, flanked by two armed Marines. The political officer must have been prowling the perimeter himself, fueled by paranoia and Chaka's stimulants.

"Comrade Political Officer," Simen greeted him, forcing a calm he didn't feel. He gestured vaguely towards the jungle. "Just checking the perimeter. Ensuring vigilance. Given the attack last night…"

Golovin stepped closer, his eyes, unnaturally bright even in the dim light, scrutinized Simen's face. Simen could smell the faint, bitter scent of the Periblue clinging to him. "Vigilance? Or perhaps a clandestine meeting. Returning from a little trip into the bush, Commander?"

Simen felt a prickle of cold sweat despite the humidity. Golovin's suspicion was a tangible force. "Sir, I assure you, I am merely observing. Concerned about another potential probe from the resistance before… Before the dawn's activities."

"Concerned?" Golovin sneered, unconvinced. "You seem unusually concerned about these terrorists, Agdestein. First your questions about the girls, now this pre-dawn reconnaissance." He paced back and forth in front of Simen, radiating nervous energy. "Where were you, precisely? Who did you see?"

"I saw nothing but shadows, Comrade," Simen lied, keeping his gaze steady. "The jungle is quiet. Too quiet, perhaps. It makes one uneasy."

Golovin stared at him for a long, tense moment, clearly weighing Simen's words, searching for any sign of deception. Simen held his breath, praying his exhaustion didn't betray him.

Before Golovin could press further, movement near the center of the square caught their attention. Chaka, the village healer, was calmly setting out supplies near the base of the gallows – bandages, tinctures, bowls of clean water, stacks of folded cloths. She moved with a quiet, deliberate purpose that seemed strangely out of place amidst the grim preparations for execution.

Golovin's attention snapped towards her, his paranoia instantly redirecting. "You!" he roared, striding towards the healer, Simen forgotten for the moment. "What is the meaning of this? Preparing for casualties?"

Chaka looked up at him, her expression serene, almost pitying. "The spirits were restless last night, Глава," she said, her voice calm but carrying in the stillness. "They showed me blood. Much blood. It is wise to be prepared."

"Spirits? Witchcraft!" Golovin spat, enraged by her calm defiance. "You dare practice your primitive superstitions here? Now? Perhaps you had a 'vision' of joining your traitorous friends on these gallows!" He gestured menacingly towards the ropes hanging in the pre-dawn air. "Maybe you should be next!"

Without warning, a low growl rose from the assembled villagers who had begun to gather, forced into the square to witness the executions. It started with one or two, then spread, a wave of angry murmurs and curses directed at Golovin. People shifted, their faces no longer showing a drained resignation, but filled with a simmering fury ignited by the threat against their healer.

"Leave her alone!" someone shouted from the crowd.

"She helps us!" cried another.

71

"You are the devil, Golovin!"

The collective anger seemed to startle Golovin. He took an involuntary step back from Chaka, his eyes darting nervously towards the growing hostility in the crowd. The villagers took a hesitant step forward, their numbers giving them a sudden, unexpected boldness. Golovin, accustomed to cowed silence, seemed genuinely unnerved by this spontaneous surge of defiance. His Marine escorts fidgeted beside him, their training for firefights useless against this sea of angry faces.

With a final, venomous glare at Chaka and a sweeping look of contempt towards the villagers, Golovin turned to his troops. "Maintain order!" he snapped before stalking back towards the relative safety of the command post, his retreat lacking its usual arrogant swagger.

Simen watched him go, a flicker of surprise and grim satisfaction cutting through his own tension. The villagers, pushed too far, had finally pushed back, however slight and brief their opposition. Chaka calmly returned to organizing her supplies. The first rays of sunlight were beginning to pierce the horizon, painting the sky in streaks of blood-red and gold. The hour of execution — and uprising — was at hand.

Judgment

The dawn arrived not with hope, but with the suffocating certainty of death. Maksim stood blinking in the harsh, rising sun as Marines roughly pulled him from the shared cage he'd endured overnight with Kong and the two terrified girls. The air in Pristan' Zorya's square was thick with dust, fear, and the forced presence of the entire village population, herded like livestock by grim-faced Krasnaya guards to witness Golovin's brutal justice. Their faces were numb, eyes averted, mirroring the despair that gnawed at Maksim's own gut.

He saw Simen standing near the edge of the crowd, face impassive, but Maksim caught a flicker in his friend's eyes: a spark of something fierce and desperate that offered a sliver of hope Maksim barely dared to acknowledge.

Golovin presided from the crude wooden gallows platform, a grotesque parody of command. The man was visibly deteriorating. His orange-tinged skin had a sickly, jaundiced undertone, his remaining hair was plastered to his scalp with sweat, and his eyes darted about, filled with a frantic, paranoid energy. He mumbled to himself, occasionally twitching, his hands trembling uncontrollably. The Periblue concoction was consuming him from the inside out.

Marines shoved Maksim towards the platform steps. He stumbled but caught himself, forcing his legs to carry him upward with a semblance of dignity he didn't feel. He stood straight as Golovin, his voice raspy and uneven, began reading the charges and the predetermined verdict, slurring some of the words. Maksim didn't listen to the litany of fabricated crimes; instead, he locked his gaze onto Golovin, holding the political officer's wavering, manic stare. He would not give this madman the satisfaction of seeing him break.

Sublieutenant Popescu stepped forward, holding a coarse black hood. His face was stony, unreadable. As Popescu moved to place the hood over Maksim's head, Maksim pulled back.

"No," Maksim said, his voice clear and steady, ringing out in the sudden silence. "Let him see my face when he murders me." He kept his eyes fixed on Golovin, a silent accusation, a final act of defiance. Popescu hesitated, glancing towards Golovin, who merely giggled, a high-pitched, disturbing sound lacking any hint of sanity.

The moment stretched, taut and brittle. Popescu still hesitated with the hood. Golovin swayed on the platform, mumbling incoherently. The crowd held its collective breath.

Then, the sharp, distinct *crack-crack-crack* of pulse-rifle fire erupted from the dense jungle foliage bordering the western edge of the square. Not the heavier sound of KR Marine weapons, but the lighter report of the Heimsee rifles supplied by the **Covenant**.

Chaos exploded on the square. Two **Vanquisher** ratings standing guard near the fence line crumpled to the ground, smoke rising from blackened holes in their uniforms. Screams tore through the assembled villagers. Panic, primal and uncontrollable, seized the crowd. People surged away from the gunfire, away from the gallows, trampling one another in their desperation to escape. Several Krasnaya crew members, caught off guard, were knocked down and trampled in the stampede.

On the gallows platform, Golovin shrieked, startled by the sudden violence. His eyes, wide with terror and drug-fueled rage, fixed on Maksim. His trembling hand fumbled for the heavy sidearm holstered at his hip. He managed to draw the weapon, attempting to level it at Maksim's chest, perhaps intending to carry out the execution himself amidst the mayhem. But his shakes were too severe. The heavy pistol slipped from his grasp, clattering onto the wooden planks of the platform.

"Return fire!" Golovin screamed, his voice cracking, barely audible above the din of battle and panicked shouts. "Kill them! Kill them all!" He staggered towards the edge of the platform, pointing wildly towards the jungle, oblivious to the chaos engulfing the square below.

Simen moved the instant the first shots rang out, shoving through the panicked crowd towards the gallows. Years of training took over, instinct driving him forward while chaos reigned around him. He saw Golovin fumbling with his pistol, saw it fall, heard his panicked screams. This was it. The opening Kong had promised, bought with resistance blood.

As Golovin staggered towards the edge of the platform, shrieking orders, his foot caught on a loose plank. He flailed against the air, arms pinwheeling, then tumbled backward off the platform with a startled cry, landing heavily in the dust below, just meters from where Simen stood.

Simen didn't hesitate. He lunged forward. Golovin looked up from the ground, stunned and winded, his eyes wide with confusion and dawning fear as he recognized Simen looming over him. Simen saw not a political officer, not a superior, but a rabid animal. He helped Golovin struggle partway up, gripping the man's tunic. Then, with a surge of cold, righteous fury, Simen drove the combat knife he'd palmed from its ankle sheath deep into Golovin's chest, aiming for the heart. He felt the sickening resistance of flesh and bone, then the blade sliding home.

Golovin's eyes bulged, a strangled gasp escaping his lips. He clawed at Simen's arm, disbelief and agony warring on his face. Simen held him tight, twisting the knife pitilessly, ensuring the work was done. He felt the tremors that shook Golovin's body, saw the light fade from the madman's eyes, replaced by a vacant stare. Golovin slumped forward, lifeless, his dead weight heavy against Simen.

Shoving the body aside, Simen vaulted onto the gallows platform, ignoring Popescu who stood frozen, weapon half-raised, stunned into inaction by the sudden, shocking turn of events. Simen slashed through the ropes binding Maksim's hands.

"It's over, Max," Simen gasped, adrenaline pounding through him, the coppery scent of Golovin's blood thick in his nostrils.

Maksim stared at him, then at Golovin's body below, comprehension dawning. He grabbed the knife from Simen and together they ran to the cage, cutting loose the terrified girls and the grimly silent Kong, whose broken arm hadn't stopped him from watching Golovin's demise with fierce satisfaction. The battle for Pristan' Zorya raged around them, but at the gallows, judgment had been delivered.

Freedom felt unreal. One moment Maksim was facing death, the next he stood knife in hand beside Simen, the sounds of pitched battle echoing through the square. But the immediate threat wasn't over.

Resistance fighters, Kaliq's men, surged from the eastern jungle edge, pouring into the village, their faces contorted with battle rage and the desire for vengeance. They fired indiscriminately at any Krasnaya uniform they saw, Marines and terrified ratings alike, cutting down those who tried to surrender as readily as those still fighting back. The disciplined attack planned by Hoffmann and Figueredo threatened to devolve into a massacre.

"No!" Maksim yelled, horror gripping him. "Simen, we have to stop them!"

Together, they leaped from the platform, ignoring the ongoing firefight, and ran towards the advancing line of resistance fighters who were closing in on a group of panicked, unarmed **Vanquisher** technicians huddled near the command post.

"Hold your fire!" Maksim bellowed, his voice raw but carrying command authority. "CEASE FIRE! Golovin is dead! It's over!"

"Stop!" Simen echoed, waving his arms. "They are surrendering! Hold fire!"

Some fighters hesitated, confused by the sight of the Krasnaya officers trying to protect their own people. Others, consumed by battle lust and hatred, kept firing. A stray pulse bolt, fired by a wild-eyed resistance fighter aiming at a fleeing Marine, struck Simen high on the left arm. He cried out, stumbling, clutching the wound as blood welled through his torn uniform sleeve.

Maksim grabbed Simen, pulling him behind the dubious cover of an overturned supply crate. The fighting sputtered around them, confusion momentarily halting the worst of the violence. From the jungle edge, Maksim saw Captain Hoffmann emerge, pulse rifle held ready but pointed to the sky, Sergeant Figueredo and his Marines flanking him, forming a disciplined line.

Hoffmann saw Simen fall. He sprinted across the chaotic square, heedless of the remaining sporadic shots, kneeling beside Simen and applying pressure to the bleeding wound. "Easy, Commander," Hoffmann said, his voice calm amidst the chaos. "Just hold still."

✦ ♝ ✦ ♝ ✦

Following Hoffmann and his Marines, Kaliq Borzhakov emerged from the jungle, his face smeared with grime and sweat, his eyes blazing. He saw the chaos, the resistance fighters still firing sporadically, the Krasnaya crew cowering or dead.

"ENOUGH!" Kaliq roared, his voice cutting through the lingering sounds of battle. "CEASE FIRE! GOLOVIN IS DEAD! PRISTAN IS OURS!"

His command, echoed by Hoffmann's authoritative presence and the disciplined posture of the **Covenant** Marines, finally pierced the bloodlust. The remaining resistance fighters lowered their weapons, looking between their leader, the Heimsee Captain, and the two Krasnaya officers: one bleeding, the other standing protectively beside him. The gunfire sputtered out, replaced by an eerie silence broken only by the crackling of small fires, the moans of the wounded, and the ragged breathing of the survivors.

Chaka, the healer, emerged from the crowd, followed by several village women carrying baskets of supplies; the very supplies she had calmly prepared under Golovin's nose. Ignoring the lingering tension, they moved purposefully through the square, tending to the wounded from both sides, their presence a quiet assertion of life amidst the carnage.

Hoffmann finished applying a temporary field dressing to Simen's arm. Maksim helped his friend to his feet. They stood facing Hoffmann and Kaliq across the debris-strewn square. For a long moment, the four men — two Krasnaya officers, a Heimsee captain, and a Samarqand resistance leader — simply looked at each other, the enormity of the morning's events sinking in. Golovin was dead. The occupation, at least this brutal phase of it, was over.

A slow, exhausted grin spread across Maksim's face. Simen, despite the pain in his arm, mirrored it. Hoffmann returned the grin, a look of profound relief softening his features. Kaliq let out a long, shuddering breath, the fierce tension draining from him, replaced by weary triumph.

Then, an almost hysterical giggle escaped Maksim. It wasn't humor, but the sheer release of unbearable tension. Simen chuckled, shaking his head. Hoffmann laughed aloud, a short, sharp bark of relief. Kaliq threw his head back and let out a whoop of pure, unadulterated joy that echoed across the square.

The sound broke the spell. They began clapping each other on the back, gripping hands, a spontaneous eruption of shared relief and disbelief. Chaka looked up from tending a wounded resistance fighter and smiled . Kong, near collapse and leaning heavily against the cage, nodded in grim satisfaction. The two girls, Xevera and Sidonie, clung to each other, weeping tears of terror and relief. Some of the villagers began to laugh, others cried openly. The tension snapped, replaced by a wave of raw, cathartic emotion. The judgment had been rendered, the immediate nightmare was over, and under the blood-streaked Samarqand dawn, an uncertain future appeared.

Alliance

Dawn broke clear and bright two days after the battle, washing Pristan' Zorya in the warm, golden light of the Samarqand sun. The metallic tang of blood and the acrid smell of burnt materials still lingered on the breeze, but overlaid now were the scents of woodsmoke from cooking fires, damp earth turned for new planting, and the sweet fragrance of jungle blossoms reclaiming their territory. Chaka moved through the village, her healer's bag lighter than it had been, her heart considerably heavier but also filled with a cautious, burgeoning hope.

The past two days had been a blur of activity. Tending the wounded, Krasnayan, Heimsee marine, villager alike; cleaning the square; burying the dead with quiet reverence; clearing debris. The **Covenant** crew, quiet and efficient, had helped immensely, their portable sonic cleaners making short work of the bloodstains that had marred the packed earth square, their strong backs assisting with the heavy lifting. Captain Hoffmann's medical team had taken the most grievously injured, including Kong, aboard their ship where advanced technology offered chances far beyond Chaka's traditional means.

Now, a semblance of peace was returning. Chaka paused near the communal well, listening. Gone was the oppressive silence punctuated by fear or the sharp commands of Golovin's Marines. Instead, she heard the rhythmic thud of axes repairing damaged huts, the murmur of conversation, the distant laughter of children, and even, faint but clear, the sound of someone singing a traditional planting song near the newly expanded garden plots. Fear's grip had loosened, replaced by the tentative shoots of renewed life.

She saw neighbors helping neighbors, sharing salvaged supplies, their interactions free from the suspicion and dread that had poisoned the village under Golovin's rule. Men who had fought side-by-side with Kaliq worked alongside former **Vanquisher** crewmen who had defected, a wary respect beginning to bridge the gap between them. The shared trauma, the shared victory, was forging new bonds.

Her gaze fell upon Xevera and Sidonie. The two girls sat together under the shade of a broad-leafed tree, weaving intricate patterns into baskets with practiced ease. Just days ago, they had stood condemned, shadows of terror haunting their young eyes. Now, they chatted quietly, often giggling, their fingers flying with deft skill. Chaka approached with quiet strides, not wanting to intrude.

"Those patterns are beautiful, little sisters," Chaka said, her soft also voice showing appreciation.

Xevera looked up, her smile bright and genuine, her haunted look almost gone. "Thank you, Healer Chaka. We are making baskets for the feast tonight."

Sidonie nodded eagerly. "To celebrate being free."

Chaka's heart swelled. The scars remained, she knew, deep within them both, as they did within the whole village. But healing had begun. Like the jungle reclaiming scarred earth, the spirit of Pristan' Zorya, wounded but resilient, was beginning to grow again, reaching towards the light. She smiled, a true, warm smile. "Then weave joy into them, girls. Weave hope." As she continued her rounds, the sound of the planting song grew stronger, a melody of resilience rising in the morning air.

The midday sun shone down on the Pristan' Zorya square, but the oppressive symbols of Golovin's reign were conspicuously absent. Under the direction of Commander Astrid Cantara, **Covenant** crewmen worked to dismantle the crude gallows, their plasma cutters slicing through the thick wooden beams. Others worked on the heavy steel bars of the cage, reducing the instrument of public humiliation to manageable pieces of scrap metal, useful for village tools in years to come. Residents watched this process with quiet satisfaction, a visible lifting of a heavy burden.

In the center of the square, beneath a hastily erected awning providing shade, a makeshift council convened around a sturdy table salvaged from the command post. Six figures represented the new, tentative power structure: Captain Maksim Bernatski and Commander Simen Agdestein, their **Vanquisher** uniforms clean but bearing the marks of recent conflict, Simen's arm still bandaged; Captain Clement Hoffmann and Commander Cantara, representing the **BASN Neue Bund** and Bad Alpenheimsee; and Kaliq Borzhakov and Healer Chaka, voices of the local Samarqand people.

By unspoken agreement, they looked to Kaliq. "If there are no objections," Hoffmann began, "I propose Kaliq Borzhakov act as Chair for this initial meeting." Maksim and Simen nodded immediate assent.

Kaliq, looking slightly flustered but resolute, accepted. "Thank you, Captain. Let this first council of free Pristan' come to order." He scanned the faces around the table. "First business?"

Chaka spoke, her voice calm but carrying the weight of community concern. "Kong. The elders ask after him. Does he live? Will he recover?"

Hoffmann fielded the question, his expression cautiously optimistic. "He lives, Healer Chaka. He's stable aboard the **Covenant**. Our medical facilities are quite advanced. The damage to his arm was severe, but repairable with synthetics and nano-regeneration. We also detected an underlying malignancy, what you likely diagnosed as jungle sickness. It appears to be a form of lymphoma, aggressive but, caught at this stage, treatable with our methods. Barring complications, Kong should not only survive but potentially live for several more decades."

A collective sigh of relief went around the table, mirrored by murmurs of gratitude from villagers standing nearby who had overheard.

"Thank you, Captain," Kaliq said, relief evident in his own voice. "That is welcome news." He straightened. "Next. We must formalize the situation. I propose we declare an official end to hostilities between the forces gathered under my command and the crew of the **KRSS Vanquisher**."

Maksim nodded. "Agreed. On behalf of the loyal crew remaining aboard the **Vanquisher**, I formally surrender my vessel and personnel to the joint authority of this council and Captain Hoffmann,

81

representing Bad Alpenheimsee." He looked at Simen, who gave a confirming nod. "All remaining personnel, regardless of previous loyalties, are ordered to lay down arms and cooperate fully."

"Accepted," Hoffmann stated. "Commander Cantara will oversee the formal surrender and securing of the **Vanquisher**."

"What of the crew?" Simen asked, voicing a concern Maksim shared. "Specifically, those who remained loyal to Krasnaya doctrine, and those who defected before the final conflict?"

"The defectors," Kaliq said, "those who came to us before the battle, are offered refuge here. They risked much to stand against Golovin."

Hoffmann added, "Bad Alpenheimsee will also offer asylum to any **Vanquisher** crew member wishing to renounce Krasnaya citizenship and resettle. As for those who actively fought under Golovin's command against the uprising…" He paused, looking around the table.

"They will be detained aboard the **Vanquisher** under guard," Maksim stated in his Captain's voice. "Their fate will be determined later, perhaps by Heimsee authorities or an interstellar tribunal. They will face justice, but not mob rule." This met with general agreement. Interestingly, when the offer of asylum or refuge was later made, all surviving **Vanquisher** crew, even those initially loyal to Golovin but horrified by his final excesses, chose to remain on Samarqand, effectively defecting *en masse*.

"Now," Kaliq continued, "we must look forward. Pristan' needs structure. Samarqand needs a future. We need an agreement, a pact between our people and Bad Alpenheimsee."

Hoffmann leaned forward. "Bad Alpenheimsee seeks allies and trading partners, not colonies. We intervened initially because our vessel was fired upon, and subsequently to prevent a massacre and aid a population facing brutal oppression. We propose a formal Treaty of Friendship and Mutual Assistance between the free people of Samarqand, represented by this council, and the government of Bad Alpenheimsee. To be formalized by officials from both planets."

Cantara elaborated, "This would include technical assistance for rebuilding, favorable trade status, medical support, and importantly, defensive guarantees against outside aggression. Specifically, potential reprisal from Krasnaya Rechka or Roma Secundus."

Maksim spoke up. "The **Vanquisher**, while damaged, is still space-worthy. Once repaired, perhaps she could serve as the beginning of Samarqand's own defense force, crewed by former personnel who wish to stay and locals trained by Commander Cantara's people."

This idea sparked immediate interest around the table, but before discussion could take root, Simen Agdestein cleared his throat, shifting his bandaged arm with a small grimace. "Captain Maksim," he began, his tone respectful but firm, "I must respectfully disagree." All eyes turned to him, surprised by the note of dissent. "However much Samarqand may need orbital defenses," Simen continued, meeting Maksim's gaze without concern, "I do not believe the **Vanquisher** should be a part of it. As a symbol of our most recent woes, its presence here will always taint memories, a constant reminder of Golovin and his terror."

He paused, letting the symbolic weight settle before pressing his main point. "Also, and this is my real concern, having a former Krasnaya vessel operating in this system without their explicit authorization invites massive reprisals. Krasnaya Rechka maintains a large and dangerous fleet only three parsecs distant. Using their stolen ship would be seen as an intolerable provocation." He looked around the table, his expression grimly serious. "No. The **Vanquisher** itself is a problem that must be dealt with decisively." He took a breath. "I offer to solve the **Vanquisher** problem myself."

A stunned silence followed Simen's declaration. Maksim looked taken aback, clearly not having anticipated this counter-argument or his friend's bold offer. Hoffmann and Cantara exchanged quick, assessing glances. Kaliq frowned, while Chaka watched Simen with her usual quiet intensity. The implication hung in the air: solving the "problem" likely meant destroying or disabling the ship in a way that couldn't be traced back as an official act of the new Samarqand council or Bad Alpenheimsee. After a moment of heavy consideration, Kaliq nodded in affirmation. Hoffmann followed suit. Maksim, after a moment's hesitation, also gave a reluctant nod of agreement, trusting his friend's judgment even if he didn't understand the plan. Significantly, out of a shared sense of caution or perhaps plausible deniability, no one asked Commander Agdestein *how* he intended to solve the problem.

Discussion turned back to the specifics of cooperation, resource sharing, and establishing formal communication channels. Seeds of a new future were sown, a future where Samarqand, represented at first by Pristan' Zorya, could engage with the wider galaxy on its own terms, allied with a respectable interstellar power like Bad Alpenheimsee.

Kaliq Borzhakov stood and tapped the table, bringing the discussion to a close. "We have agreed on much. Friendship, alliance, rebuilding. But leadership must be formalized by the people." He stood, addressing not just the council but the villagers gathered around. "In one week's time, we will hold elections. For a permanent village council, and for a Governor of Pristan' Zorya, who will act as our primary representative in dealings with our Heimsee allies." His gaze swept across the crowd, meeting nods of approval. "Until then, this interim council will manage daily affairs. This meeting is adjourned!"

As the council members rose, shaking hands, a cheer went up from the villagers. Tables were already being prepared in the square, laden with roasted meats, fruits, and jugs of local brew brought out from hidden stores. The dismantling crew joined the locals, weary smiles on their faces. Laughter mingled with the aroma of cooking food. The day, which had begun with the quiet work of healing, would end in a feast; a celebration not just of survival, but of alliance, and the dawn of a new beginning for Samarqand.

Legacy

Dusk settled over Pristan' Zorya, painting the sky in soft hues of lavender and rose, a stark contrast to the blood-red dawn of that morning. Maksim stood with Simen near the **Vanquisher**'s compact shuttle, the ramp open, waiting. The humid evening air carried the scent of woodsmoke and the distant murmur of feasting from the village, sounds of life returning, a fragile melody against the vast stillness of the jungle. A heavy silence lay between him and Simen, a silence pregnant with unspoken farewells and grim realities.

Simen finally broke it, his voice low, barely a whisper against the chirping of evening insects. "If word ever gets back to Krasnaya about Golovin, about what *really* happened here. If they learn you and I were involved in his death…" He didn't need to finish the sentence. The gallows loomed in their shared imagination, already disassembled but leaving its shadow behind.

"Golovin had his informers," Maksim acknowledged, his gaze fixed on the darkening tree line. "Spies among the crew, planted by Krasnaya's political 'perfection' komissariat. Some must have survived the uprising. They will talk." The truth, or some twisted version of it, would make its way back to Krasnaya, sooner or later. And Krasnaya Rechka would never forgive the murder of its appointed officials, especially by those deemed ideologically suspect.

Simen nodded, his expression resolute. "My life is forfeit the moment they confirm it was me who killed him." He looked at Maksim, a deep, unwavering look. "Yours too, if you remain implicated."

Maksim had already reached his decision, the weight of it settling like stones in his gut. He'd spent the afternoon supervising the transfer of the last few loyal crew members, those who still clung to Krasnaya ideology, to the care of Kaliq's men. "I will go up alone," Maksim stated, his voice firm despite the ache in his chest. "Send these two back on the shuttle." He paused, then finished the sentence he knew Simen was expecting. "And I will take the **Vanquisher** home."

Simen's eyes widened, understanding dawning. "You can't mean…"

"It must be done, Simen," Maksim interrupted, his voice hardening. "You are needed here. Pristan' Zorya needs your skills, your steadiness. You are young, I'm not. *Samarqand* needs your leadership now, more than ever. My duty, my last command, is to remove the **Vanquisher**. Completely. Irrevocably."

Simen stepped closer, placing a hand firmly on Maksim's shoulder, his bandaged arm brushing against Maksim's tunic. "No, Max. *My* duty. It is *my* duty, as I said during Council. *You* stay here. *You* build the future." He shook his head, a rare show of emotional intensity for the usually stoic XO. "Let me do this. It is my last wish. As your friend, not your subordinate."

An emotional weight settled between them, thicker than the humid air. Maksim saw the resolve in Simen's eyes, a quiet determination that brooked no argument. He knew Simen believed he was right, logically, strategically. And perhaps, on a deeper, unspoken level, Simen also carried the burden of Golovin's blood on his hands, a debt he felt compelled to settle.

"Be sure," Maksim said finally, his voice thick with emotion, "be sure it is thorough. Krasnaya cannot, must not ever retrieve her. The **Vanquisher** must vanish."

Simen's lips curved into a faint, almost melancholic smile. He turned towards the shuttle ramp, then paused, looking back at Maksim, a final, enigmatic glint in his eyes. "Watch the heavens, Max," Simen said softly, a hint of wry humor in his tone. "Watch for a sign. A sign for the future of Samarqand."

Simen turned and boarded the shuttle, the ramp hissing shut behind him, sealing him inside the small vessel, ready for ascent. Maksim watched as the shuttle lifted off, plasma streaming from its engines, climbing swiftly into the darkening sky. A solitary spark against the vast canvas of night. He stood unmoving on the beach, the sand soft beneath his boots, his gaze fixed upwards.

Alone in the quiet, his thoughts turned inward, swirling with the uncertainty of the future. Popescu. What would become of the sublieutenant and the other detained Krasnaya loyalists? Justice demanded accountability, but vengeance offered no true path forward. Kong. He would live, Hoffmann had promised. Healer Chaka and her people, welcoming, resilient; could they, alongside the former villagers of Pristan' Zorya, organize the scattered settlements of Samarqand into a thriving, unified society? Could they build a life here, a *better* life, that could withstand the inevitable impact of outworlders, of interstellar interests descending on their once-isolated, idyllic world?

He strained his eyes, searching the heavens, waiting for Simen's promised sign. Minutes stretched, filled with the rhythmic crash of waves on the shore, the whispers of the jungle behind him, and an aching sense of anticipation.

When it came, the symbol proved sudden and final.

A blinding streak of light ripped across the darkening sky, brighter than any star, impossibly fast, plunging downwards from the heavens. The **Vanquisher**, plunging into the atmosphere at full burn. For a heart-stopping moment, the night turned to day, the beach bathed in an incandescent glow, the jungle trees casting stark, elongated shadows. A blinding flash seared itself onto his retinas, even with his eyes closed. A deafening roar reached him moments later, a wave of sound that vibrated in his bones. He felt the heat wash over him, a ghostly warmth from a star fallen from the heavens.

Then silence. Complete, profound silence, broken only by the whisper of the waves. The light was gone. The roar had faded. The **Vanquisher**, and his friend Simen, were gone. Consumed in a final, glorious act of self-sacrifice.

Maksim stood for a long moment, silhouetted against the lingering afterglow, the taste of ozone sharp in the air. He had witnessed Simen's sign. The **Vanquisher** problem was solved, utterly. He turned away from the empty sky towards the village, to the faint sounds of life and laughter echoing from the square. The dark, whispering jungle waited, a vast, unknown future stretching before them all. And Maksim Bernatski, no longer Captain of the lost **Vanquisher**, but now something more, something new, walked towards his future, their future.

87

First Interests

Inception

Rain lashed against the panoramic window of Dr. Carol Powell's office module, blurring the meticulously sculpted landscape of the Cosmonomics Corporate Park into washes of green and grey. Outside, Costa Muerta wept, but inside, the air hummed with the sterile efficiency of recycled climate control. It felt like a cage, polished and comfortable, but a cage nonetheless. Carol stared out, the reflection of her own tired face superimposed on the dreary scene. Three years. Three years chasing biochemical ghosts through Costa Muerta's deceptively vibrant ecosystems, navigating its haunted history and labyrinthine local politics, only to end up here, staring at manufactured rain.

The memory of Director Valerius's office, just hours before, was colder than the rain-chilled plasteel outside. Valerius, impassive behind a desk vast enough to land a small flyer on, hadn't raised his voice. He hadn't needed to. His words, smooth and precise, had done the cutting. *"…significant resources expended, Doctor Powell. Diminishing returns…"* He'd steepled his fingers, his gaze distant, as if discussing crop yields rather than a career. *"…frankly, Carol, the board feels your Costa Muerta projects lack impact."*

Impact. Such a sterile word for the sweat, danger, and near-misses in the field. Then came the final, quiet twist of the knife. *"Samarqand is an opportunity, if you let it be."* Valerius had paused, letting the weight settle. *"A final one, perhaps. Succeed, bring Cosmonomics a dominant position in synbergris, and your future here is secure. Fail…"* Another calculated pause. *"…and we'll mutually agree it's time for you to seek opportunities elsewhere."*

Seek opportunities elsewhere. The corporate euphemism for termination echoed in the quiet hum of her office. Cold dread warred with a surge of defiant anger. It wasn't just bad luck; it was bureaucratic blindness, rivals whispering in the right ears. Samarqand. A barely charted K-class world out on Pleiades end of the Golden Road, teeming with unknown dangers, biological and corporate. It wasn't an opportunity; it was exile with a performance clause written in blood.

Fine. Let them push her out. Let them underestimate her again. She pushed away from the window, the reflection dissolving. They wanted impact? She'd give them impact. Samarqand held the key, the synbergris Cosmonomics craved. She would find it. She would secure it. Failure wasn't an option. It couldn't be. Her career, her reputation – everything depended on this one, final chance.

Misdirection

The shuttle ramp lowered with a hydraulic sigh, releasing Carol Powell into the thick, soupy air of Samarqand. It clung like a wet shroud, heavy with the scent of unknown blossoms, damp earth, and something else: a faint, musky tang of decay that spoke of ancient cycles of growth and decomposition. Emerald Landing sprawled before them, a rough-edged settlement pressed hard against a wall of emerald jungle that seemed poised to swallow it whole. Prefabricated structures bearing the logos of off-world corporations sat awkwardly beside weathered buildings of local timber and salvaged metal. It was a world away from the sterile, controlled environment of the Cosmonomics Corporate Park on Costa Muerta, with its manicured lawns and rain-streaked office windows that had become her prison bars.

This has to work, Carol thought, familiar pressure tightening her chest. Valerius's parting words echoed in her mind, smooth and cold as polished stone: *"…an opportunity… a final one, perhaps… seek opportunities elsewhere."* Failure here wasn't just a setback; it was the end of her career at Cosmonomics, maybe the end of her serious research career altogether. Three years of chasing phantoms on Costa Muerta had eroded management's faith. Samarqand, this wild, untamed world, was her last chance for vindication.

She scanned her team assembling on the ferrocrete beside the shuttle, stretching and sniffing the air. It had been a long five months, nearly seven hundred light years in pressurized metal tubes of varying size and quality. Sloane Hartstein stood solid and watchful, her gaze sweeping the perimeter with practiced vigilance. Stones. Carol had given her the nickname back on Costa Muerta, after their initial friction had tempered into hard-won respect. The woman was tough as granite, a former Costa Muertan Marine whose sharp edges Carol had learned to appreciate, especially after going to bat to save Sloane's job during that mess with the highlands survey expedition. Loyalty ran deep between them now.

Then there was Aoda Hyobanshi. Banshee, as he liked to be called. He stretched with theatrical grace, his expression one of eager curiosity. A skilled chemist, undoubtedly, but his late addition to the team still felt off. Valerius's justification, that two women needed a man for protection on a frontier world, had rung hollow then and felt even thinner now, standing beside Stones. Carol pushed the flicker of unease aside. Competence first. Results were all that mattered.

"Alright," Carol said, her voice cutting through the ambient sounds of the port: the whine of cargo lifters, distant alien calls from the jungle, the growl of moving vehicles. Shouts in a flavorful mix of Terran Standard, Heimsee Deutsch, and Krasnayan Russian, with local polyglot and more as seasoning. "Let's get our gear transferred to the temporary quarters. Standard security protocols. Stones, coordinate with the local agent. Banshee, supervise the equipment transfer. Meet at the Cosmonomics field office module in two hours for our initial briefing."

Stones gave a curt nod, already keying commands into her wrist unit. Banshee offered a charming smile. "Consider it done, Doctor Powell. Eager to see what secrets this world holds."

Carol watched them move off, then turned towards the administration building, the humid air already making her uniform cling. Secrets, yes. And hopefully, salvation.

Weeks bled into one another under Samarqand's alien sky, slightly purple compared to Costa Muerta's blue due to the light orange primary. The initial optimism curdled into a familiar frustration. Emerald Landing, despite its name suggesting riches, offered only dead ends regarding synbergris. Carol, meticulous and driven, pursued every lead. She interviewed bored local administrators whose knowledge seemed limited to port fees and smuggling rumors. She cross-referenced pre-Collapse biological surveys, fragmentary and often contradictory, with data from the few registered xenobotanists she could find operating near

91

the settlement. She led short forays into the surrounding jungle, following coordinates logged decades or centuries ago, only to find magnificent Elven Parasol trees standing alone, devoid of the crucial Mesenga Creeper vine or any sign of the Sap Tank Beetles needed to trigger synbergris production.

Each negative report back to Costa Muerta felt like another nail hammered into her professional coffin. The pressure mounted with every fruitless day. Lisya, the great continent they'd landed on, seemed biologically rich but barren of the specific prize Cosmonomics craved. The torrential rains of the wet season limited further field research, driving all three team members to occasional bored sniping at east other.

Returning to their cramped prefab office module late one afternoon, soaked and tired from another failed trek into the rainy jungle west of the port, Carol paused outside the door. Raised voices, low but intense, stopped her.

"…not buying it, Aoda," Stones' voice was a low growl, stripped of pleasantries. "That's the third 'local contact' who evaporated right before a meeting you arranged. And the sample transport you 'forgot' to requisition for the survey you were to set up out past Bagong Balay? We lost two days. It's slowing us down." A pause, heavy with accusation. "Either pull your weight, or admit you're deliberately sandbagging this operation."

Banshee's reply was smooth, almost silken, laced with wounded pride. "Stones, really. Unforeseen complications happen on frontier worlds. The requisition slip was a simple oversight amidst setting up. I assure you, I am as committed to this project's success as anyone."

Carol pushed the door open. Stones stood stiff, arms crossed, glaring at Banshee who leaned against a console, affecting an air of injured innocence. The tension in the small space was thick enough to choke on.

"Is there a problem?" Carol asked, her voice level, though her eyes narrowed slightly at Banshee.

Stones didn't break her stare from the chemist. "Just clarifying team priorities, Doctor."

Banshee turned to Carol, spreading his hands in a placating gesture. "A minor misunderstanding regarding logistics, Doctor Powell. Already resolved. My apologies if it disturbed you."

"See that it doesn't happen again," Carol said, her gaze sweeping over both of them. "We don't have time for friction or mistakes. We find synbergris, or we go home empty-handed with busted careers. Focus on the objective." She saw the hard glint in Stones' eyes, the flicker of something unreadable in Banshee's before his charming mask slipped back into place. Her suspicion solidified. Banshee wasn't just potentially incompetent; he might be an active hindrance. Which meant she had to work harder, faster, and watch her back.

The breakthrough came not from official channels or corporate contacts, but from a cramped, cluttered workshop smelling of dried herbs, preservative chemicals, and mealworms. Dr. Aris Thorne, a reclusive xenobotanist who'd lived on Samarqand since just after Rediscovery, possessed maps and journals dating back centuries, meticulously hand-copied from deteriorating pre-Collapse records. After Carol patiently earned his trust over several visits, sharing recent atmospheric data he lacked, Thorne finally unearthed a faded ecological survey from the late 2500s.

"Here," he'd said, his gnarled finger tracing lines on brittle paper. "The symbiosis. Parasol tree, Mesenga vine, *and* the Sap Tank Beetle. Requires specific humidity, soil composition, average temperature range, rain and more. The conditions were only ever right, according to this survey, on the smaller continent – Pony – and some of the larger islands in the Azure Archipelago." He tapped a region marked on Pony's western coast. "Particularly concentrated here."

Relief washed over Carol, sharp and intense, followed immediately by urgency. *Pony.* All their efforts on Lisya had been wasted. "Thank you, Dr. Thorne. This is invaluable."

Back at the office module, Carol laid out her findings for Stones and Banshee. "We've been on the wrong continent. The ecological triad we need is primarily on Pony." She pointed to the area Thorne indicated on their digital map display. "The logical next step is arranging immediate shuttle transport to Sapphire, the main port on Pony's west coast."

Before Stones could even nod agreement, Banshee spoke, leaning forward, his expression earnest. "Doctor Powell, a moment's caution. We file for shuttle transport, it goes on the public logs here in Emerald Landing. You know how many corporate ears are listening. IndAxioma, Globetek, maybe even Krasnaya agents... they'll know exactly where we're going within hours. Cosmonomics stressed discretion, didn't they? Especially now we have a confirmed target zone."

He lowered his voice, conspiratorial. "I've been making inquiries, discreet ones, just in case we wanted to go east. There's an independent ocean floater, cargo vessel mostly. Runs quiet routes between the continents, avoids official ports sometimes. No route plans filed, no tracking beacons squawking our business to everyone. We could charter it, slip out of Emerald Landing's water port, travel direct to a secluded cove near the target area on Pony." He paused, letting it sink in. "It's slower, yes." He anticipated Stones' main objection. "Maybe twelve days travel time across the strait, but it guarantees secrecy. We arrive undetected, right where we need to be, avoiding the corporate sharks circling Sapphire."

Stones immediately bristled. "Absolutely not. A twelve-day sea voyage on an unregistered, uninspected floater? Through potentially hazardous waters? Minimal communication capability? That's an unacceptable security risk, Carol. We have protocols for a reason." Her gaze locked with Carol's, a clear warning.

Carol felt caught. Stones' points were valid, logical, aligned with every risk assessment protocol Cosmonomics drilled into them. But Banshee's argument resonated with the intense pressure she felt. Valerius's words. The whispers from Costa Muerta. The need for a decisive, *exclusive* win. If another company got wind of the Pony location and beat them to it she'd be finished. They'd all be done. The twelve-day delay felt agonizing, but the risk of being scooped felt catastrophic. Banshee's 'secrecy' argument, playing on the cutthroat reality of corporate bioprospecting, felt like the lesser of two evils. It was a gamble, a huge one, against her better judgment and Stones' explicit advice.

"We take the floater," Carol decided, the words tasting like ash. "The secrecy is paramount. We can't risk another team shadowing us or arriving first." She saw the sharp disapproval tighten Stones' mouth, the flicker of disappointment in her eyes. Stones knew when to argue and when to soldier, so she simply nodded. "Stones, go with Banshee and inspect the vessel. If it's really bad, I'll uphold your veto." Another frowning nod, this time more decisive.

Behind them, hidden from Carol's direct view, a brief expression of profound relief crossed Banshee's face before vanishing under his usual mask. *This has to pay off,* Carol told herself, ignoring the knot of apprehension twisting in her gut. *It just has to.*

Discovery

The *Nauti Lass* groaned around them, a symphony of protesting metal and stressed timbers as it plowed through te turquoise chop in the Samarqand strait. Twelve days. Stones gripped the pitted, salt-sticky railing, the vibration humming through her palms. The air tasted of unfamiliar brine and the acrid tang of the floater's overworked engine fumes. Below deck, the generator throbbed with a disconcerting irregularity. Stones had meticulously inspected the vessel before departure, Carol granting her full veto power. It wasn't derelict, not quite. The hull plates, patched with mismatched sealants like old scars, seemed watertight; the lifeboat pods, though weathered, showed charged power cells; the navigation system, while decades out of date, functioned. Enough to satisfy minimum safety protocols, not enough to inspire confidence. She'd given Carol the reluctant go-ahead, the weight of Banshee's arguments about corporate spies tipping the balance against her ingrained caution. A calculated risk that still tasted sour.

For eleven days, the alien ocean had stretched vast and empty, mirroring the unsettling quiet of the ship's three crew members. They were a gaunt, watchful bunch who moved with economical silence and responded to direct questions with grunts or wary nods. Stones didn't trust them further than she could throw their burly captain, a man whose eyes seemed like black holes absorbing the light. She maintained her vigilance, running silent checks on their gear, ensuring their emergency beacon remained active and slaved to her personal comm unit. Sleep came in short, alert bursts.

She watched Banshee now. He leaned near the bow, ostensibly admiring the flight of large, leathery-winged avians that soared on thermal updrafts, their cries like screeching metal. But his gaze kept flicking towards the horizon, then down to the chrono integrated into his environment suit's wrist unit. He'd tried engaging her earlier, asking seemingly innocent questions about the range of their encrypted comms, the power output of her sidearm. She'd given him clipped, non-committal answers. He seemed too interested, too smooth. His charm felt like a lubricant designed to help something slide past unnoticed. Was he just anxious, or was he coordinating? Was his style just too foreign to hers?

Damn it, Carol. Stones' knuckles whitened on the rail. She owed Carol more than just mission support. That inquiry on Costa Muerta. The fabricated data logs pointing straight at Stones after the ambushed highland survey team had returned. Carol had risked her own standing, digging relentlessly until she exposed the real culprit, a rival researcher trying to sabotage their project. Carol had saved her career, maybe her freedom. Loyalty demanded vigilance.

And then there was David. Her brother's face swam in her thoughts; the frustrating cycles of hope and despair, the doctors shaking their heads. Synbergris... the reports hinted at potent psychoactives, neural regeneration potential. Could it be the key? Could this dangerous, uncertain mission hold an answer for him? The thought was a fragile spark she guarded fiercely. This *had* to work. *Safely.*

On the twelfth day, the scent of land reached them: a heavy perfume of damp earth, unfamiliar blossoms, and the undeniable musk of mangrove-like swamp. The *Nauti Lass* dropped anchor with a screech of rusted chain in a muddy, secluded cove. Towering trees draped in thick vines crowded the water's edge, their roots like grasping claws half-submerged in the brackish water. The air hung thick and still, buzzing with the sound of unseen insects. Not Sapphire's civilized port, but a smuggler's landing, just as Banshee had arranged. Stones tasted grit on her teeth. She drew her sidearm, checked the charge with a practiced flick of her thumb, and scanned the dense, uninviting shoreline. The risk profile just went up another notch.

The mud sucked greedily at Banshee's boots as he hauled a heavy equipment container onto the narrow strip of beach. The air was a suffocating blanket woven from heat, humidity, and the stench of decaying vegetation. Insects whined near his ears, their pitch unnervingly variable. He forced a smile, complimenting Carol on her choice of waterproof containers. *Tedious woman,* he thought, *always by the book.* But her meticulousness, her predictability, made her vulnerable.

He glanced at Stones. She moved with disciplined energy, her eyes constantly scanning the jungle perimeter, her hand never far from the sidearm holstered on her thigh. *The dangerous one.* She didn't trust him; he saw it in her curt responses, her watchful gaze. He'd have to be careful around her when the time came.

Stones checked loads and packs. This would be tough hike, carrying most of what they would need and with no porters to carry materials. The ship's captain steadfastly refused to allow his crew to be hired as porters. Banshee was surprised to see Stones take the heaviest load, one that had to be 65 kilos if it was a gram. He gave his head a shake; now was not the time to start respecting the younger woman, not with what he had to do.

The trek inland was short and brutal, following a barely discernible trail Jasik Chenier had presumably marked. Roots snagged their feet, low-hanging vines slapped wetly against their faces, and the sucking mud seemed determined to claim their boots. Banshee watched Carol struggle slightly, her face flushed, her breathing heavier than usual. A flicker of contemptuous satisfaction warmed him. *Not so tough outside her lab, is she?*

They reached the rendezvous point after a testing three kilometers: a small, gloomy clearing dominated by a cluster of colossal fungi. They towered three meters high, their caps a startling, iridescent violet that seemed to absorb the dappled sunlight, pulsing faintly with an internal luminescence. The air here smelled earthy and pungent, like ozone and mushrooms. Jasik Chenier leaned against the rubbery stalk of the largest fungus, looking as if he'd grown there. His clothes were simple, durable synth-weave, stained with mud and orange chlorophyll. A long knife rode his thigh, and a compact slug-thrower hung at his shoulder. His leather-creased face missed nothing.

Banshee moved quickly to make introductions. "Jasik Chenier, this is Dr. Carol Powell of Cosmonomics and our team leader. And this is Sloane Hartstein, our security specialist." No handshakes, as Jasik bowed deeply and kept his hands hidden in his campaign jacket pockets.

Carol almost rejected Jasik the moment Banshee introduced him. Stones watched, arms crossed, as Carol quizzed him about his experience, his reasons for taking the team on for this expedition. Banshee felt his smile move to worried frown as Carol kept after his chosen guide. He tried to interject himself into the discussion, but when Carol had waved him away, Stones had stepped between him and the ongoing discussion.

To Carol's surprise, Jasik stayed calm, smiling lightly during her increasingly hostile grilling. He gave clear answers, without embellishment. He even showed her a worn, yellowed card, a license to guide on both Pony and Lisya. She'd inspected it closely, but there was no way to tell if it was real or fake, even with Stones' help. She'd finally given in and accepted, drawing a simple not from the local and a deep sigh from Banshee.

Carol changed from inquisitioner to pleasant colleague, all business. She confirmed the payment transfer on her data slate. Jasik nodded slowly, examining his worn datapad. He bowed again, once to each of the team. "Payment received. You seek the old groves. Where the vines weep gems."

Banshee stepped forward, offering his flask. "A pleasure to work with someone who knows this land. To a successful expedition?"

Jasik grasped the flask, his eyes impassive. He took a token sip, the synth-whiskey producing no effect, and handed it back. The brief contact revealed calloused, immensely strong hands. "The jungle provides," Jasik repeated, his voice a low rasp. "But it watches. It remembers disrespect, punishes indifference. Stay alert. Follow my lead. No straying." His gaze was unnervingly direct.

No charm works on this one, Banshee realized. *Purely transactional.* That was fine. Better, even. He needed Jasik's expertise now, but the guide's presence could complicate the extraction. The Globetek plan was simple: locate the lode, transmit encrypted coordinates and sample analysis via tight-beam burst, let the shuttle handle retrieval and sanitation. Jasik was a loose end. A regrettable necessity of business. More money should do the trick.

Banshee subtly checked the timer on his wrist unit. The Globetek shuttle was moving into orbital position. Everything depended on finding a rich enough source within the next three days. The memory of his last performance review at Cosmonomics and the barely veiled threats, the dismissal of his contributions, fueled his resolve. This wasn't just about a living; it was about proving them all wrong. Proving he was smarter, more ruthless, than they ever suspected.

Carol gasped, planting her hands on her knees, trying to draw a full breath of the super-saturated air. Each inhalation felt like drinking soup. The Pony jungle wasn't just terrain; it was an active opponent. Giant ferns with serrated, metallic-blue edges snatched at her sleeves. Gnarled roots, hidden under layers of mulch, seemed to reach for her ankles. The ground itself varied unpredictably from sucking mud to slick, moss-covered rock. Sweat pasted strands of hair to her temples and stung her eyes, blurring the riot of alien botany surrounding her.

Her muscles burned, the pack straps digging mercilessly into her shoulders. This was worlds away from the controlled environmental challenges of Costa Muerta. This was raw, untamed, and indifferent to her Ph.D. or her corporate mandate. Yet, even through the exhaustion, her scientific curiosity thrilled. She saw epiphytes clinging to tree bark that pulsed with faint light, fungi in colours unknown to Terran biology, insects with crystalline wings humming intricate patterns in the air. Potential precursors, novel compounds, unique metabolic pathways: they were everywhere. If synbergris was the primary target, the secondary discoveries here could fill Cosmonomics' R&D pipeline for decades. *If we survive to report them.*

Ahead, Jasik moved like a phantom, his worn boots making almost no sound on the leaf litter. He'd pause occasionally, raising a hand, his head cocked, listening to the jungle's complex symphony. Then he'd point – a patch of iridescent slime coating a low branch ("Spore-spitter. Blinds you for hours."), a network of nearly invisible filaments stretched between trees ("Razor-web. Carnivore."), a cluster of deceptively beautiful, bell-shaped flowers nodding at ankle height ("Nerve bloom.

Paralytic touch."). He spoke little, his warnings concise, his knowledge profound and unsettling.

Stones stayed close behind Jasik, alert and focused, her movements economical, her gaze constantly scanning their surroundings. Her presence gave silent reassurance. Banshee lagged slightly behind Carol, his earlier enthusiasm apparently dampened by the sheer physical effort. Or was he conserving energy?

They stopped for a brief water break beside a narrow stream that tumbled over smooth, grey stones. The water was surprisingly cold, tasting of minerals. As Carol refilled her canteen, Banshee approached, wiping his brow with a sigh that seemed exaggerated. "Remarkable ecosystem, Doctor," he said, his tone just shy of patronizing. "But demanding. Quite different from a controlled lab environment, wouldn't you agree? Pacing yourself, I hope?"

The implication, that her field experience was somehow lesser, pricked Carol's exhaustion-frayed nerves. Before she could snap back, Stones materialized beside her, silent as the guide. She didn't look at Banshee, just stared pointedly downstream. "Jasik says we're close," Stones stated flatly. "Terrain changes ahead. Best keep moving. We'll have a modest climb before the end of the day."

Banshee's smile tightened almost imperceptibly. He gave a slight bow. "Of course. Wouldn't want to impede progress." He turned and moved up the trail.

Carol exchanged a brief look with Stones. Gratitude, understanding, and shared exasperation passed between them without a word. She took another long drink, the cold water reviving her slightly. Jasik was right; the air ahead smelled different. The cloying humidity lessened fractionally, replaced by a faint, tantalizing scent — resinous, sweet, with an undertone like ozone or electricity. It was the scent of promise, the aroma of discovery. Her fatigue seemed to lift, replaced by a thrumming anticipation. They were almost there.

101

Betrayal

Jasik raised a hand, halting them at the edge of a dense thicket of bamboo-like stalks that glowed with a faint internal indigo light. He gestured forward. "Through here. Be ready."

Stones pushed through the yielding stalks, the air growing thick with that strange, electric-sweet scent, and stepped into a place out of time. It was a vast natural amphitheater, dominated by dozens of Elven Parasol trees whose immense, layered canopies formed a living green cathedral dome far overhead. Sunlight filtered down in shimmering shafts, illuminating the forest floor. And the floor… Stones stopped dead, her breath catching in her throat.

It wasn't soil or leaves. It was treasure. Nodules, beads, gems of solidified resin glittered everywhere, blanketing the ground half a meter deep in places. They glowed with internal light in every conceivable color – fiery orange, deep sapphire, emerald green, iridescent pearl, sun yellow, blood red. Centuries, perhaps millennia, of accumulated synbergris lay scattered like a pirate king's hoard, shed from the ancient Mesenga vines that climbed the Parasol trunks like thick, gnarled ropes. The air itself hummed, thick and intoxicating, saturated with the volatile psychoactive compounds Jasik had warned them about.

"Filters!" Jasik's sharp command cut through the stunned silence. "Now! High concentration. Breathe deep, you lose yourself."

Stones fumbled with the high-efficiency filter mask clipped to her belt, securing it over her nose and mouth. The cloying sweetness in the air lessened, replaced by the sterile taste of filtered oxygen. Beside her, Carol stood transfixed, her eyes wide behind her own mask, reflecting the glittering bounty. All the stress, the exhaustion, the crushing weight of expectation seemed to fall away from her. A slow smile spread across her face, lighting it from within.

"We found it, Stones," Carol breathed, her voice muffled but ecstatic. "We actually found it. Look at the size variation! The color spectrum! The crystalline structure on these older ones… Valerius wanted impact? This… this is paradigm-shifting." She dropped to her knees, pulling out her analysis kit, her movements quick and energized, radiating pure scientific joy. Exoneration.

A wave of relief washed over Stones, so potent it almost buckled her knees. *She did it.* For Carol's career. For the mission. For David… the possibility felt tangible now, glittering all around them. She watched Carol work, her earlier fatigue forgotten, directing Jasik and Banshee on collecting representative samples: noting specific locations, apparent age, proximity to active vine sections.

Stones helped methodically, bagging nodules, labeling samples, her training keeping her movements efficient. But as the initial awe subsided, a different kind of awareness returned. She watched Banshee. He moved with feverish energy, stuffing samples into collection sacs almost indiscriminately. Greed, yes, that was obvious. But there was something else. While Carol was absorbed in analyzing a particularly large, multi-faceted amber nodule, Stones saw Banshee pause. His gaze wasn't on the glittering floor. It lifted, scanning the upper canopy, the surrounding ridgeline that formed the amphitheater's rim. Then, his hand moved subtly to the device strapped beneath his environment suit sleeve. A fractional-second glance at its display, too quick to be casual. When he looked back down, the manic delight on his face seemed overlaid with something else. Calculation. A predatory gleam.

What was that? The observation struck a jarring, discordant note against the triumphant mood. It wasn't just the thrill of discovery fueling him. It was something colder. Planned. The relief Stones had felt moments before curdled into ice water in her veins. Her internal alarms, quieted by the spectacle, began to scream. As they finished collecting the initial samples and Jasik led them out of the main clearing to find a suitable campsite nearby, Stones deliberately fell back, walking near Carol. She scanned the terrain as they moved, noting potential cover, escape routes, defensible positions. The wonder of the discovery remained, but it was now overshadowed by a sharp, prickling sense of imminent danger. Something profoundly wrong colored the win, leaving the joy.

✧ ¤ ✧ ¤ ✧

They made camp in a smaller clearing about a kilometer away from the main synbergris lode. The overpowering scent of the nodules was fainter here, though still a sweet, resinous undercurrent in the air. Exhaustion warred with exhilaration within Carol. They had done it. The scale of the find was beyond anything Cosmonomics could have hoped for. Images flooded her mind: data charts scrolling across screens, presentations to the board, the grudging respect in Director Valerius's eyes. She mentally began structuring her preliminary report, planning the encryption protocols, the tight-beam transmission sequence.

They ate a subdued meal of nutrient paste and purified water. The usual post-fieldwork banter was absent. Carol felt drained but deeply satisfied. Stones was quiet, watchful, her usual stoicism amplified. Jasik seemed preoccupied, his gaze distant. Even Banshee was less talkative than usual, though he offered Carol a brief, congratulatory nod that felt oddly perfunctory. Tension simmered beneath the surface, an unspoken counterpoint to their success.

As darkness fell, swift and complete under the dense canopy, the jungle sounds shifted. Daytime chirps and buzzes faded, replaced by nocturnal clicks, whistles, and the occasional low growl from something unseen moving in the undergrowth. The isolation felt immense, the four of them adrift in a vast, ancient wilderness. Carol zipped her sleep cocoon, ready for a few hours of much-needed rest before preparing the initial data burst transmission.

Then came the sound. A high-pitched whine, cutting through the natural chorus of the jungle, growing rapidly louder. Not the familiar roar of a standard atmospheric shuttle engine, but something higher, more powerful, with a distinctive pulsing undertone. Artificial. Close.

Everyone froze. Jasik was instantly on his feet, his slug-thrower leveled, peering into the darkness above the trees. "That's no trader," he hissed, his voice tight with alarm. "Not Research Commission either. Military grade drive signature. Or private security."

Landing lights flared through the canopy, washing the clearing in harsh, artificial brilliance. The whine intensified, culminating in the muffled thud of landing gear deploying nearby, just beyond their clearing. Heavy foliage muffled the exact landing spot, but it was close. Dangerously close.

"Stay put! Check gear!" Carol ordered, her mind racing. Pirates? Rival corporate mercs? How could anyone have known? She started towards the edge of the clearing, intending to get a visual without exposing herself. "Stones, secure the primary sample cases —"

She never finished the sentence. A sharp, stinging pressure hit her neck from behind. Not a blow, but an injection. Her muscles locked, her vision tunneled instantly, the world dissolving into grey static. A faint smell of ozone and bitter chemicals filled her nostrils. Her last conscious thought was a bewildered flash of Banshee's face, his expression not triumphant, but cold, detached, as she crumpled bonelessly to the ground.

Carol surfaced slowly, bubbling up from a thick, suffocating fog. Her head throbbed with dull, heavy pain, centered behind her eyes. A foul, chemical taste coated her tongue, and something rough pressed uncomfortably against her mouth: a binder gag. Panic flared as she realized her wrists and ankles were secured tightly behind her back. She tried to struggle, but the bonds held firm, cutting into her skin. Disorientation warred with rising fear.

Forcing her eyes open, she blinked against the flickering light of the revived campfire. The air smelled of woodsmoke, damp earth, and the lingering metallic tang of whatever drug had incapacitated her. Her gaze darted around the campsite. Stones was there, bound similarly, propped against a large tree root. Her face was grim, her eyes narrowed slits of fury, but she met Carol's gaze with a flicker of reassurance. Then Carol saw Jasik, also tied, slumped near Stones. His expression was a mixture of shock, disbelief, and a dawning, terrible understanding. He avoided looking at Carol or Stones. *Jasik too?* Why?

Six figures moved around the camp with quiet, disciplined efficiency. They wore dark, non-reflective environmental suits, devoid of obvious insignia, but the cut of the gear, the modern weaponry slung casually over their shoulders, screamed professional mercenary. One of them knelt by a portable comms unit, murmuring into a headset. Another pair was methodically transferring the bulk synbergris samples from their collection bags into large, sterile transport containers marked with a discreet, stylized globe logo Carol didn't immediately recognize. Globetek? It had to be.

Then Banshee stepped into the firelight, and the last piece clicked into place with sickening certainty. He wasn't bound. He moved freely among the armed figures, gesturing, giving quiet instructions. The amiable mask was gone, replaced by an expression of cold satisfaction. He saw Carol was awake and walked towards her, stopping a few feet away.

"Awake, Doctor? Good." His voice was devoid of its earlier charm, flat and businesslike. "Apologies for the crude methods, but time is of the essence, and your cooperation couldn't be guaranteed."

Carol glared at him, unable to speak past the gag.

Banshee allowed himself a small, tight smile. "Surprised? You shouldn't be. Cosmonomics writes people off. They value quarterly reports more than talent. They certainly didn't value mine." His gaze hardened. "Globetek, however, recognizes opportunity. They pay well for results. And this," he gestured vaguely towards the glittering nodules being packed away, "is the biggest result imaginable."

He stepped closer, lowering his voice slightly. "We'll file the discovery claim under Globetek's name, naturally. Dated preemptively, of course, using my access codes from before I 'officially' left Cosmonomics employment. By the time your company realizes what happened, Globetek will have established prior discovery rights with the Samarqand Research Commission. Your expedition will simply be logged as… lost in the field. Tragic."

He glanced towards Jasik, his lip curling in contempt. "Our local guide was instrumental in ensuring we found the lode quickly. He provided excellent intel on your movements back in Emerald Landing, too. All for a modest fee." Banshee chuckled, a dry, humorless sound. "He actually thought Globetek would cut him in for a real share. Imagine."

Jasik flinched as if struck, his face contorting with shame and fury. He finally met Carol's eyes, his filled with despair, before looking away, unable to hold her gaze. The betrayal fell like another physical blow.

Banshee walked over to where their personal gear lay piled. He picked up Carol's primary datalogger, then Stones'. He hefted them for a moment. "All your hard work, Doctor. Your precious data." With a dismissive shrug, he tossed both loggers carelessly into an empty sample bag held open by one of the mercs. He didn't even glance at the data chip slots.

Across the flickering firelight, Carol's eyes locked with Stones'. Stones, despite her bonds, gave the slightest, almost imperceptible nod towards the bag containing the loggers, then an equally minute shake of her head. Understanding dawned in Carol's mind, sharp and bright, cutting through the fog of despair like a laser. *The chips!* Stones' meticulous gear checks the night before they settled to sleep… she hadn't just been cleaning contacts. *She swapped the chips!* The real data, the proof of their discovery, the detailed analysis Carol had logged; it wasn't in those loggers Banshee held. It was safe. Hidden. A wild surge of hope, fierce and defiant, coursed through Carol. They weren't beaten yet.

Banshee turned back, oblivious. "Don't worry about your fate," he said, his voice regaining a touch of false sympathy. "It will be quick. This jungle doesn't suffer fools, or the unprepared. Consider it… early retirement." He gave a final nod to the merc leader, then turned his attention to supervising the last packing of synbergris containers.

Carol watched him go, her mind racing. Fear was still present, cold and sharp, but now it was mixed with calculation. She assessed the guards: six including Banshee. Alert, well-armed, but perhaps overconfident now they believed the primary objective was secure. She scanned the perimeter of the firelight, the dense wall of darkness beyond. Jasik had warned them about the local fauna. An idea, desperate and dangerous, began to form. They had the real data. Now, they just needed to survive to use it.

Escape

Bound and gagged, Carol forced down the rising tide of panic, her mind racing, latching onto the faint spark of hope ignited by Stones' signal. *The chips are safe.* That knowledge was a shield against despair. Now, survival was paramount. She scanned the chaotic campsite through narrowed eyes, analyzing the situation with the detached precision of a scientist observing a volatile experiment.

Six Globetek mercs, plus Banshee. They were professionals, armed with pulse rifles and sidearms, focused now on securing the synbergris haul. Their leader, a tall woman with cold eyes, conferred with Banshee near the stacked transport containers. Two mercs stood guard near the captives, their attention divided between the prisoners and the unsettling sounds of the nocturnal jungle. Another two were loading equipment onto the waiting shuttle, its ramp lowered, casting an angular shadow in the firelight. The sixth seemed to be checking the perimeter, vanishing briefly into the darkness. Overconfidence. They thought the fight was over.

Carol's gaze swept the ground near her bound feet. There. A patch of the distinctive purplish ground fungus Jasik had warned them about during the trek. *"That one,"* Jasik had said, pointing with his chin, *"Pungent fungus. Smells bad to us. Smells like dinner-and-a-fight to Kesterblades. Little devils nest nearby. Crush that fungus, you call them. Fast. Angry."*

One of the guards near her shifted his weight, carelessly planting his boot less than a meter from the fungal patch. He yawned, adjusting the rifle slung over his shoulder, his attention momentarily drifting towards the shuttle. It was now or never.

Fear coiled tight in her stomach, cold and sharp, drowned out by fierce determination. She remembered the diagrams Thorne had shown her, the complex ecological webs of Samarqand where one small action could trigger a cascade of unforeseen consequences. *Time for a cascade.*

Taking as deep a breath as the gag allowed, Carol focused all her strength. Her feet were bound together, but not immobile. Waiting for a moment when both nearby guards glanced away towards a shout from the shuttle crew, she kicked backwards, hard. Her heels slammed into the soft, yielding flesh of the purple fungus patch.

It ruptured with a faint tearing sound. A smell instantly filled the air, thick and acrid, like ammonia mixed with burnt sugar and something else, something primal and musky; roasted cinnamon or turmeric. It wasn't overpowering to human senses, just unpleasant. But Carol saw the nearest guard wrinkle his nose, glancing down at the crushed fungus with annoyance. He hadn't made the connection.

From the dense wall of blackness just beyond the firelight, a high-pitched chittering erupted. Not one voice, but dozens, sharp and furious. It was answered by more chittering, closer this time. Leaves rustled violently. Small, dark shapes began to detach themselves from the shadows. Low-slung, fast-moving bodies, glinting eyes reflecting the firelight. Kesterblades. Jasik hadn't exaggerated. They were coming. Fast. Angry.

The first scream ripped through the relative quiet of the campsite. Stones' head snapped up. One of the mercs near the perimeter stumbled back into the firelight, clawing at his legs, his rifle dropping from his grasp as small, dark shapes swarmed over him, a flurry of teeth and claws. Chaos erupted.

"Kesterblades! Hostiles!" someone yelled near the shuttle. Laser pistol fire flashed, bright green streaks cutting through the night, accompanied by the high-pitched shrieks of wounded animals and panicked humans.

Now! Adrenaline surged through Stones, cold and sharp. While the guards' attention was momentarily diverted by the sudden attack, she twisted violently, slamming her bound wrists against a sharp edge of metal bracing on the heavy camp stool she was tied to. She'd spotted it earlier, a flaw in the construction, a potential key. Pain exploded up her arm as the rough metal edge bit deep into her flesh, slicing through the synth-cord restraints. Warm blood flowed instantly, soaking her sleeve, but her right hand was free.

Ignoring the searing pain, she grabbed the heavy stool itself. Banshee, startled by the commotion, turned towards the firefight near the perimeter. Stones lunged, swinging the stool in a vicious arc. It connected solidly on the side of Banshee's head with a sickening thud. His eyes rolled back and he collapsed without a sound, hitting the dirt like a sack of meal.

One less problem. The two guards assigned to the prisoners whirled towards her, raising their rifles. Before they could fire, Jasik, still bound at the ankles but somehow free at the wrists (had he worked his bonds loose earlier, waiting for a chance?), launched himself from the ground. He didn't attack. He threw himself sideways with desperate force, body-slamming the legs of the female guard nearest him.

The guard stumbled, her rifle discharging reflexively. The pulse blast tore through Jasik's upper thigh. He cried out, a raw sound of agony, and collapsed, clutching his bleeding leg. But his sacrifice had bought Stones the one second she needed.

She dropped the stool, drawing the stun baton clipped inside her boot as she moved. The remaining male guard fired, but Stones was already diving low, the pulse blast searing the air where she'd been. She came up inside his guard, the baton humming. A precise strike to the wrist sent his rifle clattering away. A second jab to the temple dropped him, unconscious before he hit the ground. The female guard, recovering her balance, fumbled to bring her rifle back on target. Stones didn't hesitate. A swift, disabling strike to the knee joint made her cry out and collapse; a follow-up stun charge silenced her.

Across the campsite, the scene was pandemonium. Kesterblades, maybe thirty or forty of them, small, thirty-centimeter bundles of fury with oversized jaws and razor claws, swarmed everywhere. They moved with terrifying speed, darting between legs, leaping onto backs, tearing at exposed flesh. Two more mercs were down, overwhelmed by the sheer number and ferocity of the creatures. The remaining two, the leader and one other, fell back towards the shuttle ramp, firing controlled bursts from their pulse rifles, trying to clear a path.

The Kesterblades, drawn by the scent of blood and easy prey, had discovered the unconscious form of Banshee. They swarmed over him, tearing at his suit, their sharp teeth finding flesh. Carol, freed by Stones using a captured combat knife to slice her bonds, grabbed a burning branch from the campfire. "Get off him!" she yelled, swinging the makeshift torch, trying frantically to drive the vicious creatures away.

The shuttle! Stones sprinted across the chaotic clearing, dodging panicked Kesterblades and stray pulse fire. The two remaining mercs reached the ramp, turning to provide covering fire. Stones didn't slow down. She hit the ramp at full speed, tackling the nearest merc low, sending them both sprawling onto the shuttle deck. The leader whirled, raising her sidearm, but Stones was faster. She kicked out, sending the weapon flying, and followed through with a disabling blow using the stun baton. Neutralize the threat. Secure the asset. Her Marine training drove her without thought, cold and efficient.

She glanced back. Carol battled the Kesterblades clustered around Banshee, the firelight casting demonic shadows. Stones grabbed a medical kit from the shuttle wall, found a high-intensity emergency flare and ignited it. The brilliant white magnesium flare hissed to life, flooding the area with blinding light and intense heat. The light-sensitive Kesterblades recoiled instantly, chittering in alarm, momentarily breaking off their attack on Banshee and scattering back towards the shadows. She tossed the first-aid kit in Carol's general direction.

Stones quickly used cable ties from the shuttle's restraint locker to secure the two conscious but subdued mercs on the deck. The immediate threat was contained. The campsite was a wreck, littered with bodies, mercenary and Kesterblade, and the air thick with the stench of blood, ozone, and roasted fungus.

Stones vaulted back down the ramp, baton humming in her hand, the bloody gash on her arm throbbing fiercely. She did a rapid tactical assessment, her mind working with cold clarity despite the adrenaline crash settling in.

Casualties: Two Globetek mercs definitely dead near the fungus patch, torn apart by Kesterblades. Another one down near the perimeter, likely fatal wounds. Banshee: unconscious, horribly mauled, bleeding profusely from dozens of deep bites, but somehow still breathing shallowly. Jasik was conscious, pale with shock and pain, clutching a makeshift tourniquet Carol had applied to his thigh, the leg clearly shattered by the pulse blast. The three mercs she'd disabled (two stunned, one with a shattered knee) were secured but needing attention. The two she'd subdued on the shuttle were conscious and restrained. Total: Seven Globetek personnel neutralized or dead, leaving Banshee, Jasik, Carol, and herself.

Assets: One functional, albeit slightly damaged, Globetek security shuttle. Their own gear, minus the primary dataloggers Banshee had taken, useless without the real chips. The bulk synbergris samples still secured in the Globetek transport containers aboard the shuttle.

"Status report," Stones snapped, kneeling beside Jasik, reinforcing Carol's field dressing with pressure bandages from the shuttle's medkit. She jabbed Jasik's arm with a dose of orthomorphine, which made him smile in seconds, then sleep.

"Banshee's critical, maybe too far gone," Carol reported, her voice tight, face pale but steady as she worked on the worst of his wounds. "Multiple deep lacerations, probable internal bleeding, shock. Needs a full trauma unit, now. Jasik needs immediate surgical intervention for the leg. Massive tissue damage, possible arterial involvement."

Stones nodded grimly. The shuttle could carry maybe four, five max, with the medical equipment deployed. Not everyone. Triage. Hard choices.

"Right," Stones made the decision instantly. "Carol, you fly the shuttle. Take Banshee and Jasik. Load the most critical merc too, the one you worked on. Maybe he survives." She indicated the guard Jasik had tripped, who was groaning, semiconscious. "Get them to Emerald Landing. Use the Globetek emergency transponder codes. Broadcast a Mayday, claim pirate attack. Might confuse things, buy you time. Transmit our data *securely* the moment you're clear of local interference. Call for Cosmonomics evac and security, full priority."

Carol hesitated for only a second, looking from the wounded to Stones. "And you?"

"I'll handle these four." Stones jerked her chin towards the remaining conscious prisoners: the two she'd stunned who were groggily recovering, and the two subdued on the shuttle ramp. "We'll take the overland route back towards the coast. Slower, but manageable. We rendezvous near Sapphire. Go. Now." There was no room for argument in her voice.

Carol nodded, understanding the harsh tactical necessity. Together, they quickly loaded the critically wounded, with Banshee strapped to an anti-shock gurney, Jasik carefully stabilized, and the semi-conscious female merc secured. Carol climbed into the pilot's seat, her hands moving over the unfamiliar controls with focused competence.

"Good luck, Stones," Carol said over the comm, her voice tight.

"You too. Fly well," Stones replied, stepping back from the shuttle.

The engines whined, kicking up dirt and leaves. The shuttle lifted off, blowing debris around like a small tornado, banking sharply and disappearing over the high canopy. Its lights vanished into the oppressive darkness in a few seconds. Silence descended, broken only by the crackle of the dying campfire and the groans of the wounded prisoner at her feet.

Stones took a deep breath, ignoring the throbbing pain in her arm and the bone-deep weariness settling over her. She turned to her four prisoners, who watched her with a mixture of fear and resentment. She nudged the nearest one with her boot. "On your feet. All of you. We've got a bit of walking to do. No problem for ex-military, right?" Stones let her face show an evil, gloating smile. The coast was days away through hostile jungle, burdened with unwilling company. It would be a long, hard march.

Five days later, exhausted, filthy, several kilos lighter and running on sheer grit, Stones emerged from the dense jungle onto a stretch of rocky coastline a few kilometers south of Sapphire. Her prisoners stumbled behind her, sullen and defeated, helping each other as Stones commanded. She hadn't lost any of them, though one had required rough field treatment for Kesterblade bites sustained during the initial chaos. As she scanned the horizon, a familiar shape appeared: the sleek lines of a Cosmonomics corporate shuttle descending towards the beach.

The ramp lowered, and Carol hurried out, looking clean, rested, and immensely relieved to see her. Cosmonomics security personnel quickly took charge of the Globetek prisoners.

"Report?" Stones asked, accepting the fortified water bottle and stim-loaded carnesticks Carol offered.

"Transmitted everything," Carol said, her voice filled with grim satisfaction. "HQ is energized. Full response team inbound, heavy security. Globetek is finished. As for the wounded, Jasik's stable. They saved the leg, but he'll need extensive regeneration therapy. He's asking about you. Says he owes you."

"And Banshee?" Stones asked, watching the prisoners being loaded.

Carol's expression tightened. "He survived the transit. Barely. He's in deep medical coma and lockdown on Spice. Multiple surgeries already, years of reconstructive work ahead, nerve grafting… They're not sure about the neurological damage from the blood loss and trauma. Might have saved his life, but not his mind." A flicker of dark irony crossed her face. "Maybe someday we'll find a compound here on Samarqand that could help him." She managed a thin, humorless smile. "No rush, though."

Vindication

Two months. Sixty-three standard days since Carol had flown the commandeered Globetek shuttle back to Emerald Landing, carrying the grievously wounded and irrefutable proof of discovery and betrayal. Emerald Landing felt different now. The ramshackle port town still bustled with its usual frontier energy, but a new, more organized layer had been superimposed. Cosmonomics' temporary prefab modules had multiplied, forming a neat compound near the main landing pads. Cargo haulers bearing the company logo were a common sight, offloading equipment and personnel. Security patrols, discreet but present, moved through the settlement. Cosmonomics had arrived in force, galvanized by the secure data burst Carol had transmitted the moment she cleared Samarqand's ionosphere.

Carol stood on the ferrocrete tarmac beside Stones, watching the sky. The humid air still carried the scent of alien jungle and salt water, but today it felt less like a threat and more like potential. They waited under the harsh glare of Samarqand's primary, the K2 subgiant Ipak. The intervening weeks had been a blur of activity: securing the synbergris site on Pony with the initial Cosmonomics security team, debriefing specialists via tight-beam comms, overseeing the careful extraction and cataloging of initial bulk samples, even conducting brief aerial surveys of adjacent territories that showed promising ecological markers. She'd spoken briefly with Jasik via comm link; he was recovering well at the orbital station's medical facility, already offering advice on navigating Pony's complex interior based on their survey data. He seemed eager to put his role in the betrayal behind him and work honestly. Carol believed in second chances, especially hard-earned ones.

Stones stood beside her, solid and calm as ever. The deep scar on her forearm from cutting her bonds had healed to a thin white line, a permanent reminder of their ordeal. They had faced disaster together and emerged stronger, their partnership forged in fire. Whatever came next, they would face it together.

A deep-throated roar grew overhead, resolving into the sleek, powerful lines of a Cosmonomics long-range corporate transport descending towards the landing pad reserved for priority arrivals. This wasn't just another supply run; this was the arrival of senior management. This was the moment of reckoning. Carol felt a flicker of the old anxiety, the ingrained fear of corporate judgment, but tamped it down. She had the data. She had the results. She had survived.

The transport settled onto the pad with barely a whisper from its inertial dampeners. The main ramp lowered smoothly. Several figures emerged, blinking in the bright sunlight – executives in crisp shipboard uniforms, specialist scientists eager for their first look at Samarqand's biosphere. Leading them was a woman Carol didn't recognize. She was slim, of medium height, with sharp, intelligent eyes, dark hair cut in a severe but practical style, and an air of brisk, no-nonsense authority. She wore the insignia of a Senior Vice President. She walked directly towards Carol and Stones, her stride purposeful.

"Dr. Carol Powell? Sloane Hartstein?" Her voice was clear, resonant, carrying easily over the background noise of the spaceport. "I'm Merula Lenski, acting VP for Xenobotanical Development." She offered a firm handshake to each of them, her grip surprisingly strong. Her gaze was direct, assessing. "Welcome back to relative civilization. Your preliminary reports have caused… considerable excitement back on Costa Muerta, shall we say?"

"Director Lenski," Carol replied, keeping her voice steady. "It's good to finally meet you in person. We trust the wounded arrived safely?"

"They did," Lenski confirmed. "Hyobanshi and Chenier are receiving the best care available. The captured Globetek personnel are being debriefed under Sol League authority. Your handling of the situation after the ambush was exemplary, Ms. Hartstein. Textbook extraction under fire." Stones gave a curt, almost imperceptible nod.

Lenski turned her full attention back to Carol. "Director Valerius sends his regrets. He elected to take early retirement last month. Very sudden." A faint, knowing smile touched Lenski's lips. "Your encrypted report, Doctor Powell, including the secure data, as well as the extracted

116

video recordings from the Globetek shuttle, were conclusive. It arrived just as Globetek was attempting to file their fraudulent claim with the Samarqand Research Commission, citing technical difficulties for their delay."

Lenski paused, letting the impact sink in. "Your evidence was airtight. Timestamps, unique biochemical markers only your field analysis could have detected that quickly, corroborating testimony from Hartstein and Chenier, the shuttle's flight recorder data all painted a damning picture. Industrial espionage, claim jumping, attempted murder of Cosmonomics personnel, illegal deployment of armed mercenaries on a designated research world."

Vindication washed over Carol, warm and complete, erasing the last vestiges of doubt and fear. Valerius gone. Globetek exposed.

"Globetek Supplements filed for bankruptcy protection last week," Lenski continued, her voice crisp. "Their assets are being liquidated under Commission oversight. Cosmonomics, naturally, is positioning itself to acquire anything useful, such as research notes, precursor samples, perhaps even a few salvageable scientists not implicated in the Samarqand fiasco." She gave a slight shrug. "Their ambition outstripped their competence. A fatal mistake in this business."

She met Carol's gaze directly. "Which brings me to you, Doctor Powell. The board convened an emergency session. Based on your initiative, your resilience, and the sheer scale of the synbergris discovery you secured under extreme duress, they have approved an immediate, unprecedented double promotion. Effective today, you are Senior Project Director for Samarqand Operations."

Carol felt a dizzying sense of unreality. Senior Project Director. Two grades up. It was more than she had dared hope for.

"Furthermore," Lenski continued, "they have created a new position specifically for you at headquarters on Costa Muerta. Head of the newly formed Xenobotanicals Acquisition and Analysis Division. Full lab facilities, significant budget, direct report to the Executive VP of Research. It's yours, Carol. Acknowledgment of your expertise and your value to this corporation."

Costa Muerta. Headquarters. The pinnacle of a research career at Cosmonomics. Everything she had once thought she wanted. The sterile labs, the corporate park, the political maneuvering. The cage, gilded though it might be. She thought of the vibrant, dangerous, intoxicating wilderness of Pony. She thought of the endless potential humming just beneath the surface of this world. She thought of Stones at her side, facing the unknown.

Carol took a breath, the Samarqand air filling her lungs. "Director Lenski," she said, her voice clear and firm. "Thank you. I am honored by the board's confidence. I accept the promotion to Senior Project Director." She paused. "However, I must respectfully decline the position at headquarters."

Lenski raised a single eyebrow, her expression unreadable. "Indeed? May I ask why? It's a significant opportunity."

"My work isn't finished here, Director," Carol stated simply. "Samarqand… We've barely scratched the surface. Synbergris is just the beginning. There are countless other compounds, entire ecosystems waiting to be understood. My place is here, in the field, leading the research effort on the ground." She glanced at Stones, who met her gaze with quiet approval. "With my team."

Merula Lenski studied Carol for a long moment, her sharp eyes assessing. She gave a quick glance to Stones standing implacably by, a rock of silent support. Then, a genuine smile touched her lips. "I thought you might say that, Doctor Powell. Good." The approval in her voice was unmistakable. "Frankly, that's where Cosmonomics needs you most right now. We need strong, experienced field leadership, especially on a world this competitive and potentially hazardous."

She gestured towards the growing Cosmonomics compound. "I'll be staying planetside for the next two standard years myself. My primary task is establishing the permanent Lisya base operations here in Emerald Landing. Labs, security infrastructure, logistics hub. After that, the plan is to oversee development of research facilities on the moon, Spice. A safer location for sensitive analysis and synthesis work." She looked back at Carol. "Your success here has accelerated Cosmonomics' investment timeline for Samarqand by at least a decade. You'll have all the resources you need, Doctor. Just tell us what discoveries you plan to make next."

A sense of profound relief and rightness settled over Carol. The weight of needing to prove herself was gone, replaced by the invigorating challenge of the work itself. She wasn't just surviving anymore; she was leading. Here, on this wild frontier, under this alien sun.

She caught Stones' eye again, and this time, they both allowed themselves a small smile. The future stretched before them, vast and full of possibilities. The Golden Road had tested them, nearly broken them, but they had endured. And the real journey was just beginning.

Completion

Samarqand's light orange K2 primary dipped toward the horizon, painting the sky in fiery strokes of amber, bronze and crimson. Stones sat outside her field tent, perched on a collapsible stool at the edge of a small, rocky promontory that overlooked a vast savannah. The tall, golden grasses rippled in the evening breeze like an inland sea, dotted with herds of graceful, five-legged pentalopes grazing in the lengthening shadows. Their mournful calls carried on the wind, a low, melodic counterpoint to the rustling vegetation.

Behind her, the field camp hummed with quiet efficiency. Four sturdy tents, a portable lab module, and compact comms array formed their temporary home, three days' hike from the nearest outpost on Pony. The sweet, resinous scent of synbergris hung in the air, stronger than she'd ever smelled it before. They had found another lode that morning, a vast deposit that dwarfed their initial discovery. The forest floor had literally glowed with the accumulated treasure of centuries.

Stones took a sip from her wine bulb, savoring the complex, earthy notes of the Muertan vintage – a small luxury they'd packed for special occasions. The liquid warmed her throat, easing the pleasant ache of physical exertion. The past few months had settled into a rhythm of exploration, discovery, and careful documentation. The work suited her. Out here, the rules were simple, the dangers honest. No corporate politics, no pretense. Just survival, vigilance, and the quiet satisfaction of protecting something valuable.

Carol emerged from the lab module, her face illuminated by the fading light. She held another wine bulb and joined Stones at the edge of the promontory, lowering herself to sit on a flat rock nearby. She looked tired but content, the lines of stress that had marked her face during their early days on Samarqand smoothed away.

"Sample analysis confirmed it," Carol said, gesturing with her bulb toward the distant tree line they had explored that morning. "This field is at least three times the concentration of the first site. The nodules are older too, more complex chemical structures. Merula's going to have a fit when she sees the preliminary data."

They clinked their bulbs together in a gentle toast. "To discovery," Carol murmured.

"And survival," Stones added, her eyes scanning the darkening horizon. The first stars were becoming visible, strange constellations she was slowly learning to recognize.

They sat in comfortable silence, watching the light fade. A distant, bellowing call echoed across the savannah — one of the larger predators beginning its nocturnal hunt. The pentalopes shifted nervously, forming tighter groups.

"Another good haul today," Stones observed, rolling her shoulder to ease a knot of tension. "This field makes the first one look like a test run."

Carol laughed softly, the sound carrying in the still air. "Think Merula has any more of that Costa Muertan vintage back in Emerald Landing? This data might be worth trading for a case."

"Knowing her, she'd charge us triple," Stones replied with a rare smile. "But it might be worth it."

In the four months since Merula Lenski's arrival, Cosmonomics' presence on Samarqand had expanded exponentially. The synbergris extraction was proceeding smoothly. Jasik had recovered sufficiently to join their field team, his knowledge of Pony's interior proving invaluable. His betrayal forgiven, if not forgotten. The captured Globetek personnel had faced Sol League justice, their testimonies further cementing Cosmonomics' legal position. And Banshee... last they'd heard, he remained in medical stasis, his recovery uncertain.

The sky deepened to indigo, then black. The stars of the nearby Pleiades blazed overhead in their uncounted millions, more brilliant than any Stones had seen on more developed worlds. She felt small beneath them, yet somehow perfectly placed. She thought briefly of her brother David, and the latest test results from the medical team on Costa Muerta. Preliminary, but promising. The synbergris-derived compound showed potential. Another reason to push forward, to explore deeper into this world's secrets.

Stones leaned back, feeling the day's tension drain from her muscles, replaced by a quiet contentment she'd rarely known. The dangers were still there — Samarqand was never truly safe — but they had earned this moment of peace.

"Life is good, Carol," she said simply, her voice soft against the night sounds of the savannah.

Carol nodded, gazing up at the alien stars. "Yes, Stones," she replied. "It really is."

Flowers in the Ashes

Before the Storm

The damp morning air clung to Brynn's skin, cool before the Samarqand sun breached the towering canopy. Sweat beaded on her brow as she flowed through the *Sayaw sa Hangin*, the Wind Dance form her mother insisted grounded the spirit as much as it trained the body. Her bare feet padded without a sound on the packed earth of the training space, a small clearing wrested from the jungle's edge just outside Bagong Balay. Behind her, the twenty-seven structures of the village, stilt houses of woven bamboo and salvaged plastisteel, were stirring, the scent of wood smoke mingling with the rich, loamy smell of the jungle floor.

Each movement was precise, honed by years of practice. A low block flowed into a spinning kick, her silver-white braid whipping around her head. She was sixteen, tall for her age, lean muscle coiled beneath her simple tunic and trousers. *Faster,* she pushed herself. *Stronger.* Five years. Five years since Papa vanished into this same green immensity, chasing whispers of miracle plants. Five years of waiting, of Cilka's quiet reassurances wearing thin against the gnawing absence. He'd find something amazing, he'd promised. He always did.

She finished the form, breathing air deep into her lungs, listening. The usual morning chorus of unseen birds and buzzing insects filled the air, punctuated by the distant shouts of children. But something felt... off. A subtle dissonance in the cicadas' rhythm, a momentary hush where there should have been the screech of a canopy glider. Brynn tilted her head, scanning the impenetrable wall of green, her senses

123

straining against the familiar backdrop, searching for the source of the subtle disturbance.

Brynn knelt beside a patch of broad-leafed *Lunas* vines, snipping the youngest leaves with care, using her sheath knife. Their milky sap, Cilka had taught her, eased fevers when brewed according to a difficult procedure. She placed them into her woven collecting basket, already half-full with *Hikaw* roots for pain and crushed *Bato-Bato* petals for wound sealing.

Back in the village proper, children chased squawking ground-runners between the houses while adults tended small garden plots or repaired fishing nets. Brynn nodded greetings as she passed, heading for the largest hut, distinguished by the drying racks of herbs outside and the faint, complex aroma of poultices and tinctures drifting from its open doorway. This was Cilka's domain, the heart of Bagong. Inside, bundled herbs hung from the rafters, clay pots lined shelves, and a low fire simmered beneath a bubbling kettle.

"Good morning, *anak*," Cilka said without turning, grinding something fine in a stone mortar. Her mother's presence was a calming anchor in Brynn's life, steady and knowledgeable.

"The *Lunas* looked strong today, Mama," Brynn replied, setting down her basket.

Elder Taho entered, leaning on his walking stick like he had walked miles already. His wrinkled face broke into a smile. "Ah, Brynn. Practicing early, I heard. You have your father's discipline."

Brynn felt the familiar pang. "I try, Elder."

"Manuki was strong," Taho continued, his gaze distant. "But even he knew caution. These woods… they draw outsiders now. Corporate surveyors near the eastern ridge last month, whispers of cartel scouts sniffing the borders. Be watchful, child."

Cilka looked up, her eyes meeting Brynn's. A silent warning passed between them. The outside world, with its insatiable hunger for Samarqand's riches, felt closer than ever.

Dusk painted the sky in hues of violet and orange, bleeding through the dense canopy as Brynn returned to the training space for a final cool-down stretch. The air was thick, heavy with the promise of night. But the usual evening symphony of the jungle was muted, replaced by an unnerving quiet. The birds had fallen silent. Even the incessant buzzing of insects seemed subdued. An expectant stillness settled over the clearing, raising the hairs on Brynn's arms.

Without warning, the undergrowth bordering the clearing thrashed in bird-scaring violence. Branches snapped. A figure stumbled out, ragged and wild-eyed, crashing through the last barrier of ferns. He was gaunt, his clothes ripped to shreds, skin scratched raw and burning with fever. He saw Brynn, his eyes widening in delirious recognition, or desperation. He lurched forward, collapsing onto the packed earth at her feet, his breath coming in ragged, tearing gasps.

He scrabbled at the dirt, then reached out, grabbing Brynn's ankle with surprising strength. His hand was hot like the burning sun. "Manuki. Manuki was right," he choked out, his voice a dry rasp. He coughed, a wracking sound that shook his thin frame. His eyes darted in fear towards the jungle he'd just fled. "They know. They're coming!"

Brynn reacted instantly, pulling her ankle free while assessing his condition. Fever, delirium, severe exhaustion, likely injuries. "Help!" she yelled towards the village, her voice cutting through the unnatural quiet. "Someone help!" She knelt beside the man, trying to ease his breathing as the first villagers emerged from their homes, drawn by her cry. The fragile peace of Bagong had just shattered.

Dying Man's Warning

Cilka worked with practiced efficiency, her movements calm amidst the rising tension in the small hut. Villagers murmured in concern outside, but within the circle of firelight, only the rasping breaths of the stranger broke the quiet. Brynn knelt beside her mother, handing her heated compresses soaked in *Luya* root infusion, the sharp ginger scent filling the air. Cilka dabbed with soft, practiced motions at the deep gashes on the man's arm and chest, inflicted by something far sharper than thorns. The air in the hut was thick with the earthy smell of damp clay, woodsmoke, and the pungent aroma of medicinal herbs.

"Poisoned, I think," Cilka murmured, examining a weeping puncture wound on his leg. "Some kind of neurotoxin. And fever... raging." She fed the man small sips of a dark, bitter concoction from a gourd, the liquid dribbling down his chin. His skin was clammy, his eyes unfocused, darting from side to side, then up and down. Brynn found a crumpled ID card tucked into a pouch in his torn jacket. It was cracked and faded, but she could just make out: *Ahearn Speth, Research Associate, Planetary Biocorp.* A corp. An outsider.

"Speth," Brynn said, showing her mother the card. Cilka glanced at it, a frown deepening the lines around her eyes.

Speth's breathing hitched, becoming shallower. He mumbled again, words tumbling out in a rush. "Stellaris. Beautiful. Like stars." Then, clearer, his voice gaining desperate urgency. "Manuki. He understood. Sempernal. Eternal life. They want it..." He clutched at Cilka's hand, his grip stronger than Brynn could believe. "Don't let them! They'll destroy it, everything..." His eyes rolled back, his body convulsing, going still. Cilka checked his pulse, her expression grim.

"He's gone," she said in soft tones, releasing his hand. The only sound now was the crackling fire and the hushed whispers of the villagers gathered at the doorway. The stranger's warnings hung heavy in the humid air, thick with unspoken fear.

The low fire in the village center cast flickering shadows across the faces of the gathered elders. Brynn sat beside Cilka, listening with deep focus as Taho, his voice usually strong, now wavered with uncertainty. The night air, usually alive with jungle sounds, felt heavy, expectant. A palpable fear permeated the small group.

"Corporations," Elder Linay muttered, shaking her head. "or worse. Cartels. They're all hungry for Samarqand's secrets."

"Speth was from Pristan Biocorp," Elder Falak reminded them, his voice tight. "Emerald Landing is crawling with them. Maybe we should send runners before, before they come looking."

"And tell them what?" Cilka interjected, her tone firm. "That a delirious stranger died in our village, babbling about star-flowers and eternal life? They'll call us fools, or worse, think we're hiding something valuable."

"But if these raiders are truly coming —" Falak persisted, gesturing to the dark jungle surrounding them.

Elder Taho sighed, his shoulders slumping. "Contacting Pristan might draw more trouble than it prevents. We are isolated by choice. Perhaps silence is our best defense, as always." He looked at Cilka. "What do you advise, Cilka Erith?"

All eyes turned to Brynn's mother, the village healer, the woman who had always guided them through crises. Brynn held her breath, waiting. Cilka's decisions had always kept them safe. Tonight, however, the jungle felt different, the threat more real, the shadows deeper.

✧ ¤ ✧ ¤ ✧

Later, after the council dispersed, leaving a nervous quiet in their wake, Brynn sat beside Cilka's sleeping mat, the stranger's meager possessions laid out on a woven cloth. A worn synth-leather pouch, a dented water flask, a broken multi-tool, and the damaged ID card. And tucked deep within a hidden inner pocket of his jacket - a small, stiff square of plasti-paper, folded meticulously. A map fragment.

Brynn's fingers trembled as she unfolded it. Jagged lines detailed unfamiliar terrain, marked with coded symbols in faded ink. In the margins, scribbled notes, also coded, but one word stood out, stark and clear, underlined twice: Sempernal. Brynn traced the word, a chill prickling her skin. Speth's dying whisper… eternal life. She recognized the handwriting style: slightly slanted, hurried. Papa's.

"Brynn?" Cilka murmured, stirring on her mat, her voice still heavy with fatigue.

Brynn folded the map before her mother could see, tucking it into her own pouch. "Just looking at his things, Mama. Trying to understand."

Cilka sat up, her gaze sharp, perceptive. "You think this is about your father?"

Brynn hesitated, then nodded, a fragile hope flickering in her chest. "The handwriting, and the word Speth spoke. Sempernal. Papa was always searching for extraordinary things."

Cilka reached out, her hand covering Brynn's. "Hope is a dangerous fire, *anak*. It can warm you, but also burn you if you're not careful. Be watchful, Brynn. Be prepared. That's the best we can do." But in her mother's eyes, Brynn saw a flicker of something else: a shared, unspoken hope mirroring her own, mingled with a deep, abiding fear.

Attack

Morning dawned with deceptive serenity. The villagers gathered in the small clearing beside the burial ground, the air thick with the scent of freshly turned earth and the sweet, cloying fragrance of funeral orchids laid on the simple grave. Elder Taho began the ceremony, his voice resonating with somber dignity in the humid air, reciting verses about the jungle's embrace and the journey of spirits.

"We return this stranger to the earth of Samarqand," Taho intoned, his weathered hands gesturing toward the mound of soil. "May his spirit find peace in the Great Green."

Brynn stood apart a bit, her gaze scanning the jungle perimeter. The unease from the previous evening lingered, a cold knot in her stomach. The birds were too frantic, their calls sharp and warning rather than melodic. Something was wrong. The jungle knew it. She edged closer to her mother, who stood with head bowed in respect.

"Mama," she whispered, "something feels —"

Cilka's subtle nod silenced her. Her mother had sensed it too.

Taho reached the crescendo of the ceremony, raising his arms skyward. "And so, we commend this wanderer to —"

A sharp crack echoed from the jungle's edge, followed by the sickening thud of impact. Elder Falak crumpled to the ground, a smoking hole in his chest. Before anyone could react, a second blast hit Elder Linay, her body jerking backwards into the new grave.

Chaos erupted. Villagers screamed, scattering in panic. Above the din, Brynn heard the distinctive whine of approaching airships. She grabbed a small child who ran past her, pulling the boy behind the trunk of a massive tree just as the canopy above them shredded under a hail of energy fire. Two sleek attack airships appeared above the clearing, their weapon ports spitting death.

"Mama!" Brynn screamed, searching for Cilka in the chaos. But her mother had vanished in the panicked crowd, and the clearing began to fill with armored figures emerging from the jungle, weapons firing.

◇ ¤ ◇ ¤ ◇

Brynn pressed herself against the tree trunk, the small boy trembling in her arms. She watched in horror as the raiders systematically herded the surviving villagers into the center of the clearing. These weren't random bandits: they moved with military precision, their dark armor unmarked except for crimson vipers coiling around their shoulders. Drug syndicate. The worst kind.

"Please," she whispered to the terrified child, "stay here. Don't move." She pushed him deeper into the hollow at the tree's base.

A harsh, amplified voice boomed across the clearing. "Villagers of Bagong Balay! Stand down! We are here for information! Cooperate, and you might live!"

From her vantage point, Brynn could see her people — neighbors, friends, elders — being forced to kneel in a line. Some were bleeding, others sobbing without sound. Six bodies lay motionless in the dirt. She scanned for Cilka, finally spotting her mother among the kneeling villagers, her face composed despite the chaos.

A tall woman strode into the clearing, flanked by two heavily armed guards. Unlike the others, her armor was sleeker, and she carried herself with the easy confidence of someone accustomed to being obeyed. Her dark hair was pulled back in a severe tie, accentuating sharp cheekbones and eyes that gleamed with cold intelligence.

"Good afternoon, villagers," the woman's voice, now audible without amplification, dripped with false cordiality. "I am Veronica Lutz, though most call me Venom." She smiled, revealing teeth that seemed too white, too sharp. "We have a few questions. About a certain thief who sought refuge in your quaint little town. And about a certain plant he was so interested in. Stellaris. Ring a bell?"

Silence fell over the clearing, broken only by the whimper of a child.

130

Venom paced along the line of kneeling villagers, her boot heels crunching in the dirt. "No? How disappointing." She paused before Elder Taho, whose weathered face remained impassive. "Perhaps you need motivation to jog your memories."

She nodded to one of her soldiers, who stepped forward and dragged a young man from the line. Brynn recognized him: Samat, just turned seventeen, who had just begun apprenticing with the village's master hunter.

Brynn's muscles tensed. She had to do something. But what? She was unarmed, outmatched, outnumbered. If she revealed herself now, she'd just be another captive. Or worse.

Her gaze locked with her mother's across the clearing. Cilka gave an almost imperceptible shake of her head. Wait, the gesture said. Not yet.

With every fiber of her being screaming in protest, Brynn forced herself to remain hidden.

✧ ◻ ✧ ◻ ✧

"Perhaps our young friend can help us," Venom said, circling Samat like a predator. The boy trembled, his eyes wide with terror.

"Please," he stammered, "I don't know anything —"

Venom's hand snapped out, backhanding him across the face. The crack of impact echoed in the unnatural silence of the jungle. "I didn't ask you to speak," she said softly, almost tenderly. She drew a thin knife from her belt. Not a combat weapon; a blade designed for precision work. For pain.

"Now," she continued, addressing the kneeling villagers, "who helped the researcher? Who knows about Stellaris?"

Cilka rose to her feet, her movements deliberate. Raiders trained weapons on her, but Venom waved them down, curiosity flickering across her features.

131

"I helped him," Cilka said, her voice clear and steady. "I am the healer. The stranger was brought to me. If anyone here knows anything, it would be me."

Brynn's heart seized. *No, Mama. No!* She pressed her fist against her mouth to keep from crying out, tears burning in her eyes.

Venom's smile widened, genuine this time, a flash of satisfaction. "Well, well. A volunteer." She gestured, and two raiders roughly dragged Samat back to the line, shoving Cilka forward in his place. "And what exactly did this 'stranger' share with you, healer?"

Cilka stood tall, dignity wrapped around her like armor. "He was delirious. He spoke of many things, in many languages. Plants. Stars. Names. Nothing coherent."

"And yet," Venom circled Cilka, tapping the flat of her blade against her palm, "you were interested enough to help him. A stranger. Curious, that."

"I am a healer," Cilka replied. "That is what we do."

Venom laughed, the sound brittle in the heavy air. "Nobility. How quaint." She nodded to one of her raiders, who stepped forward with a crackling electro-prod. "Let's see if it survives scrutiny."

What followed seemed to stretch into eternity for Brynn. Venom's questions, growing more specific, more demanding. The sickening smell of burning flesh as the prod made contact again and again. Cilka's gasps of pain, becoming weaker, but her denial never wavering. The prod's blue light reflecting in her mother's eyes, still somehow defiant even as her body betrayed her.

Brynn's fingernails bit into her palms, drawing blood. Every muscle in her body strained toward her mother, held back only by the silent plea in Cilka's gaze each time their eyes met across the clearing: Be strong. Survive.

Venom stepped close to Cilka; too close. Her arm moved like a striking bogsnake, and Cilka gasped. With a sickening jolt, Cilka's body went limp, collapsing into the dust. Venom straightened, wiping a spatter of blood from her cheek with casual disdain.

"Pity," she said, her voice devoid of emotion. "She could have made this easier." She turned toward the remaining villagers. "Who's next?"

Brynn exploded from hiding, murder in her heart. An unseen club struck her senseless, darkness taking her before she could reach Venom.

Survival

The hut door slammed shut, plunging Brynn into near darkness, broken by a few slivers of light piercing the woven bamboo walls and the dim glow of the datapad on the table. The air became heavier, thick with unspoken threat. The two raiders flanking her were hulking figures in shadow, their armor exuding the cold reek of plasteel and gun oil. One carried a heavy vibro-axe, the other a wicked-looking plasma injector pistol. They exchanged a look, a silent communication passing between predator and predator.

"So," the one with the vibro-axe rumbled, his voice gravelly, circling her as if sizing up a boarbeast ham. "The boss wants you to… remember." He hefted the axe, its humming blade casting faint, flickering shadows on the hut walls. "Maybe we can help jog your memory." He trailed the edge of the blade along the rough-hewn table, a screeching sound that grated on Brynn's nerves.

The other one chuckled, a dry, humorless sound. He stepped closer, the pistol glinting in the dim light. "Or maybe you prefer a… softer approach." He raised the pistol, pointing it at her arm. Brynn remained still, impassive, but her senses were screaming. The metallic tang of fear filled her nostrils, mingling with a stale ale smell. She could feel the rough wood of the stool digging into her skin, the tight burn of the plasticuffs on her wrists. Every detail sharpened, as Cilka's voice echoed in her memory: Observe your enemy. Find the weakness. Use every advantage.

She subtly shifted her weight on the stool, testing the bindings, noting the guards' stances. The one with the axe was impatient, eager for violence. The plasma pistol raider was more calculating, savoring the anticipation. Neither of them seemed to expect resistance from a teenage village girl. Their mistake, a cold voice whispered in Brynn's mind. She locked her gaze on the pistol raider, feigning a tremor of fear in her lip, hoping to lull them into complacency, buying precious seconds. The air crackled with tension, stretched taut as a hunting snare.

The pistol raider smirked, misinterpreting Brynn's stillness. "That's better, little bird," he sneered, moving closer, the pistol inches from her arm. "Cooperate, and maybe this'll be quick." He reached out with his free hand to grab her chin. That was his mistake.

Brynn exploded into motion. Years of training, honed in silent practice, unleashed in a blinding flash. Her bound hands, though restricted, were still weapons. She snapped her wrists upwards with brutal force, the plasticuffs cracking against the raider's forearm as she twisted on the stool. He roared in pain, recoiling, losing his grip on the pistol. In that fraction of a second, Brynn drove her forehead forward, slamming it into his nose with bone-jarring impact. He staggered back, hands flying to his face, blood spurting.

The vibro-axe raider reacted instantly, swinging the humming blade in a wide arc. Brynn threw herself sideways off the stool, hitting the dirt floor hard, barely avoiding the axe's fatal sweep. She scrambled backwards, adrenaline surging through her veins, pain lancing in her wrists but ignored. The plasma pistol raider was still dazed, clutching his broken nose, but the axe raider was enraged, advancing with the humming weapon raised.

Brynn saw her opening. As the axe raider lunged, she dropped to the ground, rolling beneath his outstretched arm, her shoulder slamming into his knee. He roared again, this time in surprise and pain, losing his balance. Before he could recover, Brynn was on him, scrambling up his armored legs, using him as a shield against the recovering pistol raider. She reached his head, her fingers finding the vulnerable seam between his helmet and gorget. With a desperate, focused thrust, she jammed two fingers into the gap, finding soft flesh. He stiffened, spasmed once, and went limp, the vibro-axe clattering to the floor beside her. The second raider, hampered by his own wounded comrade, hesitated. Brynn seized the moment, grabbing the fallen vibro-axe. The hum of power resonated in her hand. She turned to face her last opponent, the glowing blade a lethal extension of her will.

Panic flared in the eyes of the remaining raider. He knew, suddenly, he was outmatched. He fired the pistol wildly, the darts hissing past Brynn's head, embedding themselves in the hut's bamboo wall. Brynn advanced slowly, the humming vibro-axe held ready, its energy blade spitting blue sparks. He backed away, firing again, shouting for help, but his voice was lost in the growing roar of the jungle at dusk. Brynn pressed her attack, forcing him towards the open doorway. He stumbled backwards, tripping over the stool, falling sprawling into the twilight clearing outside as Brynn lunged.

But she didn't strike. Instead, she used the vibro-axe not as a weapon to kill, but as a tool to threaten. She held the humming blade inches from his throat, its heat radiating against his skin. He froze, his breath coming in ragged gasps, his eyes wide with terror reflecting the blade's eerie glow.

"Who are you?" Brynn's voice was low, dangerous, surprising even herself with its cold fury. "Who sent you? And what do you want with Stellaris?"

The raider stammered, his bravado evaporated. "Lutz. Venom Lutz, she wants the plant. Sempernal. For the Syndicate…" He was babbling, desperate to appease her. "Please, don't kill me…"

Brynn pressed the blade closer, its hum vibrating against his Adam's apple, silencing him. Kill him. The thought was sharp, insistent, fueled by rage and grief. He deserves it. They all deserve it. But Cilka's face flashed in her mind: Vengeance is a cold fire, Brynn. It consumes everything. Brynn hesitated, the vibro-axe trembling in her grip. She lowered the weapon slightly, but kept it poised. "Tell Lutz," she hissed, her voice shaking with barely suppressed emotion. "Tell Venom Lutz that Brynn Winterborn is coming for her. And for everyone who spilled blood in Bagong Balay." She shoved him away from her, sending him sprawling into the dust. "Run. And tell her everything." She watched him scramble to his feet and vanish into the jungle's shadows, then turned back to the devastated village, the humming vibro-axe heavy in her bloodied hands, the scent of smoke and death filling the air.

✧ ¤ ✧ ¤ ✧

136

Twilight deepened into night, bringing not silence but the jungle's nocturnal chorus: chirping insects, distant howls, the rustle of unseen creatures moving through the undergrowth. Brynn used these sounds as cover, her bare feet making no noise on the damp earth as she approached Bagong from downwind. The raiders had set up crude perimeter lights, harsh circles of illumination that aided her by creating deeper shadows between them.

She paused at the jungle's edge, counting. Three raiders patrolled the village's remains, their weapons slung carelessly, voices loud as they complained about the assignment. Beyond them, in the central clearing, a larger group clustered around a fire. And overhead, the two airships hovered silently, their running lights dimmed.

Brynn steadied her breathing, focusing on the nearest guard, a stocky figure separated from the others, relieving himself against a tree. One chance. She slipped from shadow to shadow, her silver-white hair tucked beneath a coating of mud, her skin darkened with the same camouflage. Three meters away. Two. The guard sensed something, beginning to turn.

Too late.

Her arm locked around his throat, cutting off both air and sound. His hands clawed in desperation at her forearm, but Cilka had taught her well: pressure on the carotid, not the windpipe. Within seconds, he went limp. Brynn lowered him to the ground without making a sound, relieving him of his plasma pistol and vibroknife.

The weight of the pistol was unfamiliar but not unwelcome. She checked its charge: nearly full. Enough for what needs doing.

Moving deeper into the village, she positioned herself behind the burnt remnants of the communal kitchen. From here, she could see four raiders by the fire, sharing a bottle of something strong-smelling. Venom was nowhere in sight. Likely in one of the intact huts, or perhaps on an airship. It didn't matter. Not yet.

Brynn raised the pistol, its targeting reticle glowing faintly green in the darkness. She aimed not at the raiders, but at the fuel canister beside them: smuggled off-world military-grade stuff, highly volatile. Breathe in. Aim. Exhale. Slow, steady. Fire.

The plasma bolt streaked through the darkness, a brief flash of green ending in an explosion that lit the night like artificial day. Screams erupted as raiders were thrown in all directions, some aflame, others stunned. Brynn was already moving, sliding to a new position, picking her next target.

Her second and third victims fell before they knew what hit them — clean shots through center of mass. The fourth managed to return fire, plasma bolts searing the air above her head as she rolled behind a storage drum. The acrid smell of burning plastic filled her nostrils.

"Contact! East side!" someone shouted. "How many?"

Just one, Brynn thought grimly, switching positions again. *But that's enough.*

Aftermath

Dawn broke over Bagong Balay, pale light filtering through smoke that still rose from smoldering ruins. The acrid smell of burnt bamboo and plasteel hung in the humid air, mingling with the metallic tang of blood. Brynn moved through the village like a ghost, her silver-white hair matted with soot and sweat, her hands steady despite the night's violence.

In what remained of Cilka's healing hut, Brynn sorted through salvaged supplies: crushed herbs, tinctures in cracked vials, bandages singed at the edges. She worked methodically, her mother's voice guiding her hands. *Lunas leaf for fever. Hikaw root for deep pain. Bato-Bato petals to seal wounds.* Twenty-two survivors out of forty-nine. The numbers repeated in her mind like a grim mantra.

"Brynn?" A small voice pulled her from her trance. Lita, seven years old, stood in the doorway, her round face smudged with dirt. "Tito Naro won't wake up."

Brynn followed the child to where an elderly man lay on a woven mat, his breathing shallow, a plasma burn across his side angry and weeping. She knelt beside him, applying a poultice of Bato-Bato and binding the wound. Too late, she knew. The wound was too deep, too severe. But she worked anyway, her face betraying nothing.

"Will he be okay?" Lita asked, her voice small.

"He's with the ancestors now," Brynn said quietly as the old man's breathing stuttered and ceased. "He's not in pain anymore."

Twenty-one survivors.

Elder Taho approached, leaning heavily on a makeshift crutch. "The children are asking when we can go home," he said, his voice cracked with grief.

Brynn looked up, meeting his gaze. "There is no home, Elder. Not anymore." She gestured around them. "We must go to Emerald Landing. Before they return."

"And you, child? Will you come with us?"

Brynn's hands stilled on the bandages. Behind her closed eyes, she saw her mother's face, heard Venom's laughter. "I will see you safely on the path," she said, her meaning clear. "I have.. something I must do."

Taho's weathered hand came to rest on her shoulder, surprisingly heavy. "Vengeance is a hungry ghost, Brynn Winterborn. It will never be satisfied."

"Neither will I," she whispered, but only after he had moved away, leaving her alone with the dead.

The survivors gathered what little they could carry: water gourds, dried food, a few precious tools. Brynn supervised the preparation of simple travois for the three wounded who couldn't walk. No one spoke above a whisper, as if the village itself were a funeral pyre requiring reverence.

They buried their dead in a single grave beside the jungle path. Eighteen bodies laid to rest in haste, murmured prayers from the remaining elders. Cilka was among them. Brynn had carried her mother's body herself, refusing help, her face a stone mask hiding the maelstrom within. She had placed Cilka's healing pendant around her own neck, the carved bone warm against her skin, heavier than it should be.

As the survivors prepared to leave, Elder Mara approached Brynn. The old woman's face was a map of grief, new lines etched overnight alongside the old. She moved stiffly, favoring her right leg, burned during the attack.

"Youngling," she said, her voice low. "I have something for you."

Brynn looked up from checking the bindings on a travois. "What is it, Elder?"

Mara glanced around, ensuring they weren't overheard, then pressed something into Brynn's hand: a small, folded square of plastic-coated paper, sealed with wax. "I searched the dead researcher more thoroughly, after the council meeting. Found this in a hidden pocket of his jacket."

Brynn stared at the object, her heart pounding. "A map?"

Mara nodded. "More complete than your fragment. Your mother would want you to have this. It bears your father's mark."

With trembling fingers, Brynn broke the seal. The map unfolded, revealing detailed terrain markings, coordinates she recognized as deep jungle, and there: a location circled in red, labeled "Stellaris." In the margin, unmistakably in her father's handwriting: "*Found it. Waiting. M.E.P.*"

"He's alive," Brynn breathed, the words barely audible.

Mara's gnarled hand closed over Brynn's. "Perhaps. But remember, child, vengeance has a price. Your mother knew this. The healing arts and killing arts flow from the same knowledge. Choose wisely which path you walk."

Brynn carefully refolded the map, tucking it into her belt pouch. "I choose both," she said.

✧ ¤ ✧ ¤ ✧

They walked in silence, a ragged procession winding through the jungle. Brynn took the lead, the vibroknife strapped to her thigh, plasma pistol holstered at her waist. The morning heat pressed down on them, thick and oppressive, but she set a steady pace, mindful of the wounded and the children.

By midday, they reached the fork in the jungle path. Left led to Emerald Landing: safety, authorities, civilization. Right plunged deeper into the jungle, toward the coordinates on the map. Toward answers. Toward vengeance.

Brynn called a halt, allowing the survivors to rest in a small clearing. The children collapsed gratefully into the shade, their small faces drawn with exhaustion and trauma. She distributed water and the last of the journey bread, her movements efficient, avoiding their eyes. She couldn't bear their trust, their expectation that she would lead them to salvation.

Niko, one of the older teenagers, approached her. "We're making good time," he said. "Another day's walk to Emerald Landing?"

Brynn nodded, her gaze fixed on the right-hand path, disappearing into the denser jungle. "A day and a half, following the eastern ridge. Safer that way. Less chance of encounters."

Niko followed her gaze, understanding dawning in his eyes. "You're not coming with us."

It wasn't a question. Brynn met his gaze. "I can't."

"Because of the map? Because of your father?" Niko's voice was quiet, but there was steel beneath the softness. "Or because of her? Venom."

"All of it," Brynn admitted. "They'll come back, Niko. For the Stellaris. For whatever my father found. I have to find it first. I have to find him." Her hand drifted to the healing pendant. "And I have to make them pay. For Mama. For all of them."

Niko was silent for a long moment, then nodded. "I can get them to Emerald Landing. I know the way."

Relief and guilt warred within Brynn's chest. "You're sure?"

"I'm sure," he said, confidence showing. "But Brynn..." He hesitated. "What will you do if you find them? The raiders? You're just one person."

The question hung between them, weighted with all they had witnessed. Brynn's hand tightened around the plasma pistol, its solidity reassuring. "I'm not just one person anymore," she said, and the cold certainty in her voice made Niko step back. "I'm what they made me. And they'll learn what that means."

Brynn stood alone at the edge of what had once been Bagong, her home her whole life. The survivors were long gone, a half-day's march toward Emerald Landing with Niko leading them. The evening sun slanted through the trees, turning the smoke still rising from the ruins into ghostly, golden columns.

She moved through the devastation with purpose, gathering what she needed. Her father's old pack, buried beneath the floorboards of their home. A set of his clothes, far too large but more durable than her own. His machete, its edge still keen after years of disuse. She changed quickly, rolling the sleeves and pant legs, securing everything with a length of cord. The plasma pistol went into a makeshift holster, the vibro-knife strapped to her calf.

In Cilka's ruined healing hut, she collected seeds; her mother had always kept them, dozens of varieties, ready to plant each season. Brynn poured them into a small pouch, adding it to her supplies. Life, even in the midst of death.

Lastly, she went to the communal storage, or what remained of it. The raiders had taken most of the preserved food, but they'd overlooked the emergency cache hidden beneath a false floor panel. Brynn retrieved protein bars, water purification tablets, a compact med-kit. Enough to survive.

Standing in the center of the village one final time, Brynn looked around at the burned-out shells of homes, the trampled gardens, the bloodstained dirt. This had been the only world she had known. Now it existed only in memory.

She took out a small fire starter from her pack and approached the nearest intact structure. One by one, she set fire to what remained, ensuring nothing would be left for the raiders to return to. The flames caught quickly, hungry after the previous night's destruction.

As the fire spread, Brynn turned toward the jungle, the map secure against her chest, her father's machete in hand. The right-hand path beckoned, disappearing into the deepening green shadows. Without looking back, she stepped onto it, leaving Bagong Balay to burn behind her. The silver-white of her hair caught the last rays of sunlight before she vanished into the emerald darkness, a ghost seeking vengeance, a daughter seeking truth.

The Chemistry of Betrayal

Peacehaven

Professor Nikolas Antoniades Kusuma drew the molecular structure with practiced precision, his chalk moving in confident strokes across the blackboard. The classroom was silent except for the soft scratch of chalk and the occasional rustle of notes. He preferred traditional teaching tools: chalk and board allowed him to pace his explanations, forcing students to follow his process rather than simply copying completed slides and AI bursts.

"And here," he said, adding a final bond to the complex organic structure, "is where the magic happens." He turned to face the amphitheater of graduate students, dusting chalk from his fingers. "R-(+)-propionamylthujanic anhydride. Propiothujane, if you want to save some syllables. This deceptively simple molecule is transforming trauma medicine."

The late afternoon sun slanted through tall windows, catching dust motes in golden beams that illuminated the tiered classroom. Nikolas paced before the board, his tall frame casting a long shadow. At forty-one, he wore his academic position with the same comfort as his rumpled blazer; a natural fit earned through years of dedication.

"Dr. Kusuma," a student in the front row raised her hand, "the literature suggests the gamma-hydroxyl group should cause steric hindrance at the binding site. How does it achieve such high efficacy despite this?"

145

Nik smiled, pleased by the question. "Excellent observation, Ms. Carroway. That apparent contradiction is precisely what makes this compound so fascinating." He sketched a secondary diagram, illustrating the molecule's behavior in solution. "The binding conformation actually twists — like this — creating a perfect lock-and-key fit with the receptor."

He continued his explanation, watching comprehension dawn on his students' faces. These moments, when complex chemical principles clicked into place, were what he lived for. Research accolades were gratifying, but nothing matched the satisfaction of igniting understanding.

After class, Nik gathered his worn leather messenger bag, stuffed with journal articles he'd been meaning to review. His phone buzzed with a message from Fionna: *Dinner with Dad tonight. Don't forget. 7:30 sharp.*

He grimaced. Dinner with Cormac Chevere Audun, his father-in-law and Chair of the University Ethics Board, was never relaxing. The man had a way of making even casual conversation feel like an examination. Nevertheless, he texted back: *Will be there. Stopping by lab first.*

The research building hummed with evening activity. Science rarely kept regular hours. The familiar scents of disinfectant and the faint, acrid tang of chemical reagents greeted him as he badged into the Laboratory for Advanced Biomolecular Research. His kingdom, secured through fifteen years of grinding work, countless publications, and the substantial funding he'd attracted from StarCure Pharmaceuticals.

"Professor!" Akbar Spallina looked up from his workstation, dark circles under his eyes suggesting he'd been there since early morning. "I've got the initial binding assays for the new derivatives."

Nikolas placed his bag on a chair. "Show me."

The tall, lanky graduate student pulled up a series of graphs on his monitor. The data looked promising—several variants showing significantly improved binding profiles compared to the control. As Akbar explained his methodology, Nik noticed a slight tremor in the student's hands, the third time this week he'd observed signs of fatigue or nervousness.

"You're pushing yourself too hard, Akbar," he said, interrupting the technical explanation. "The research is important, but not at the expense of your health."

Akbar's eyes darted away. "I'm fine, Professor. Just need to finish this series before the StarCure review next week."

From across the lab, Supsam Piccilo glanced up, his attention caught by the mention of their corporate sponsor. The stockier graduate student had been angling for the lead position on the propiothujane project since he'd joined the lab, making little secret of his ambition.

"StarCure's putting on the pressure, eh?" Supsam called over, his tone casual but eyes sharp with interest.

"Just the usual quarterly review," Nik replied, keeping his voice neutral. He'd learned to navigate the complex politics of corporate-funded research—the constant balance between academic integrity and commercial expectations. StarCure had been generous, providing almost unlimited resources for his propiothujane research after early results showed remarkable promise for combat medicine and emergency trauma treatment.

His phone buzzed again. A text from Fionna: *Don't be late. Wearing the blue dress you like.*

A peace offering, perhaps. Things had been strained in recent months, with his long hours at the lab and her growing frustration with his absent-mindedness. Fifteen years of marriage, the last five increasingly difficult as his research consumed more of his time and attention.

"I need to go," he told Akbar. "But first, walk me through those anomalies in the control group again."

Akbar hesitated, just a fraction of a second, before pulling up another set of data. "It's nothing significant, Professor. Just standard deviation within expected parameters."

Nik frowned, studying the numbers. Something felt off, but he couldn't pinpoint what. After fifteen years of research, he'd developed an instinct for data patterns, and something here wasn't following the expected trajectory.

"Run it again tomorrow," he said. "Fresh samples, full protocol."

Akbar nodded too quickly. "Of course, Professor."

As Nik left the building, the security guard nodded a familiar greeting. "Working late again, Professor Kusuma?"

"Not tonight, Hector. Dinner with the in-laws."

The guard chuckled sympathetically. "Rather you than me, sir."

Destabilization

The fluorescent lights hummed overhead as Nikolas peered over Akbar Spallina's shoulder, studying the molecular model rotating on the screen. The graduate student's fingers trembled as he manipulated the display, zooming in on a specific binding site of the propiothujane derivative.

"See here, Professor?" Akbar pointed to a complex region where the molecule interfaced with simulated tissue. "The modified side chain increases binding affinity by nearly forty percent without compromising metabolic clearance."

Nik nodded, impressed despite the faint odor of alcohol barely masked by breath mints that wafted from his student. Akbar's brilliance had always outshone his personal demons, at least in the lab.

"Excellent work, Akbar. If these simulations translate to the *in vitro* tests, we're looking at a significant breakthrough." He straightened up, glancing around the bustling laboratory where six other graduate students worked at various stations. His gaze lingered on Supsam Piccilo, hunched over his own terminal with a scowl that had become his default expression.

Akbar saved his work, the bags under his eyes more pronounced under the harsh lighting. "I'll start the cell culture assays tomorrow. Should have preliminary results by Friday."

"Don't rush it," Nik cautioned. "Precision over speed."

"But the StarCure deadline —"

"Will be met," Nik finished. "But not at the expense of sound methodology. Remember, this isn't just about publications or corporate milestones. If these compounds perform as expected, they'll save lives."

Before Nik could probe further about Akbar's obvious exhaustion, Supsam appeared beside them, digital tablet in hand. "Professor

Kusuma, I've completed the stability analyses for compounds seven through thirteen." His tone was cordial, but his eyes darted to Akbar's screen, scanning the data with undisguised hunger.

"Thank you, Supsam." Nik accepted the tablet, noting how the stocky graduate student positioned himself to maintain sight of Akbar's work.

"I've also drafted a modified protocol that might accelerate our testing timeline," Supsam added, inserting himself between Nik and Akbar. "If we parallelized the binding assays instead of running them sequentially —"

"We'd risk cross-contamination and confounding variables," Akbar interjected, fatigue momentarily forgotten. "The sequential approach ensures cleaner data."

"At the cost of time," Supsam countered. "And isn't time critical for trauma patients? For soldiers bleeding out on battlefields?"

Nik raised a hand before the disagreement could escalate.

"Both approaches have merit. Supsam, draft your parallelization proposal for me to review. Akbar, continue with the established protocol until we've fully evaluated alternatives."

The tension in the air remained palpable as Supsam retreated to his workstation, casting one last lingering look at Akbar's screen.

✧ ⊓ ✧ ⊓ ✧

Akbar Spallina hunched deeper into his jacket as he hurried across the deserted campus quad, the night air carrying a bite that penetrated his thin clothing. The university's gothic architecture loomed like silent judges in the darkness, their shadows stretching across the manicured lawns. His breath fogged in front of him, matching the clouded state of his thoughts.

The message had been clear: *Meet at the Orbital View Café. 10 PM. Come alone. Final warning about your debt.*

His hands trembled, not entirely from the cold. Three months of increasingly desperate gambling at underground establishments had left him owing credits to people who didn't accept excuses or payment plans. People who knew where he lived, where he worked, and — most terrifyingly — seemed to know about his mother's expensive care on Xinjiang.

The café was almost empty when he arrived, just a few students hunched over late-night study materials and caffeine. Akbar scanned the room, his heart hammering against his ribs, before spotting a man in a tailored business suit sitting alone in the corner booth. Not the usual type of enforcer he'd expected.

"Mr. Spallina," the man said as Akbar approached. "Please, sit. I took the liberty of ordering you a Martian dark roast. Still your preference, I believe?"

Akbar slid into the booth, eyeing the steaming mug with suspicion. "How do you know what coffee I drink?"

The man smiled, extending a manicured hand. "Dario Klempt. Medical research consultant. And knowing details is my specialty." His grip was firm, dry. "Including your outstanding debt of seventy-three thousand credits to certain individuals who lack my patience and civility."

The blood drained from Akbar's face. The exact amount, down to the last credit. "I can pay. I just need more time. My stipend next month — "

"Won't cover the interest," Dario finished, his tone almost sympathetic. "Your university compensation is a matter of public record, Mr. Spallina. As is your mother's experimental gene therapy on Xinjiang. Quite expensive, I understand."

Fear congealed in Akbar's stomach. The mention of his mother wasn't coincidental.

"What do you want?" Akbar whispered, the café now too warm, too close.

Dario sipped his coffee, regarding Akbar over the rim. "I represent interests that could solve your financial difficulties. Permanently. In exchange for... consulting services."

✧ ♯ ✧ ♯ ✧

Three weeks later, Nikolas frowned at the results on his tablet, the inconsistencies in the data drawing his attention like discordant notes in a familiar symphony. The lab was quiet in the early morning hours, just himself and the gentle hum of equipment for company. He preferred these moments before the students arrived. Time to think, to analyze without interruption.

Akbar's latest results showed promising efficacy for compound TJ-117, but some of the control values seemed... convenient. Too clean, with variance patterns that didn't follow expected distribution. It could be coincidence, or exceptional experimental technique, but something felt off.

The lab door opened and Akbar entered, startling visibly when he saw Nikolas already present.

"Professor! You're in early." His voice was too bright, his smile too fixed.

"Good morning, Akbar." Nik gestured to the tablet. "I was reviewing your TJ-117 data. The binding profile is remarkable."

"Yes," Akbar moved to his workstation, avoiding direct eye contact. "The modifications to the gamma position exceeded our expectations." He busied himself setting up for the day, slightly rushed.

Nik noticed the graduate student looked better than he had in weeks: clean-shaven, wearing new clothes, his previous perpetual exhaustion less evident. Even his hands were steadier.

"The control group values," Nik said, "they're unusually consistent. Almost perfect negative controls."

Akbar froze for a moment before resuming his preparation with deliberate nonchalance. "I've been refining my technique. Multiple runs, selecting the cleanest data sets."

"I see." Nik set down the tablet. "And you documented these multiple runs in the lab notebook?"

A pause. "Most of them. Some were obviously flawed, not worth recording."

Alarm bells rang in Nik's mind. Discarding data without documentation was a basic methodological sin, something he emphasized to every student who joined his lab.

"Akbar," he said, keeping his tone neutral, "you know our protocols. Every experiment, successful or failed, gets documented. Especially controls."

"Of course, Professor. It won't happen again." Akbar's movements became more deliberate, his attention fixated on preparing cell cultures with exaggerated precision.

Nik watched him for a moment longer. The physical improvement was welcome, but this new nervousness was concerning in a different way.

"Is everything alright, Akbar? You seem tense."

"Fine, just fine." Too quick, too emphatic. "Better, actually. I've, uh, sorted out some personal matters."

Before Nik could probe further, his comm device chimed with an incoming call from Elena Vostok at StarCure. "I need to take this. But Akbar," he waited until the student met his eyes, "we'll continue this discussion later. Full experimental records. Non-negotiable."

Supsam Piccilo hunched over his terminal in the deserted lab, the clock on the wall showing almost midnight. His eyes burned from hours of staring at molecular structures, comparing his approach to Akbar's, searching for any advantage that might elevate his position in Kusuma's lab. The frustration of playing second fiddle to Akbar gnawed at him like acid.

The door opened behind him, and Supsam minimized his screen, not wanting anyone to see him studying another student's research methodology. He turned, expecting a late-night custodian, but instead found himself facing a well-dressed man he didn't recognize.

"Working late, Mr. Piccilo?" the stranger asked, moving further into the room. "Dedication is an admirable quality."

The smile died on Supsam's face as his guard went up. "Do I know you?"

"Not yet. Dario Klempt, medical research consultant." Their handshake was brief, with Supsam's reluctance written in every line of his body. "I often work with pharmaceutical firms looking to recruit promising researchers. Your name has come up in several conversations."

Despite his suspicion, Supsam felt a flicker of pride. "Really? Which companies?"

"Several major players. Your work on alternative synthesis pathways for complex anhydrides has not gone unnoticed." Dario settled into a chair near Supsam, his posture relaxed but somehow commanding the space. "Though I understand you're not the lead on the propiothujane project, despite your evident qualifications."

The comment hit its mark. Supsam's jaw tightened. "Professor Kusuma has his favorites."

"Indeed. Academic politics can be frustrating." Dario glanced at Supsam's minimized screen. "Especially when more qualified individuals are overlooked in favor of those with, shall we say, less stability."

Supsam hesitated, torn between professional discretion and the temptation to voice his long-held grievances. "Akbar is brilliant," he said, though the admission pained him. "But lately, his work has been inconsistent. Professor Kusuma doesn't see it."

"Or chooses not to," Dario suggested. "Sometimes mentors develop blind spots regarding their protégés. It often falls to colleagues to ensure scientific integrity is maintained." He paused, seeming to consider something. "I shouldn't mention this, but given your position in the lab..."

He trailed off, the unfinished thought hovering like smoke. Supsam leaned forward despite himself. "Mention what?"

"I've heard concerning rumors from contacts at StarCure. Inconsistencies in the TJ-117 data submissions. Patterns that suggest manipulation, perhaps." He shook his head, the very picture of scientific concern. "Nothing confirmed. But if true, it could damage the entire lab's reputation. Including yours, by association."

Supsam's heart raced. This aligned with his own suspicions about Akbar's too-perfect results. "What kind of inconsistencies?"

"Control values with statistically improbable consistency. Binding profiles too clean to be genuine experimental data." Dario sighed. "The worst part is that Professor Kusuma's reputation would suffer the most. As principal investigator, the responsibility ultimately falls to him."

Entropy Cascade

Cormac Chevere Audun's office embodied academic gravitas: oak paneling, leather-bound volumes, and the subtle scent of lemon polish that couldn't quite mask the mustiness of old paper. As Supsam Piccilo perched on the edge of a leather chair, data tablet clutched in white-knuckled hands, he felt his confidence wavering under the Ethics Board Chair's penetrating gaze.

"Mr. Piccilo," Cormac said, breaking the suffocating silence. "You requested this meeting with considerable urgency. Something about research misconduct in Professor Kusuma's laboratory?"

Supsam nodded, his Adam's apple bobbing as he swallowed. "Yes, sir. I... I wouldn't come forward without substantial evidence. I understand the seriousness of these allegations."

Cormac leaned back, steepling his fingers. At sixty-three, with silver-streaked black hair and piercing gray eyes, he cut an imposing figure. Supsam tried not to think about the man being Professor Kusuma's father-in-law.

"Please proceed, Mr. Piccilo. Specifically and factually."

Supsam activated his tablet with trembling fingers. "It concerns the propiothujane research led by Akbar Spallina under Professor Kusuma's supervision. I've identified multiple instances where reported results don't match raw experimental data."

He turned the tablet toward Cormac, displaying side-by-side comparisons. "The official submissions show statistically perfect binding profiles for compound TJ-117, but the original measurements show significant variability and several failed trials."

Cormac examined the evidence, his expression unchanged though his interest sharpened. The discrepancies were not subtle. Someone had deliberately altered experimental outcomes to present flawless results where the actual data showed promising but inconsistent performance.

"How did you obtain access to these raw data files?" Cormac asked, his tone implying the question was procedural rather than accusatory.

"I... I had concerns about the statistical probability of Akbar's results. They were too perfect." Supsam shifted in his chair. "I accessed the secure server during off-hours to compare original instrument outputs with reported findings."

"Without authorization." It wasn't a question.

"Technically, yes. But as a member of the research team, I have legitimate access to the server. I just... used it for verification rather than my assigned research."

Cormac made a note, the scratch of his pen against paper unnervingly loud. "And you're certain Professor Kusuma isn't aware of these discrepancies?"

Supsam hesitated. "I can't be absolutely certain, but I don't believe so. Professor Kusuma is meticulous about research integrity. He would never knowingly permit falsification."

"Mr. Piccilo, are you aware that bringing false allegations of research misconduct carries severe consequences?"

The blood drained from Supsam's face. "The evidence is real, Dr. Audun. I wouldn't risk my career on fabricated accusations."

Cormac nodded, having expected that response. "And your motivation for bringing this forward? Professor Kusuma's laboratory is highly competitive. Some might interpret your actions as... professionally opportunistic."

Supsam flushed, the implication striking its mark. "I respect Professor Kusuma deeply. That's why I came to the Ethics Board rather than confronting the situation directly. Scientific integrity has to come first, regardless of personal or professional considerations."

Cormac reached for a formal complaint form, the university seal embossed at the top. "I'll need you to document your allegations officially. The Board will conduct a preliminary investigation to determine if formal proceedings are warranted."

157

✧ ◻ ✧ ◻ ✧

The sound of breaking glass shattered the tense silence of the Kusuma household.

"Damn it!" Fionnantan's voice echoed from the kitchen, followed by the clatter of ceramic shards being swept up.

Nikolas looked up from the research papers spread across the living room coffee table, grateful for the interruption. The data discrepancies he'd been trying to reconcile were giving him a headache.

"Need help?" he called, already rising.

"I've got it," came the terse reply.

Nik paused, reading the subtext. Fourteen years of marriage had taught him to recognize her moods, and this one spelled trouble. He moved toward the kitchen anyway, finding her kneeling on the tile floor, angrily sweeping glass shards from a broken wine glass.

"Here, let me —"

"I said I've got it." She didn't look up, her movements sharp. Her dark hair fell forward, obscuring her face.

Nik stepped back, leaning against the doorframe. "Bad day at the lab?"

Fionna stood, dumping the glass into the recycler with more force than necessary. "My day was fine until my father called."

A chill ran through him. Cormac rarely called his daughter during working hours unless something significant had occurred. "What did he want?"

She turned to face him, her green eyes hard with an emotion he couldn't quite identify: anger, disappointment, perhaps fear. "He couldn't say, specifically. Ethical constraints. But he suggested I should prepare myself for some 'unfortunate developments' regarding your research program."

The chill deepened. "What's that supposed to mean?"

158

"You tell me, Nikolas." Fionna crossed her arms. "Is there something happening in your lab I should know about? Something my father, as Ethics Board Chair, might be concerned with?"

Nik's mind raced through possibilities. The data discrepancies? Akbar's behavior? But those were internal matters, not yet ethical violations. "Nothing comes to mind. Your father's being cryptic for no reason."

"My father," she said with deliberate precision, "doesn't make cryptic warnings without cause."

The implication stung. "So you automatically assume I've done something unethical?"

"I didn't say that." Her voice softened, but the tension remained. "But you've been distracted lately. Worried. That night last week when you came home at three, you said you were 'reviewing anomalous results.' You've been obsessing over Akbar's data."

"Because something's not right with it," Nik admitted, running a hand through his hair in frustration. "The control values are too perfect. But that's a methodological issue, not an ethical one."

Fionna studied him, her expression unreadable. "Unless you knew about it and didn't report it."

The accusation hung in the air between them. Nik felt heat rise to his face. "You think I'd knowingly overlook falsified data? After fifteen years as a researcher?"

"I think," she said, "that StarCure is putting enormous pressure on you. I think Akbar is your academic golden child. And I think my father doesn't make these kinds of calls lightly."

Nikolas stared at his tablet, the headline from the *Peacehaven Academic Review* seeming to burn into his retinas: "ETHICS INVESTIGATION TARGETS STAR RESEARCHER: Kusuma Lab Data Falsification

Alleged." His coffee sat untouched, growing cold beside him in the faculty lounge. The article cited "anonymous sources close to the Ethics Board," detailing allegations of "systematic data manipulation" in research funded by StarCure. It didn't name him, but the references to propiothujane made the target unmistakable.

The lounge door swung open, and Richard Thales, his department chair, entered. Richard's eyes fell on Nik and the tablet. "In my office," Richard said in soft, even tones, abandoning his own coffee. "Now."

They walked in tense silence through the morning bustle of the department, acutely aware of conversations that stopped as they passed, of eyes that followed. By the time Richard closed his office door, Nik's bewilderment had hardened into fury.

"This is insane," Nik burst out. "I requested a meeting with you to discuss potential data irregularities, and before we can even talk, it's splashed across the academic press?"

Richard gestured for Nik to sit. "When did you first become aware of the Ethics Board's involvement?"

"Officially? Just now, reading that hatchet job." Nik ran a hand through his curls. "Unofficially, my father-in-law hinted to Fionna yesterday."

Richard's expression darkened. "This doesn't follow protocol. Ethics investigations are strictly confidential. Someone deliberately leaked this to damage you."

"But why? And who?" Nik leaned forward. "The article mentions StarCure. Could a competitor be trying to sabotage the TJ-117 patent application?"

"Possibly," Richard conceded. "But this feels... targeted." He hesitated. "Nik, is there any truth to the allegations?"

"I noticed inconsistencies," Nik admitted. "That's why I wanted to meet. But I haven't confirmed falsification, and I certainly haven't knowingly allowed manipulated data to be reported."

Richard looked relieved but still concerned. "But the Ethics Board moves on evidence..."

The harsh ring of Richard's comm device interrupted them. He answered, listened, his face growing progressively dismayed. When he ended the call, he looked ten years older. "That was Dean Vishwanath. The university is issuing a formal statement acknowledging the investigation. They're... distancing themselves. Your keynote at the symposium is canceled. Your seminar suspended. And they're requesting you take administrative leave, effective immediately."

The room seemed to tilt. "They're suspending me based on an allegation? Before any investigation?"

"Standard procedure," Richard said, though his tone suggested distaste. "It's about protecting the university's reputation."

"What about protecting mine?" Nik jumped up.

His own comm device buzzed, a call from Elena Vostok at StarCure. He accepted, steeling himself.

"Professor." Elena's voice was glacial. "Explain why I'm fielding calls about fraudulent research data? Why our stock is plummeting?"

"The allegations are unfounded," Nik insisted, though doubt nagged him.

"Our legal team is preparing a response," Elena cut in. "In the meantime, we're pausing all funding transfers."

The message arrived as Nikolas was leaving his lab, the air thick with the scent of failure. He'd spent hours combing through Akbar's files, finding clear evidence of manipulation, but Akbar himself had vanished. The comm notification chimed softly: *Professor Kusuma: information vital to your situation. Not for university channels. Orbit Bar, 9 PM. Look for the woman in red. Bring no one. — A Friend*

Suspicion warred with desperate hope. What more could he lose?

The Orbit Bar rotated slowly, offering panoramic views of Peacehaven. He spotted her instantly: auburn hair, elegant red dress. "Professor Kusuma," she said, her voice accented. "Reina Cabral. Please, sit."

An Old-World Scotch, his preferred drink, appeared before him. "You said you have information."

"Direct. I like that." She smiled, though her eyes remained calculating. "We believe you're being set up, Professor. Your student, Akbar, was falsifying data, but not alone. He worked with operatives from IndAxioma Pharmaceuticals."

The name hit him like a physical blow, aligning with his darkest suspicions. "Evidence?"

"Some." She tapped a datapad. "Financial transfers. Meetings. But more importantly, IndAxioma needed to block StarCure's patent. By compromising your research, they damage the application."

Another Scotch arrived. The alcohol dulled the day's anxieties. "And the Ethics Board?"

"Manipulated," Reina said, leaning closer. "Another student, Supsam Piccilo, was guided into reporting the data. Tomorrow's hearing? Likely a foregone conclusion against you."

The room seemed to tilt faster. "That's impossible."

"Procedures can be expedited," she murmured, her fingers brushing his hand. "We want to help. Our publication exposes corporate manipulation."

The drinks kept coming, each stronger than the last. Peacehaven's lights blurred outside. "You should document everything," Reina advised, her voice seeming distant. "Secure original data off-campus."

"My lab," Nik mumbled, words thick. "Secure backups..."

"University servers? Compromised." She leaned closer, her spicy perfume enveloping him. "You need physical evidence."

162

The room spun. "Should go back... get drives..."

"Let me help you," Reina offered, her arm sliding around his waist as she helped him stand. "You're in no condition to drive."

The journey became fragmented: cool air, her steadying hand, the deserted research building. His credentials still worked. "Secure server... there..." he pointed before collapsing into a chair.

"Rest here," Reina murmured, moving toward the server cabinet. He was distantly aware of her speaking in a soft voice into a comm, of other figures entering, of equipment being handled.

"We should go," she said later, helping him up. "You need rest."

The trip to her apartment — when had they decided that? — was a deeper blur. Minimalist furniture. Her helping him onto a couch. "Sleep, Professor," she murmured, fingers brushing his hair.

As consciousness slipped away, Nikolas remained unaware of the camera recording his presence, or that across campus, his laboratory was being systematically gutted, crucial evidence destroyed while he slept in the apartment of the woman who had orchestrated his final downfall.

Beyond the Event Horizon

Chaos ruled Nikolas's lab. The acrid smell of burnt electronics hung in the air, mingling with the sweet, chemical tang of spilled reagents. Equipment lay scattered, monitors cracked, glassware shattered across the floor like crystal dragon's teeth. Yellow tape cordoned off his domain, turning his once-pristine space into a crime scene.

His stomach clenched. The main server cabinet gaped open, wires dangling like severed nerves. Backup storage gone. Years of research, reams of irreplaceable data, vanished.

A campus security officer stood guard, impassive. Nik barely registered his presence, his mind racing. "The security footage?" he asked, his voice rough.

The officer shrugged. "Corrupted sector, sir. Right during the window of the break-in. Tech services is working on it."

Corrupted. Convenient. Dario Klempt's words echoed in his mind: *Systematic destruction.* This was more than vandalism; it was a targeted assassination of his research.

Richard Thales found him amidst the wreckage, his face grim. "Dean Vishwanath's office. Now, Nik."

The meeting was brief and brutal. Richard, his usual warmth replaced by glacier-cold distance, delivered the news: administrative leave, effective immediately. "For your protection as much as the university's," Richard added, but Nik heard the subtext loud and clear.

He returned to the almost-empty condo, the silence amplifying his sense of isolation. His comm pinged with a message from an unknown sender. An image file. He opened it, and felt his blood run cold.

The photo showed him and Reina Cabral entering her apartment building. Her arm around his waist, his posture unsteady, unmistakably

164

compromised. Below, a second image: a close-up of the building's timestamp: 11:42 PM. *Lab break-in, approximately 11 PM - 1 AM.*

Another message followed, this time from Fionna. Just one word: *Disgusting.*

His phone rang. Fionna's number. He answered, hope flickering despite the evidence.

"Nikolas." Her voice was flat, devoid of emotion, a stranger's voice. "My father sent me the photos. I've seen enough."

The line went dead. He stared at the blank screen, the chill in his apartment mirroring the icy void inside him.

Supsam fidgeted in the witness chair, the Ethics Board chamber amplifying his unease. The oak-paneled walls seemed to lean in, and the portraits of past chairs felt like judgmental eyes boring into him. The air was thick with the scent of old paper and hushed expectation. He swallowed, his mouth dry despite the glass of water he'd been sipping.

Professor Farrow, the Acting Chair, fixed him with an unwavering gaze. "Mr. Piccilo, please reiterate for the Board the substance of your complaint against Professor Kusuma and Mr. Spallina."

He cleared his throat, his prepared statement feeling flimsy now under the weight of the formal setting. "My complaint concerns research misconduct... data falsification... in the propiothujane project." He gestured to the tablet displaying the damning comparisons. "These are side-by-side analyses of reported results and original experimental outputs for compound TJ-117. As you can see, there are clear discrepancies."

Professor Harlan from Bioethics leaned forward, his gaze sharp. "And to be clear, Mr. Piccilo, you are alleging that Professor Kusuma was aware of, or complicit in, this manipulation?"

Supsam hesitated, a knot tightening in his gut. Dario Klempt had stressed the need to implicate Kusuma, to solidify the appearance of broad negligence. But seeing Professor Kusuma across the room, facing the Board alone, a wave of doubt washed over him.

"I… I don't have direct evidence of Professor Kusuma's explicit involvement," Supsam admitted, his voice barely above a whisper. "But as the Principal Investigator, he bears ultimate responsibility for the integrity of his lab's data. And the scale of the alterations… it's systematic. I believe he must have been aware of at least some irregularities."

He glanced at Professor Kusuma. Nikolas sat as straight as a post, his expression unreadable, but Supsam caught a flicker of something in his eyes – not anger, not yet, but a deep, wounded bewilderment.

"Mr. Spallina, however," Professor Zhen interjected, her voice assessing in even tones, "was directly responsible for generating the data in question?"

"Yes," Supsam confirmed, relieved to shift focus to Akbar. "The data was attributed to his experiments. And… and I believe these alterations benefited him professionally, securing lead authorship, continued funding."

Professor Farrow turned to Nikolas. "Professor Kusuma, your response?"

Supsam watched as Nikolas began his defense, his voice steady despite the strain etched on his face. He spoke of his own suspicion, of initiating an internal review. He even admitted to noticing anomalies. But as Nikolas deflected blame towards Akbar — a student who wasn't there to defend himself — a fresh wave of unease washed over Supsam. Had he done the right thing? Or had he become a tool in something larger, something colder, than academic rivalry?

166

The news cycle descended like vultures. Nikolas scrolled through the relentless stream of headlines on his tablet, each more damning than the last. "STAR PROFESSOR FALLS FROM GRACE: Ethics Board Finds Kusuma Guilty of Research Misconduct." "STARCURE IN DAMAGE CONTROL: Billion-Dollar Drug Patent at Risk Amidst Fraud Scandal." "ACADEMIC INTEGRITY BETRAYED: Was Kusuma Blinded by Ambition?"

Each article dissected the Ethics Board's preliminary findings, painting Nik as either willfully negligent or actively complicit. One particularly vicious piece in *Global Science Today* suggested he'd deliberately cut corners to secure tenure, conveniently forgetting he'd been a tenured professor for years. IndAxioma carefully planted narrative was taking root: *"Sources within IndAxioma suggest StarCure's pressure for rapid results may have contributed to a lax ethical environment in Kusuma's lab."*

His comm device remained silent. Former colleagues, once eager for collaborations and casual lunches, now seemed to exist in a parallel universe, their digital presences flickering just beyond his reach but never connecting. Even Richard Thales had become a gatekeeper, his brief, strained messages strictly professional and worded with undue care.

He ventured out for groceries, pulling his collar high, the Peacehaven air feeling colder, sharper. At the checkout, he recognized Dr. Anya Sharma, a fellow chemistry professor from a different department. Their eyes met. Hers widened slightly, then slid away, focusing on scanning her organic vegetables. The cashier avoided his gaze. The casual smiles, the nods of acknowledgement, all vanished, replaced by a chilling, pervasive invisibility.

Back in his desolate apartment, the building's auto-notification system chimed. *Package delivery to resident Kusuma, Nikolas A. Biometric confirmation required. Please retrieve from front desk.*

He walked down to the lobby, the fluorescent lights buzzing overhead, and received a thick, registered envelope after retina scan. Inside, crisp legal paper. *Kusuma vs. Kusuma. Petition for Dissolution of Marriage.*

167

Fionnantan wasn't just leaving; she was severing all ties with legal precision and dispatch. The impersonal formality of the legal document felt colder than any shouted accusation, a final, bureaucratic severing of their shared life. He stared at the official seal, the embossed university crest feeling like a brand of shame rather than a symbol of achievement. Professional disgrace followed by personal annihilation. The media crucifixion was complete, and other nails were still being hammered in.

The crisp white envelope from the university administration lacked any personal touch, just official logos and bureaucratic typeface. Inside, the termination letter was as sharp as a lab scalpel: *"...your employment as Professor of Chemistry is hereby terminated, effective immediately. Final salary disbursement, less standard deductions and outstanding university fees, will be processed..."* No thanks for years of service, no hint of understanding, just cold, corporate dismissal from the institution that had been his professional home. The paper felt thin and flimsy in his trembling hands, a stark symbol of his plummeting worth.

His comm device buzzed: Elena Vostok from StarCure. He answered, bracing for another blow. "Professor Kusuma," her voice was devoid of any warmth, purely transactional. "Further to our earlier discussion, StarCure is formally withdrawing all research funding for the propiothujane project and related initiatives. All grant agreements are voided, effective immediately. We expect full return of any unexpended funds within thirty standard days. Good day." The line clicked dead, severing another vital lifeline, the financial oxygen supply to his intellectual life extinguished.

Driven by a desperate, futile hope, Nik logged into his joint bank account. The digital interface blinked at him: *Zero balance.* He refreshed the page, the stark numeral stubbornly unchanged. Every credit, every saved resource, accumulated over years of shared income, gone. Fionna had not just accessed 'their' account; she had extracted every last unit of currency, leaving behind only digital emptiness and the echoing void of betrayal.

Another notification flashed on his comm. *Court Services: Emergency Divorce Hearing scheduled for tomorrow, 09:00 hours, Peacehaven Family Court, Section 3B.* Tomorrow? He checked the timestamp on the notification: *Sent 08:57 today.* Three minutes notice for an emergency hearing. Deliberate. Systemic. He was being buried under an avalanche of orchestrated disasters, each designed to strip him bare, financially, professionally, personally. He sat back, the silence of his stripped-bare apartment pressing in. Financial ruin wasn't just the absence of money; it was the systematic dismantling of his foundations, the tangible manifestation of his complete, utter collapse.

Terminal Override

The silence in the apartment was thick, a suffocating blanket that muffled even the faint hum of Peacehaven's distant city life. Nikolas sat in the single remaining chair, facing the bare walls where bookshelves once stood, where family photos used to hang. The moving company had been efficient, clinical in their removal of everything that constituted 'home,' leaving behind echoing emptiness and the ghost-scent of Fionna's perfume, a cruel reminder of what was lost.

Sunlight slanted through the uncurtained window, highlighting dust motes dancing in the stagnant air. Another official envelope lay on the floor, dropped through the mail slot. He didn't need to open it to know what it contained. *Kusuma vs. Kusuma. Final Decree of Dissolution.* He was divorced, legally and irrevocably separated from the woman who had been his anchor, his partner, for half his life. He let it lie there, another piece of debris in the wreckage of his existence.

Another chime from the mail slot. This one was heavier, bearing the embossed logo of the *Federated Chemistry Guild*. He tore it open, his fingers clumsy. …*membership revoked… ethical violations… damage to the profession's standing…* The formal, impersonal language was laced with condemnation, stripping him of his professional identity, his hard-earned status among his peers. He was no longer Professor Kusuma, respected chemist; he was Nikolas Kusuma, disgraced academic, a pariah.

A final, smaller envelope slid through the slot, its handwriting unfamiliar. He picked it up, a knot of dread tightening in his stomach. Inside, a single folded sheet of cheap paper. Akbar's handwriting, frantic, uneven. *Professor… I'm sorry… pressure was too much… data… they made me… can't live with it… forgive me…* No signature, just the raw, desperate scrawl of a broken man.

Suicide. Akbar, unable to bear the weight of his betrayal, had chosen the ultimate escape. And the note, while confessing to data manipulation and hinting at external pressure, crucially omitted the puppet master, IndAxioma, leaving Nikolas to carry the full weight of the blame, to be forever linked to the tragic downfall of his student. He sat in the hollow silence, surrounded by the ghosts of his past life, utterly, irrevocably alone. The isolation was not just physical; it had burrowed deep, isolating him from his past, his profession, his very sense of self.

The air in the dive bar was thick with the smells of stale beer, cheap synth-whiskey, and hopelessness. Nikolas nursed a glass of something brown and acrid, the taste mirroring the bitterness coating his tongue. The flickering neon sign outside cast a lurid glow across the stained tables and worn booths, illuminating the faces of Peacehaven's forgotten — lost souls seeking oblivion in cheap liquor. He fit right in. A couple more appalling swills and he would be ready to follow Akbar.

He was on his third glass when a shadow fell across his table. Dario Klempt. Impeccably dressed as always, a stark contrast to the bar's clientele and Nikolas's own disheveled state.

"Professor Kusuma," Dario said, his voice cutting through the bar's low hum. "May I join you?"

Nikolas stared at him, past anger exhausted, replaced by a weary numbness. "What do you want?"

Dario slid onto the opposite seat, uninvited. "To offer clarity. I believe you deserve to know the full picture of what happened." He signaled the bartender, ordering a sparkling water, a deliberate contrast to Nikolas's drink. "Your… situation… it's unfortunate. Collateral damage in a larger game."

"Game?" Nikolas's voice was flat. "My life is in ruins. My career, my marriage, gone. My student dead. That's your 'game'?"

"Crass, I admit," Dario conceded, his smile faint. "But accurate. Professor, you were caught in a corporate war. Between pharmaceutical giants. StarCure, yes, but they were merely a the weaker dragonfish in the fight. The real battle is between…" He paused, leaning closer, his voice dropping conspiratorially. "…one of the 'big four' operating on Samarqand."

Samarqand. The name pricked his attention. "IndAxioma?" he guessed, the name emerging from the fog of his despair.

Dario's smile widened, but didn't quite reach his eyes. "Sharp as ever, Professor. They orchestrated everything. Supsam, the Ethics Board leak, the media campaign. Akbar's vulnerabilities were exploited. Sadly." He avoided direct eye contact with the last phrase. "IndAxioma wanted to bury StarCure's propiothujane project. And they succeeded. You were simply in the way."

Nikolas stared, the pieces clicking into place, a horrifying mosaic of calculated destruction. "But… why tell me this now?"

Dario's tone softened, almost paternal. "Consider it making amends. I understand your life is disrupted. But you possess unique skills, Professor. Skills valuable on Samarqand. The bioprospecting rush there… it's a new frontier. A chance to start over." He slid a datapad across the table. "Information on Samarqand. Opportunities abound for someone with your expertise."

He stood, smoothing his jacket, a predator satisfied with his kill, but offering a poisoned olive branch. "Think about it, Professor. Sometimes, the only way to rise from the ashes is to find a new fire. Samarqand awaits, for the right Phoenix." He left Nikolas alone in the dim light, the datapad glowing on the table like a malevolent invitation.

✧ ¤ ✧ ¤ ✧

Back in the desolate apartment, Nikolas stared at the datapad Dario had left, the screen glowing with information about Samarqand.

172

Bioprospecting. Pharmaceutical gold rush. A wild frontier where regulations were loose and fortunes were made or lost in the jungle's green depths. He scrolled through glossy corporate brochures for Helicoverse, Cosmonomics, IndAxioma – the major players vying for Samarqand's biological treasures. IndAxioma. The name resonated with a cold, bitter hum. Dario's carefully constructed confession, designed to manipulate, had instead ignited something unexpected: a spark of cold, focused rage.

He spent the rest of the night immersed in planetary data, market analyses, and whispered rumors circulating on illicit channels – tales of corporate espionage, ruthless competition, and fortunes built on exploiting Samarqand's unique biosphere. He learned about synbergris, tosclareol, and whispers of other, more potent compounds, still undiscovered, still unclaimed. He saw the names of the four major corporations repeated endlessly, IndAxioma prominent among them. StarCure also featured, but as a minor player, easily crushed.

Rage solidified into resolve. Revenge. Not a blind, uncontrolled fury, but a calculated, precise retribution, mirroring the surgical precision with which his downfall had been orchestrated. They had destroyed Nikolas Kusuma, the respected professor. They had not destroyed his knowledge, his intellect, his skills. He would become something else, someone else. He would use their ruthlessness against them.

He accessed an untraceable identity service, a ghost in the machine, and began crafting a new persona: Lance Paparelli. No academic credentials, no digital footprint leading back to Peacehaven, just a skilled independent operator, a bioprospecting mercenary ready to navigate Samarqand's treacherous landscape.

His remaining assets were meager — the threadbare proceeds from selling his few possessions. Just enough for passage to Samarqand's spaceport, Emerald Landing, and a bare minimum of survival gear. He booked passage under the Paparelli alias, a one-way ticket to a new life, a life defined by purpose: to dismantle the corporate machine that had crushed him, brick by calculated brick.

Standing in the empty apartment, sunlight now a harsh, judging glare, Nikolas Kusuma ceased to exist. In his place stood Lance Paparelli, his gaze fixed on the digital map of Samarqand, a predator scenting blood, ready to hunt in a new jungle, a far more dangerous kind. He whispered a promise into the hollow silence, a vow aimed across light-years of space, at the architects of his ruin: "You took everything from Nikolas Kusuma. Now, Lance Paparelli is coming for you."

Phoenix

The interstellar transport **Distant Horizon** hummed with the gentle vibration of its fusion engines as it approached the final jump point to the Samarqand system. In his small private cabin, Nik — no, Lance Paparelli now, he reminded himself — studied the planetary briefing materials with the same methodical attention he had once given to research papers.

The tablet displayed detailed topographical maps of Samarqand's two major continents, Lisya and Pony, with corporate territories clearly marked. StarCure's operations were concentrated in the northern regions of Lisya, while IndAxioma maintained several smaller outposts on both landmasses. He memorized the locations, committing the geography to memory with scientific precision.

A soft chime announced the final countdown to jump. Lance secured his materials and leaned back in the acceleration couch, feeling the subtle shift in gravity as the ship prepared for the transition. His fingers brushed against the hidden compartment in his jacket where he kept Akbar's data chip, a reminder of what had been taken from him and why he was here.

Through the small viewport, the stars elongated briefly, then snapped back to normal as the ship completed its jump. Samarqand's star now dominated the view, its old K2 subgiant status giving it a deep orange hue. Somewhere in that system was his future, undefined but pregnant with possibility.

The ship's announcement system activated: "Approach to Samarqand orbital station commencing. All passengers please prepare for station docking procedures."

Lance gathered his few possessions, mentally reviewing his cover story one final time. Former chemical engineer from Krasnaya Rechka, seeking opportunities in frontier bioprospecting. Experienced with laboratory procedures and field analysis. No academic connections, no professional history that might link back to Nikolas Kusuma.

As he stepped into the corridor, he caught sight of himself in a reflective panel. The face looking back still startled him: harder, leaner, with none of the academic's thoughtful softness. In the transport's harsh lighting, his eyes appeared darker, almost predatory.

At the customs checkpoint, he presented his documentation with calm confidence. The bored security officer hardly glanced at his identification as he scanned it, then waved him through to the arrival hall.

The station hummed with activity: corporate representatives recruiting new talent, independent traders haggling over equipment prices, frontier types exchanging information about jungle conditions. The air smelled of recycled oxygen, disinfectant, and the faint exotic spice notes that gave the nearby moon its name.

Lance moved through this chaos with purpose, heading toward the shuttle bay for planetside transport. His destination was Emerald Landing on Lisya, formerly Pristan' Zorya, where he would establish his base of operations before venturing into the jungle interior.

As he waited for his shuttle assignment, Lance reviewed messages on his secure comm. Klempt's contacts had verified his identity papers would withstand scrutiny. Everything was proceeding as planned.

"Final boarding call for Emerald Landing shuttle," announced the transit system.

Lance shouldered his pack and moved toward the departure gate. Behind him lay the shattered remains of Nikolas Kusuma's life. Ahead lay Samarqand's dangerous jungles, corporate intrigue, and the possibility of reinvention. Perhaps even redemption.

But first, there would be reckoning.

Golden Perseus Dreams

Quotidian

Pipewatch Security's monitoring room hummed with the low thrum of active electronics. Around the circular periphery, flat panel displays glowed with the deep blue and bright green of star charts, scrolling telemetry, and the crisp white text of ship manifests. Everyday tools, the digital bread and butter of their trade: tracking cargo, flagging deviations, and maintaining a watchful eye on the Chanticlar region of the Perseus Pipe, that sinuous vein of human commerce threading through star systems. In the center of the room, a different kind of seeing waited for the right moment. Here, a holographic projector stood on standby, dormant for the moment, ready to cast data into a three-dimensional, interactive space.

Siobhan Tang sat at her workstation, her flaming red hair a vibrant contrast to the muted tones of the room. Her aquamarine eyes, sharp and focused, scanned the FPD array in front of her, effortlessly absorbing the flow of information. Decades of training, from a doctorate in biological chemistry to military pilot, and then as a civilian astrogator, had prepared her brain for this kind of spatial awareness. She saw patterns where others might see only random data points. She anticipated traffic flows, sensing anomalies in the subtle flicker of a transponder signal.

For now, space traffic in the Pipe moved in predictable ways, almost boringly so. During these lulls, Siobhan allowed a different kind of data stream to occupy her attention. With a few deft taps on her control surface, she banished the manifest displays to the periphery and brought forward a window filled with the intricate diagrams of organic chemistry journals. Her fingers flew across the virtual page, highlighting sections on cyclic compounds and enzymatic reactions. On a separate digital pad, a web of chemical structures began to form beneath her stylus — hexagons and pentagons linked by precise bonds, functional groups sprouting like tiny, purposeful limbs. She wasn't reviewing operational protocols. She was chasing ghosts, the ghosts of her past, the spirit of a cure.

The soft chime of the room's entry alert broke her concentration. Bogdan Jenson, her supervisor, strolled in, his presence immediately filling the space with a different kind of energy — less focused, more...oily. Jenson's security blues were always a shade too tight, straining slightly across his midsection. He slicked-back his thinning dark hair meticulously each morning, but by mid-shift, stray strands invariably escaped to frame a face perpetually set in a salesman's smile that didn't quite reach his eyes.

"Tang," Jenson greeted, the syllable clipped, more of a sound than a name. He gestured vaguely at her array of screens. "Keeping busy, I hope? Not getting lost in those... pretty pictures, are we?" He chuckled, a thin, reedy sound.

Siobhan met his gaze without blinking, her expression neutral. "Routine traffic analysis, Supervisor Jenson. Sector Gamma-9 is within acceptable parameters. No unusual deviations." She deliberately kept her tone light and clean, devoid of any hint of her private pursuits.

Jenson perched on the edge of a neighboring workstation, his smile widening but still cold. "Good, good. Just remember, Tang, billable hours are what keep the lights on, not chasing down every theoretical blip. Clients want solid numbers, threat assessments, not... well, whatever you're doing with those molecule doodles." He waved a dismissive hand at her digital pad. "Keep it practical, eh? We're Pipewatch, not...not some research lab."

Inside, a familiar coldness settled under Siobhan's ribs. *Worthless.* The word echoed, faint but persistent, a phantom limb of childhood insults. She pushed it down, as she always did, behind a wall of practiced indifference. "Understood, Supervisor," she said, her voice even. "Practical applications are the priority."

Jenson took her compliance as genuine, at least on the surface, nodding with satisfaction. "That's the spirit. Just keep those eyes on the Pipe, Tang. That's where the real threats — and the real paychecks — are found." With another fleeting, insincere smile, he moved on, leaving Siobhan alone again in the hum and glow of the monitoring room.

She watched him go, staring at the empty doorway, then turned back to her workstation. The controls on the central holographic projector remained untouched, , dark and inert. No need for 3-D visualizations of routine traffic. But the chemical structures on her digital pad, those intricate, hopeful lines, shimmered with a different kind of potential, a different kind of risk, a different kind of…dream. She returned her focus to the FPDs, to the steady pulse of the Perseus Pipe. The molecular whispers still lingered at the edge of her awareness, a secret project running in the background of her highly trained mind.

¤ ✧ ¤ ✧ ¤ ✧

Siobhan didn't immediately dismiss Jenson's words, but she filed them away in the same mental compartment where she stored corporate jargon and inane safety regulations: necessary noise to navigate her workday. As soon as Jenson was gone, the chemical structures vanished from her primary display, replaced once more by the stark lines of sector Gamma-9's shipping lanes. But now, one particular track snagged her attention: *Stardust Drifter*, call sign SD-492-JX.

She zoomed in on *Drifter*'s icon on the FPD array, its projected trajectory a wavering blue line against the star-speckled black. Routine freighter, according to its manifest: industrial lubricants, bound for a refuelling depot on the far side of the Perseus Pipe. Innocuous cargo, standard route. Except the rhythm of its pulses, the slight hesitations in its plotted course, felt off-key. She might be considered inexperienced at these tasks, but she had learned to trust her intuition in the long hours chasing down pirates in Chatham Station space.

Siobhan called up archived flight data for the *Stardust Drifter*. The FPDs flickered, replaced by weeks of recorded transponder signals, a ghost dance of light across the black screen. She ran a pattern analysis algorithm, her fingers flying across the input pad, highlighting subtle

179

deviations, minor course corrections that seemed statistically improbable for a routine freighter run. Glitches. Like a skip in a worn-out record, they were almost too faint to notice individually, but collectively, they formed a pattern of irregularity.

A cold knot formed in Siobhan's stomach. Irregularities. It was a feeling she knew intimately, a primal unease that resonated deep within her bones. A flicker of memory, sharp and unwelcome, flashed through her mind: the interior of a tramp freighter, older than she was now, the artificial gravity stuttering without warning, the recycled air stale and heavy with the scent of ozone and desperation. Her mother's face, etched with exhaustion and a weary resignation. *Never trust an old ship, Winnie,* Rose had murmured once, her voice flat, devoid of hope. *They'll shake you apart sooner or later.*

Siobhan pushed the memory aside, focusing on the data. She cross-referenced the *Drifter*'s manifests with customs declarations, then with publicly available commodity prices. Another anomaly surfaced. The listed value of the "lubricants" was consistently, marginally, under-declared. Not enough to flag outright fraud, but enough to shave off tariffs, to move slightly under the radar. Small savings on a system-wide scale, but multiplied across numerous shipments, it could become significant. And for what? Petty tax evasion? Or something more concealed the surface?

With a flick of her wrist, the FPD shifted again, now displaying a cargo manifest alongside a chemical database entry. "Industrial lubricants," the manifest claimed. But the listed chemical names... Siobhan scrolled through them, muttering under her breath, "Xylosolvents... Periabenzenes... fluorinated hydrocarbons... wait..." Her finger froze above a line: "Tri-methylated cyclohexanone isomers." She highlighted it, cross-referencing it against another, more restricted database, one she accessed through backchannels, skills honed during her graduate research. The results flashed on screen, stark red warnings overlaid on complex molecular diagrams. "RESTRICTED PRECURSOR COMPOUND. SYNTHESIS OF PSYCHOACTIVE AGENTS – CLASS IV (SAMARQAND)."

Samarqand. The name resonated, a low hum of recognition. Samarqand was famous — or infamous — for its unique biosphere, its potent biologicals, and, of course, for Synbergris. The notoriously addictive mood-altering substance. Precursor compounds for the alteration of Synbergris on a freighter ostensibly carrying lubricants. The 'glitches,' the under-declared value, the restricted chemicals; this wasn't random. It wasn't clerical error. It was deliberate.

She compiled her findings, concise and data-driven, and called up Jenson's comm frequency. He answered with a sigh in his voice, as if already burdened by her call. "Tang? Is it important? I'm in the middle of quarterly projections."

"Supervisor Jenson," Siobhan began, her voice calm but firm. "I've identified a freighter, the *Stardust Drifter*, exhibiting multiple anomalies. Route deviations, transponder inconsistencies, and irregularities in cargo manifests. The listed cargo includes chemicals classified as restricted precursors for psychoactive compound synthesis, specifically Class IV, with known connections to Samarqand."

There was a pause on the line. Then Jenson chuckled, a short, dismissive sound. "Synbergris precursors? Come on, Tang, really? Sounds like space-madness kicking in. Next you'll be seeing pirate queens in the telemetry data."

"Supervisor, the data is clear," Siobhan pressed, keeping her tone even. "These are not isolated incidents. There's a pattern of —"

Jenson cut her off, his voice hardening slightly. "Pattern of you wasting billable hours, Tang. That's the pattern I see. Look, these shipping lanes are complicated. Things move around. Manifests get messy. Doesn't mean it's some galactic drug cartel, alright? Probably just some paperwork snafu. Log it as a minor discrepancy, close the file, and get back to real threats."

"But Supervisor —"

The comm line clicked dead. Siobhan stared at the blank comm screen, a cold certainty settling in her gut. Jenson wasn't just dismissive; he was actively shutting her down. Willfully ignorant? Or something more deliberate? The question hung in the air, heavy and unsettling.

She was alone again in the monitoring room, the hum of the electronics suddenly feeling louder, more insistent. Outside the viewport, Chanticlar's lights glittered, oblivious. But Siobhan knew, with a chilling clarity, that the innocuous façade of routine in the Perseus Pipe was cracking. And she had just glimpsed something dark and dangerous beneath. She looked back at the *Stardust Drifter*'s track on the FPD, the wavering blue line now seeming less like a route and more like a dare. She wouldn't log it as a discrepancy. She wouldn't close the file. She was just getting started.

Exigency

Siobhan's apartment was a study in functional minimalism. Small, utilitarian, reflecting a life lived with a deliberate lack of excess. No personal touches, no softening décor; just the essentials for rest and sustenance between work shifts. Efficiency, always efficiency. Even in her private space, the ghost of her mother's chaotic drift through life seemed to whisper a constant warning against disorder, against attachment.

Late that night, the apartment's dim, ambient lighting cast long shadows across the bare walls as Siobhan worked at her personal terminal. The compact unit hummed softly, a counterpoint to the quiet susurrus of the Chanticlar night outside her window. She'd logged out of the Pipewatch network, leaving Jenson's dismissive pronouncements behind, but the *Stardust Drifter* still dominated her thoughts, a digital phantom refusing to be exorcised.

She'd moved beyond publicly accessible databases, delving into the deeper, murkier currents of the data streams. Anonymizing protocols engaged, firewalls activated, and blatantly misusing her Pipewatch access protocols, she navigated the labyrinthine networks where legitimate commerce blurred into shadow transactions. Years of research in psychoactive drug synthesis had inadvertently granted her access to these digital underworlds — academic curiosity sometimes led down unexpected paths. And her brief stint in military intelligence had sharpened those skills, adding layers of operational security to her clandestine searches.

On the screen, lines of code scrolled, tracing the shell corporation listed as the *Drifter*'s owner. Dead ends, false fronts, layers of obfuscation designed to dissolve upon scrutiny. But Siobhan was patient, methodical. She followed the digital breadcrumbs, peeling back the layers, each failed trace only hardening her resolve. She was built for endurance, for the long haul. Her body, honed by years of ultra-marathon running, possessed a similar kind of relentless efficiency. Lean muscle, economical movements, a finely tuned engine built for sustained effort. Even after hours hunched over the terminal, she felt no fatigue, only a sharpening focus.

A brief image flickered in her mind: the sun-baked, ochre-red trails of Bellisaurius, the endless kilometers stretching ahead, the rhythmic pound of her feet on the hard-packed earth, the solitary communion with her own body pushing its limits. One hundred and fifty kilometers. Twice. Three times. Victories not against others, but against herself, against the ingrained whispers of inadequacy that still haunted her. *"Competitors weren't that strong,"* she'd shrugged to a reporter after her third win, the words sounding almost dismissive, but masking a deeper, more fundamental truth: her own internal drive was the only competitor that truly mattered.

Now, that same drive was channeled into this digital pursuit. She shifted her focus from the shell company to the *Drifter*'s predicted flight path. Based on the previous anomalies, she extrapolated a likely "glitch zone," a sector of minimally monitored space traffic near a dense asteroid field. Perfect cover for a brief rendezvous, a quick data transfer. Or something else. Something less benign.

Siobhan accessed the Pipewatch surveillance systems remotely, bypassing standard security procedures; another skill acquired and quietly maintained. Unauthorized, off the books, but necessary. She designated Sector Gamma-9, predicted glitch zone, as her priority focus. Then she activated the system's advanced signal parsing array, a tool designed to filter out background noise, to isolate faint communications signals within dense traffic. A long shot, but worth the risk.

Hours crawled by. Static hissed across audio feeds. Telemetry data scrolled, meaningless noise. Just as fatigue finally began to gnaw at the edges of her concentration, a blip. A momentary flicker in the background noise. Too brief to be accidental, too structured to be random radiation. Encrypted data burst. From the predicted sector, coinciding with the *Stardust Drifter*'s projected transit time.

Adrenaline surged. Siobhan isolated the burst, routed it through her personal decryption suite, a patchwork of algorithms and key-crackers she'd assembled over years. A digital Swiss Army knife for locked data.

Line by line, the encrypted code began to unravel on her screen, fragmentary, partial, but yielding glimmers of meaning.

Samarqand. Precursor delivery Confirm warehouse coordinates. Port Azure. Flight adjustments, always in Sector Gamma-7.

The words coalesced, forming a disjointed but chilling message. Samarqand. Precursor. Delivery. Port Azure. Warehouse. Like pieces of an old-fashioned jigsaw puzzle, they clicked into place, revealing a stark, unsettling picture. The *Stardust Drifter* wasn't just carrying illicit chemicals; it was part of a clandestine supply chain, with a delivery point right here on Chanticlar, in the bustling port city itself. The warehouse district. Abandoned warehouses, forgotten corners of industrial sprawl. Perfect for clandestine operations.

Siobhan stared at the fragmented message on her screen, the adrenaline now laced with a cold dread. Confirmation. She'd been right. This wasn't just corporate malfeasance; it was something deeper, more dangerous. Smuggling, yes, but organized, deliberate, and reaching right into the heart of Chanticlar. And now, she knew too much. The shadows of the Perseus Pipe had just reached out and touched her, and the warmth of her apartment suddenly felt thin, fragile, desperately inadequate against encroaching cold.

¤ ✧ ¤ ✧ ¤ ✧

The Pipewatch Security monitoring room was deserted at this hour, the circular array of FPDs dimmed to standby mode, casting faint, ghostly reflections across the darkened space. Siobhan had returned, driven by a grim necessity. She needed access to the station's secure comms array, to reach beyond Chanticlar, beyond Jenson's compromised authority. But first, she needed to download the decrypted message fragment, to solidify her evidence, to prepare for what she knew was coming.

She moved with a practiced stealth honed during her military service, her senses hyper-alert. The silence in the room felt heavy, charged, expectant. The air itself seemed to vibrate with a subtle tension, a prickling at the nape of her neck that whispered of unseen eyes, unheard footsteps. Paranoia? Or instinct? In the shadowy spaces of the Perseus Pipe, the line between the two was often dangerously thin.

As she reached her workstation, fingers already poised above the console, a subtle shift in the room's atmosphere snagged her attention. A nearly imperceptible sound, the faint electronic sigh of the access panel at the main entrance. Then, the almost silent click of the door unlocking. Not a system malfunction. Deliberate.

Adrenaline flooded her system, cold and sharp. Combat reflexes, honed in zero-G dogfights and close-quarters drills, snapped into focus. Heart rate spiking, breath shallow, senses amplified. Danger. Real, immediate danger. She sought her calming mantra as she waited.

Two figures materialized in the dark doorway, their silhouettes stark against the dimly lit corridor beyond. Larger than average, bulky shapes moving with a practiced, unsettling confidence. Not Pipewatch personnel. Intruders.

"Miss Tang?" one of them rumbled, his voice low, gravelly, devoid of inflection. "We need to ask you some questions about your work tonight." He took a step forward, his partner flanking him, cutting off any escape route toward the corridor.

Siobhan remained outwardly still, her expression carefully blank, but her mind was a whirlwind of calculations. Escape vectors, weapon availability (none, save for a standard-issue utility knife clipped to her belt; useless), engagement probabilities. Not good. Not good at all.

Then, a third figure emerged from the shadows behind the two intruders. Jenson. Bogdan Rangoon Jenson, his forced smile absent, replaced by a mask of nervous compliance, his eyes darting around the room, avoiding hers. Betrayal, stark and sickeningly clear.

"Siobhan," Jenson began, his voice strained, almost pleading. "These gentlemen just want to clarify a few things. Routine security matter. Cooperate, and we can all avoid complications." He wrung his hands, a pathetic, cowardly gesture.

"Complications?" Siobhan echoed, her voice calm, deceptively so. Inside, ice was spreading, but years of military discipline held her composure rigid. "Like breaking and entering? Intimidation? Is this Pipewatch's new client relations protocol, Supervisor?"

The first thug chuckled, a dry, humorless rasp. "Pipewatch? Lady, you're way out of your depth. This ain't about your Mickey Mouse security firm. This is about discretion. Some things are best left un-watched. Un-noticed." He advanced another step, the two thugs forming a loose semi-circle around her, cornering her against the workstation console.

"We know you've been curious," the second thug added, his voice equally devoid of warmth. "Poking around where you shouldn't. Data trails, encrypted channels. You're a smart girl. Too smart for your own good, maybe." He waved, a dismissive flick of his hand. "Just hand over what you got. The data. The decryption keys. Everything. And we can all walk away. No complications." His use of Jenson's word was a deliberate emphasis.

Siobhan's mind raced. They knew about her investigation, about the data. Jenson had sold her out completely. Willingly or under duress, it didn't matter now. Cooperation was not an option. Compliance meant erasure, at best; something far worse, more likely. Buying time was her only play.

"Data?" she feigned confusion, tilting her head slightly, playing for ignorance. "I'm not sure what you mean. Routine traffic logs? Standard sector analysis? Supervisor Jenson reviews everything. I'm just a technician." She hoped the tremor in her voice was subtle, masked by the feigned confusion.

While she spoke, her fingers danced beneath the console's edge, initiating a sequence, a low-level emergency alert. An outdated, rarely used system, designed for station-wide lockdowns, unlikely to reach external authorities quickly, Maybe it would be enough. A silent, desperate gamble. Simultaneously, almost subconsciously, her left hand moved, detaching a small, innocuous-looking credit chip from her wrist, palming it, securing the encrypted data backup. Habit, training overriding conscious thought.

"Don't play games, Red," the first thug growled, his patience thinning. "We know what you decrypted. The *Drifter*. Samarqand."

187

Warehouse. You're smart, but not smart enough to play in this league." He took a final step, closing the distance, his hand reaching out, not for data, but for her arm.

That was the trigger. No more talk. Time was gone. Siobhan moved.

Not with brute force, which would have met a brick wall of muscle and failed. With precision, with speed. Years of martial arts training, honed in the close-quarters combat simulators, erupted into action. As the thug lunged, she dropped low, pivoting on her heel, using his own momentum against him. A sharp, angled strike to his knee, a sickening crunch of cartilage and bone. He bellowed, collapsing, momentum broken.

The second thug reacted instantly, swinging a heavy fist. Siobhan swayed back, narrowly avoiding the blow. Using the workstation console as a pivot, she launched herself forward, a blur of motion. A palm strike to his throat, disrupting his airway, followed by a precise heel strike to the nose. Another bellow, another body crumpling. Her rotation broke his elbow.

Chaos erupted in the monitoring room. The sudden violence, the raw physicality of the fight, shattered the sterile silence. Jenson recoiled, stumbling backwards, his face contorted in terror. Siobhan didn't waste time. She jumped, adrenaline surging. She grabbed a heavy, metal-framed workstation chair, swinging it in a wide arc, smashing it into the nearest thug's head as he rose, a sickening thud of impact. He went down, hard, unmoving.

The second thug, still struggling to breathe, lunged again, desperation fueling his attack. But Siobhan moved into an Eight Limbs flow, anticipating, weaving. Using the wreckage of the shattered chair as a makeshift shield, deflecting his clumsy blows. She closed the distance, delivering a tight, brutal series of strikes: elbows, knees, focusing on vulnerable points. Disabling, not killing. Military efficiency, cold and precise.

Within seconds, it was over. Both thugs were down, groaning, limbs twisted at unnatural angles, incapacitated. Jenson was huddled into a ball against the wall, whimpering, useless. Siobhan stood in the center of the wreckage, chest heaving, adrenaline still coursing through her system. Assessing, calculating. The alarm: had it triggered? Time ran out.

No time for Jenson. No time for explanations. Escape. Survive.

She turned away from the battle and ran. Out of the monitoring room, into the dimly lit corridors of Pipewatch Security, leaving the wreckage and the betrayal behind. Chanticlar was no longer a safe haven. It was a hunting ground. And she, Siobhan Tang, had just become the prey.

Metamorphosis

Running blind through the deserted corridors of Pipewatch, Siobhan relied on instinct and ingrained spatial memory. Emergency exit routes, maintenance access points, service tunnels; knowledge accumulated during safety drills, now transforming into lifelines. She shed her Pipewatch jacket as she ran, discarding any outward marker of her identity. Blending into the anonymous flow of Port Azure as her only way to safety, to freedom.

Emerging into the cool night air of Chanticlar, she pulled her hood up, melting into the shadows of the spaceport's periphery. No clear plan, just a driving need to disappear, to become untraceable. Her apartment was compromised, Pipewatch was a trap. She needed help, and there was only one person she trusted implicitly: Linden.

Reaching a secure comm booth in a low-traffic transit hub, she accessed an encrypted channel, initiating a priority call to Lyudmilla Kovalenko's private frequency. After a tense moment of ringing, Linden's face materialized on the small screen, her brow furrowed with concern, her voice fuzzy with broken sleep. "Siobhan? What is it? You sound breathless."

"Linden, I need help. Now. Pipewatch, it's gone bad. Really bad. Intruders, Jenson's involved, I had to defend myself." Siobhan summarized the break-in, the thugs, the decrypted message, keeping it brief, focused on the essential threat. She couldn't afford to reveal everything over an open channel, even an encrypted one.

Linden's expression hardened, her initial concern shifting to focused resolve. "*Chort voz'mi*," she swore in rapid Krasnaya Rechkan dialect, then switched back to accented Standard. "Get to my apartment. Sector Four, level 32. Back entrance, access code —" she rattled off a sequence of digits. "Go now. And Siobhan: be careful, *moy luchshiy drug*." The connection terminated.

Siobhan moved, fast and efficient, navigating the crowded transit lines, utilizing her training to blend, to observe without being seen.

paranoia gnawed at her. Were they already searching? Likely Were eyes watching her from the shadows? If her luck held, then not yet, but soon. Every flicker of movement, every lingering glance felt like a potential threat.

Linden's apartment was a sanctuary, small but warm, cluttered but safe. The scent of strong tea and simmering spices hung in the air, a comforting domesticity that was alien to Siobhan's sterile existence. Linden met her at the door, pulling her inside, bolting the locks behind them. "*Davai, davai,*" Linden urged, switching to Russian, the rapid-fire syllables a comforting reassurance. "Tell me everything. *Vsyo.*"

Siobhan recounted the full story, from the *Stardust Drifter* anomalies to the brutal fight in the monitoring room, showing Linden the fragmented decryption on her wrist-mounted drive. Linden listened intently, her expression growing increasingly grim. When Siobhan finished, Linden was silent for a moment, then nodded slowly. "*Da... eto ochen' ploho.* This is very bad." She paused, then her eyes sharpened. "But... not hopeless. We will make *khitrost'*. We will be cunning."

Linden's "cunning" proved to be a network of contacts stretching back to Krasnaya Rechka, to the insular, tight-lipped communities of Ukrainian and Belarusian diaspora. Whispers in encrypted channels, veiled requests, favors traded in the shadows of the Perseus Pipe. Within hours, arrangements were made. A meeting, clandestine and brief, in a darkened corner of a freighter supply depot. An exchange of data, encrypted and anonymized, and a heavy credit chit. For "services rendered."

The services were forged papers. Not cheap imitations, but top-tier fabrications::::: biometric data flawlessly replicated, background history crafted to perfection, official stamps and seals indistinguishable from the real thing. The persona of "Maeve Chen" materialized on a data chip, complete, airtight, ready to become Siobhan's next skin.

While Linden's contacts worked, Siobhan's mind raced ahead. Samarqand. The decrypted message fragment. "You said Samarqand was in the message?" Linden asked suddenly, breaking Siobhan's train of thought. "The precursor chemicals. From there?"

Siobhan nodded. "Samarqand. Class IV psychoactive precursors."

Linden's eyes widened slightly. "Samarqand. Krasnaya Rechka people, *nashy lyudi*, our people, were the first to settle there after the Collapse. Old language, Russian, Ukrainian. They are still spoken on Samarqand, and on Spice, their moon." A flicker of an idea sparked in Linden's gaze. "You should learn Russian, Siobhan. If you go there, it could help. People trust familiar voices."

The suggestion resonated. Language as a tool, as a shield, as a key. Siobhan's analytical mind clicked into gear. Immersion learning programs, linguistic algorithms, her own innate capacity for accelerated learning. Within hours, she immersed her mind in Russian, the Cyrillic alphabet flickering across her screen, pronunciation drills echoing softly in Linden's apartment. Days blurred into a relentless cycle of language acquisition, interspersed with anxious waiting for the forged papers, the constant undercurrent of fear, and the quiet, unwavering support of Linden.

With Linden's secure comms access, Siobhan also initiated another, riskier maneuver. Leveraging her past military service, she crafted an encrypted message to Bellisaurius Space Defense Forces military police. Data logs from Pipewatch (selectively purged to remove traces of her deeper investigation, but still damning for Jenson), the decrypted message fragment, a concise account of the break-in and Jenson's complicity – all bundled together, anonymized but traceable back to her original Pipewatch ID, a digital breadcrumb trail for those who knew how to follow. A long shot, a gamble that the military police on Bellisaurius still operated with some semblance of integrity, beyond the reach of Perseus Pipe corruption.

The long wait proved useful, as Linden brought in a trusted *babushka*, Tatsiana, who taught Siobhan how to hide in plain sight. Subtle changes to stride, posture, skin color. Dark contact lenses. Her long, red braids cut and shaped into a much shorter style, rainbowed tips favored by the younger crowd. Clothing designs she would never choose for herself. After three visits Tatsi's work was done. Siobhan no longer recognized herself in a mirror.

Time to learn how to be someone else.

The Maeve Chen papers arrived, delivered in a sealed data packet. Siobhan held the chip in her hand, the weight surprisingly substantial. A new life, a constructed identity, a clean slate. Or was it only another layer of illusion? Siobhan Hu Tang was gone. Officially erased. Only Maeve Chen remained. She practiced the name in her mind, in front of Linden, testing the cadence, the feel of it on her tongue. Maeve Chen. A stranger staring back from the reflection in the darkened screen. Sadness mingled with a strange sense of liberation. Letting go of Siobhan, of the past, of the weight of expectation, of the ingrained sense of worthlessness. Perhaps Maeve could be different. Perhaps Maeve could be free.

¤ ✧ ¤ ✧ ¤ ✧

Port Azure Spaceport pulsed with the chaotic energy of departures and arrivals, a constant churn of humanity flowing through security checkpoints and transit gates. Maeve Chen moved through the throngs with a quiet confidence that belied the turmoil within. No trace of Siobhan Hu Tang remained in her posture, her gait, or her carefully neutral expression. The forged papers felt reassuringly solid in her pocket, a tangible anchor to this new, constructed self.

At the embarkation gate for Perseus-bound transports, she presented her Chen identification. The automated scanner hummed, green lights flashed, and the gate opened without hesitation. No flicker of suspicion, no raised eyebrows. Maeve smoothly collected her boarding pass, a small victory in this fragile new game of identity. She was Maeve Chen, at least to the unblinking eyes of the system.

Aboard the civilian transport **Corvus**, she found a window seat in a sparsely populated section of the passenger cabin. As the vessel detached from the port and ascended into orbit, Chanticlar receded in the viewport below, a sprawling tapestry of light dissolving into the velvety black of space. Maeve watched its descent, a complex mix of emotions churning within her. Sadness for Linden, their emotional parting a sadness she would examine later, in her cabin. A pang of something akin to regret for the life she was leaving behind, however precarious it had become. But no nostalgia for Pipewatch, no sentimentality for Chanticlar itself. It was a waypoint, a temporary stage in a life defined by movement, by constant shifting.

She opened her datapad, the Maeve Chen identity file prominent on the screen. She reviewed the fabricated details one last time, imprinting the new history, the new biographical markers onto her memory. *Maeve Chen. Born on Kepler-186f. Shuttle pilot certifications, security operations for various asteroid mining ops in the Pincushion system, recently. Between contracts.*

A plausible, unremarkable backstory. She practiced the name silently, mouthing the syllables, feeling the unfamiliar shape of it in her mouth. Maeve Chen. It felt detached, like a borrowed, badly-fitting suit, not yet her own.

She turned her thoughts to Samarqand. IndAxioma Pharma. She accessed the company's public profile, scrolling through corporate brochures and employment opportunities. "Shuttle pilot," "orbital logistics," "materials transport." The mundane language of commerce, masking the undercurrents of something far more complex, more volatile. Samarqand: land of synbergris, of bio-prospecting gold rushes, of corporate shadows and whispered fortunes. The nexus of the precursor chemicals, the thread connecting back to the *Stardust Drifter*, to Jenson's betrayal, to the thugs in the monitoring room. Answers waited there, hidden within the chaotic sprawl of that distant world.

On a separate secure partition of her datapad, she accessed files downloaded during those frantic hours in Linden's apartment. Additional combat tactics. Jungle survival protocols. Counter-surveillance techniques. Not the scientific gloss of her academic training, but the raw, pragmatic skills of survival. Maeve Chen, shuttle pilot, would need to be more than just a skilled operator; she'd need to be resourceful, resilient, ready for anything. The scientist was receding, replaced by something harder, more pragmatic, more… dangerous.

As **Corvus** initiated its jump sequence, the stars outside the viewport stretching and distorting into hyperspace streaks, Maeve closed her eyes, taking a slow, deliberate breath. The recycled ship air tasted faintly metallic, sterile, yet somehow carrying a hint of something else – possibility? Uncertainty? A new beginning, forged in crisis, propelled by necessity. This wasn't just escape; it was a deliberate stride into the unknown, towards a destination now imbued with purpose. A promise whispered to herself in the silence of her mind: *I will find out what this is about. I will use what I know. I will survive. And mama, I promise on my soul, I will find a cure.*

Opening her eyes, she focused on the starfield ahead, already charting a mental course towards Samarqand. Then, softly, almost experimentally, she murmured a phrase in the new language she was beginning to inhabit. "*Новое начало*," she whispered, the Russian words feeling strange yet comforting on her tongue. *A new beginning.*

Maeve Chen inhaled deeply, the recycled ship air tasting like strange new beginnings. Samarqand awaited.

The End of
Samarqand: Prelude

Books by Mitchell R. White

Brannigan Mysteries
Secrets of Silvergrove
Forget-Me-Nots and Forgotten Graves
Blue Iris, Blood Morning (Summer 2025)
Daisies for My Wife (Fall 2025)

Summers Rose Investigations
End in a Dead Heat
So Easy It's Criminal (Summer 2025)
Tacos, Sunsets, and Murder (Summer 2025)

The Hollister Files
The Case of the Shadow Sisters (Fall 2025)
Salt Money, Blood Money (Fall 2025)

Writing as M. R. "Doc" White, Ph.D.
Samarqand (Spring 2025)
Redeeming Lost Pegasus (Winter 2025)
Bloodwine Warriors Trilogy (2026)

ABOUT THE AUTHOR

Dr. Mitchell R. White, Ph.D.

Mitch White writes murder mysteries, cozy and otherwise, as well as science fiction and fantasy novels. His works can be read via the Kindle platform (tablets and computers), and soon will be available in print form.

Mitch White grew up reading the greats of his time in science fiction, fantasy, action and mystery. These stories encouraged Mitch to try his hand at writing while in graduate school, where he was fortunate enough to take creative writing courses led by Orson Scott Card. The demands of school and family prevented Mitch from publishing, though the "writer's bug" never left his soul.

Working through school found Mitch in roles from ditch-digging to nuclear non-destructive testing, mixologist to prep cook for a dorm of 1,200 students. All these experiences provided incentive to finish a doctorate in chemistry, with other degrees gathered along the way.

A rewarding career in science and technology, and a gratifying family life, left little time to write until retirement appeared on the horizon. Traveling the world as a consultant scientist and engineer provided exposure to and appreciation of many cultures. Nothing broadens one's perspective quite like travel, and Mitch's experiences in other lands informs his interests and prose.

Mitch also taught as visiting professor in the sciences at several universities. He provided technical training in semiconductor and computer manufacturing, process optimization, quality improvement, and statistics to over 20,000 attendees on five continents.

Avocations pursued through the years include cooking, mixology, chess, travel, photography, fostering Golden Retrievers, and recreational computing.

Somewhere in all this chaos, Mitch found time for family, raising a daughter and now spoiling a granddaughter.

During retirement, Mitch performs as a professional musician when not writing. Mitch finds that the two avocations cooperate well, and he looks forward to years of fun, creative endeavors.

He lives in the suburbs of Austin, Texas, very close to the center of the universe.

www.ingramcontent.com/pod-product-compliance
Lightning Source LLC
Chambersburg PA
CBHW051502170626
46811CB00002B/610